Miss Fanshawe's Fortune

The Brides of Mayfair

Book Two

LINORE ROSE BURKARD

LILLIPUT PRESS

OHIO

MISS FANSHAWE'S FORTUNE
Copyright © 2020 by Linore Rose Burkard
Published by LILLIPUT PRESS
OHIO 45068
www.LilliputPressllc.com

Publishers Cataloging-in-Publication Data
Name: Burkard, Linore Rose, author
Title: miss fanshawe's fortune / by Linore Rose Burkard
Description: 1st edition
Summary: A young woman's mysterious past must be unraveled for her to gain fortune and respectability—and the hero's love—in this traditional Regency Romance.

Identifiers: Library of Congress Control Number: 2020911586
ISBN : 978-1-7333111-7-5 (print) / ISBN: 978-1-7333111-6-8 (ebook) /
Subjects: 1. Fiction—Romance, Historical, Regency   2.Fiction—Romance, Clean and Wholesome

Cover Adapted by *J.Blair Design*

Printed in the United States of America

What Readers Are Saying

"Wonderful novel! Vividly drawn characters, an intriguing mystery, and humorous and sparkling dialogue reminiscent of Heyer, as if the author was laughing as she wrote it. Fans of traditional Regency romance will love this book!"
Camille Elliot, Author, *Prelude for a Lord*

"Burkard sweeps us into the world of Regency England with rich detail and the language of the day. Highly enjoyable!"
Kathleen Rouser, Author, *Rumors and Promises*

"A *delightul* read! And the sweet romance! Call it exquisite torture...*sigh* ...you'll just have to read it for yourself. "
Nicole Sager, Author, *The Heart of Arcrea*

"Well done—a cracking read! Was great for lockdown too."
Charlotte H., UK Reader

"Whoa. This is a Dickensian Regency that will have you learning as you laugh, wonder, and swoon with the story."
Becky Lewis, VINE VOICE

"Burkard's tale is off and running with Frannie's future hanging in the balance. Readers of Burkard know she immerses you in the Regency. She writes with relaxed panache, and the comic moments, of which there are plenty, will make you laugh out loud."
L.K. Simonds, Author, *All In*

"Another gem in the *Brides of Mayfair* series! It was difficult to put down...(and) reminiscent of Georgette Heyer's novels. Highly recommend."
D.E. Taylor, Reviewer

I absolutely enjoyed Burkard's second book in The Brides of Mayfair series! The characters make up a delightful menagerie and I found myself chuckling at their wittiness while enjoying the moments of mayhem.
Anne Payne, Reviewer

"This plot reminded me very much of a Georgette Heyer novel, and I couldn't put it down.... Words fail me as to how much I loved Sebastian's character. If only he was real...!"
Brittany A. Searfoss, VINE VOICE

"A refreshingly clean Regency romance, complete with an antagonist you LOVE to hate. A delight from beginning to end. The only drawback was that in ended too soon!"
R. Kaye, Reviewer

"I found myself coming to the defense of young Miss Fanshawe several times. Talk about placing yourself in a story. I was there!"
Judith Blevins, Reviewer

"Quite the tangle! If you are looking for a good, clean, intriguing, regency romance, look no further".
Deb Mitchell, Reviewer

"Loved it!! ...Hooks you on the first page. It has just enough twist and turns to keep you turning the pages. This book was an absolutely joy to read".
Ann Ferri, Reviewer

"The story captures from the beginning and holds the reader throughout...Watching the gradual defrosting of (the hero's) heart through to the final scenes was very well scripted. I think this was the first time I have ever uttered 'Awh.' while reading!"
AM Daniele, Reviewer

Special Back-of-the-Book Features

- Timeline

- Mayfair Map (the Arundells' Home)

- Bonus Excerpt, *Before the Season Ends*

- Bonus Excerpt, *Forever, Lately: A Regency Time Travel Romance*

- Reader's Glossary of Regency Terms

Dedicated to
Charlotte H.,
My friend in the U.K.
who knows why I call her my secret weapon.

CHAPTER ONE

Edward Arundell suspected from the moment he almost ran her down on Monmouth Street, that Miss Fanshawe would be trouble. He had merely a few more corners to conquer before reaching the house on King Street, and had just rounded the bend to Monmouth when a young woman in a delicate sprigged muslin and a straw, beribboned hat, holding a single valise, and with a corded trunk at her feet, stepped lightly into the road. If he hadn't been such a sure hand at the reins, he'd never have managed to pull up the team in time to skirt around her. But with a hair's breadth to spare, he missed her and roared past.

He should have kept right on roaring. The curricle he commanded at top speed was not his own, first of all, and if he didn't reach home before his elder brother Sebastian awoke and discovered the theft (for surely he would call it that) he'd be in for a monstrous combing and quite possibly lose his monthly stipend. The combing he could take with fortitude. But losing his stipend was an unthinkable horror.

To complete his journey he needed only to bear left onto Grafton Street, angle quickly right onto Gerrard's, then make the razor-sharp turn onto Prince's in order to come up directly by the mews off King. He would have stabled the horses and got in the house before Sebastian would know the difference. Only he didn't keep on. The devil made him turn, he supposed, to spy the sweet vixen he'd missed by mere inches and see her drop senseless in the street.

He was no saint, by Jove. But even he, a young sprig intent on making a wave among a set of wave cutters, had no choice but to slow the team, swallow an oath that flew to his lips, and return to the scene of the almost crime. At this early hour, only two passersby were on hand, and they hurried to surround the prostrate young woman. These lost no time in hailing Edward, begging him to be so kind as to take the poor thing in his chariot to the nearest inn or coffee house.

With a heavy heart, Edward allowed them to lift the young lady, and then her valise and trunk, into the curricle. She came to as he drove off, sinking his spirits yet further, for now he would have to apologize prettily, perhaps even take her somewhere across the metropolis—who knew? By the time he got back to King Street with Sebastian's curricle, his elder brother would be in rare form. And if he cut off Edward's stipend, which was by any standard already too meager to keep him looking all the crack, he'd be utterly dashed and done in.

He slowed the team to a stop in front of The Boar's Head Inn and turned apologetically to his slim, dark-haired young victim. After craning her neck to get a good look at the establishment, the young lady turned to him with large brown eyes infused with gratitude, eyes that would melt a sterner man's heart. "Thank you, sir," she said quietly. Colouring, she added, "I—I believe I nearly swooned!" He looked past a riot of curls that had escaped her bonnet and met those luminous orbs with a suddenly gentle disposition.

"But you did swoon," he assured her. "And it was on my account. Please—please—allow me to—to—." He motioned with his head to the inn, but when the innkeeper emerged from inside the brick building dusting off an apron and followed by a porter, a sudden better thought occurred to Edward.

If he took this lovely creature into the inn to revive her with some refreshment, it would cost him something. More, he'd be detained and not get home before Sebastian—that starched shirt!—would discover his transgression. He'd been given set downs before on account of borrowing the curricle. With this infraction, he and his brother'd go to loggerheads and upset Mama. Or Edward would have to deliver a Canterbury story deep enough to satisfy the pope. In the few seconds it took for the servant to reach him, extending a hand for the ribbons to walk the horses to the mews, he'd made a decision.

"Allow me to offer you breakfast," he said magnanimously, turning only to dismiss the man with a curt nod. "My mother and elder brother are home, and there is no trouble at all in bringing a guest, I assure you." With an apologetic air, he added, bowing his head, "I beg your pardon. Edward Arundell, at your service."

"Miss Fanshawe," said Frannie with a nod of the head. "Pleased to meet you." Normally she would have left it at that. Normally she wasn't given to a display of emotions but the excitement and danger of her situation must have had her in its grip, for she added in a gush, "But oh, Mr. Arundell, you've no notion of my troubles! I have endured the most horrifying experience!"

Edward looked at her fairly amazed. "It's but nine o'clock.

Have you already had the most horrifying experience?"

She nodded, with large, pained eyes. "Yesterday. I'm afraid I've been at sixes and sevens ever since, wandering in town like—like a nomad."

"Surely you didn't wander the streets all night," he said, half in disbelief and half in awe.

She shook her head, resulting in a ripple of curls that framed the bonnet. "I lodged at an inn, but I left this morning determined to return to my father's house and—"

"You didn't run from home!" Edward pronounced. Such an impropriety on the part of a proper looking young woman quite astonished him.

"No, indeed!" she said imploringly, her large eyes pinned upon his. "But my only relations that I know of—I suppose it was my aunt—turned me away!"

"Do ye' not know your aunt?" Edward asked, with narrowed eyes.

"I never laid eyes on her before yesterday. You see, I was brought up by my mother and Mrs. Baxter," she explained. "But they are both gone now, and I have suffered the very worst sort of ill usage by—by this lady! It is quite abominable."

"Bad luck," he said feelingly, regarding her now with a benign expression, his entire sympathies instantly on her part. Miss Fanshawe was certainly under the hatches. He'd found himself at the bottom end of deep scrapes for most of his eighteen years, so that a fellow sufferer he regarded almost as a fellow in arms, though he wasn't a military man.

"Not to fret," he assured her. "My uncle's a baronet," he said importantly, "and my brother's his heir." Miss Fanshawe's eyes widened.

This satisfied Edward, who had yet to discover a commoner who wasn't impressed with a tie to nobility, whether high or low as to the scale of titles. Sir Hugo would scarcely know him by sight, but that was not to the point. The connexion was real, but tenuous because of an ancient feud between Sir Hugo Arundell and his mama; a mysterious affair that remained shrouded in reticence, with the result that Edward's family rarely saw the baronet. Nevertheless, claiming the relation was social proof that Edward found uncommonly useful and irresistible, therefore, to make known.

He nodded toward King Street. "Whatever your troubles, Sebastian'll sort them out."

"Is that the brother you spoke of?"

Edward nodded. "My elder by nine years." In a disgruntled voice he added, "Thinks he's my father, I daresay."

Frannie's large eyes filled with hope. "Could it be—do you indeed think he will champion my cause? I find myself quite friendless. I own it is a nasty kettle of fish and I haven't the faintest idea how to proceed in it. But I prayed earnestly for divine assistance. I believe it was Providence that brought you to me!"

Edward would not have put it that way, but he gave her a wry glance while slapping the ribbons lightly to start off. "What sort of trouble is it?"

She swallowed, and said emphatically, "A mystery. Which I must get to the bottom of as soon as possible! My future, my entire fortune is at stake!"

Respectfully, and trying not to appear too curious, Edward asked, "And is that fortune very large?"

"Quite large, I am told." She said philosophically, "Mrs.

Baxter assured me that it must be in excess of £30,000 by now."

"Lud, that is a fortune," he acknowledged gravely, and rather in awe. "Mrs. Baxter?"

"The dear lady who raised me after my mama died." At this, Frannie blinked back tears. "She has only gone to her rest a fortnight ago."

"I say," Edward mumbled, sincerely. "Poor Miss Fanshawe."

Frannie stifled her tears with a handkerchief, turning to give him a look of gratitude for his understanding, her eyes large and dark and long-lashed. Edward sucked in his breath. Miss Fanshawe was first-rate, his friends would say. A pearl of the first water.

"But that is only part of my trouble. The worst of it is what happened since her passing!"

He turned the final corner onto King Street. With any luck they'd be in the house before Sebastian had summoned his valet. Good thing his elder brother wouldn't countenance appearing at breakfast unshaved. But he turned to Frannie and said warningly, "Sebastian can be devilish unfriendly in the morning; he grows less formidable as the day wears on."

After a moment Frannie asked curiously and a little troubled, "Why would that be? If a gentleman is good-natured and amiable, he ought to be so always unless there has been provocation. He ought to be steady in his character, day or night."

"He don't sleep well," Edward explained matter of factly. He gave her a serious look. "Don't get in the vapours if he ain't amiable right off."

Frannie frowned. "I assure you, I am not in the habit of

getting in the vapours."

"But you swooned earlier," pointed out Edward, "though you weren't injured by me."

Frannie sniffed again. "That's only because…because I haven't eaten for a whole day. And the fright of that close call—." She turned to him, her eyes dawning with recognition. "Injured by you? Was that you? Thunder! It was this carriage that almost killed me?"

Edward's heart lurched. "Dash it, Miss Fanshawe, I meant no harm! Only I was—I am—in the deepest pickle; couldn't afford to lighten the pace! I daresay an apology will hardly answer, but I am sorry."

Frannie regarded him silently for a moment. "And you did return to rescue me." In another moment her eyes brightened. "You are forgiven, Mr. Arundell. I maintain, it would have been worse for me had any other carriage nearly blown me down. Not many gentlemen would see their way to helping a stranger! That must compensate for one small moment of terror."

Edward swallowed, and hoped sincerely that his brother would indeed be able to untangle whatever ravel she was in. He owed her that.

He pulled up to the house. It was ungentlemanly not to assist her down, but he needed to get the curricle stowed and out of sight. Frowning, he explained that he had only to get the horses in the mews himself—didn't wish to disturb a servant!—and would be right back with her valise, but was silenced by the arrival of a dour-faced Sykes, Sebastian's man. Glancing disapprovingly at Edward, Sykes assisted the lady from the carriage. After ordering a footman to lift down the young woman's portmanteau, he looked back upon

Edward with his peculiarly frigid gaze.

"Look here, Sykes, you needn't tell him—"

"He knows, sir," said Sykes, in the deep, gloomy voice that always reminded Edward of a mausoleum.

"Dash it all!" Edward took a deep breath. "So be it."

Sykes took the ribbons and handed them to a groom who had emerged from the servants' entrance, while Frannie looked nervously and questioningly at Edward. Edward climbed down and went around to the pavement where he offered her his arm. They walked, Sykes following with his singularly disapproving mien, to the door. Edward said bracingly, "Sebastian's a crusty fellow, but he won't dare comb me over in your presence." The words were more for his own assurance, it seemed, than Miss Fanshawe's. Escorting her inside, he hoped it was true.

CHAPTER TWO

"It must seem irregular to you," Frannie said apologetically, allowing him to usher her in ahead, "to accept such kindness, to come into your home on so short an acquaintance!"

A small, squat, but dignified little man hurried toward them and took Edward's things, and then Frannie's. He was not the usual butler to be found in an upper-class establishment, or most anywhere for that matter. In place of the long legs and fine calves that butlers and footmen were sometimes chosen for—because they showed off the breeches of livery to a turn—this man was thick set and muscular; not what you would call elegant by any standard. But he performed his office and was thanked by Edward as he bowed shortly to Frannie before Edward turned them toward the stairs.

Sykes, holding the valise, said, "Is your guest staying, sir?" His sepulchral monotone echoed in the hall. Edward could not understand for the life of him, how Sebastian could stand such a dull plate for a servant. Why, if he, Edward, had a gentleman's gentleman, it'd be a man with spirit, with conversation and suggestions. An energetic being, not a walking tomb like Sykes. Flustered at the unexpected question, however, he replied, "Yes, yes. Tell my mother.

She'll direct you to which bedchamber she wants for Miss Fanshawe."

With both servants gone, Edward looked timorously at the young woman. "Are you stopping elsewhere? I suppose I should have asked you first, if you were wishing to stay."

But she answered, smiling, "It is exceedingly generous of you to put me up. Indeed, I have no lodgings in the city. You see, it was part—part of my troubles; that I ended up without a place to lay my head. And my purse was nabbed—and—and—" Her eyes watered at this, and Edward, alarmed, said, "None of that now. As I said, we'll get it sifted for you." He brought her to the morning room, which thankfully, neither his mama nor brother had as yet entered. Frannie looked with appreciation through its arched window at a small garden behind the house, a welcome spot of greenery in the city.

The sideboard, with delicious aromas wafting from an assortment of covers, beckoned, and lifted her spirits further. She'd been feeling the lack of nourishment, for she'd had nothing since her purse was snatched. Edward offered her a plate, and she chose what she wanted. When they were both seated with breakfast before them, *eggs en cocotte* and rolls, butter, a pot of chocolate and one of tea, he eagerly dug in but glanced her way, and stopped chewing.

"Is something amiss?" he asked.

"Do you not—" she hesitated. "That is, do you mind if I give thanks?"

Edward hurriedly put down his fork. "Forgive me. Not at all." *Sebastian must like this one*, he thought with satisfaction as Frannie said a heartfelt prayer of thanks. Indeed, it rather astonished him, for she gave thanks for the *mercy* of having *almost* been run down, for it led him to help her. Such a detailed prayer from the heart was not something he often heard. Must be a Methodist, he thought, instantly resolving to say nothing of it to Sebastian, a staunch Anglican.

When she'd done, he dug back in to his food, being famished. He'd been out half the night in pursuit of a fly-by-nighter, a man who'd promised to sell him a bang up equipage, a smart gig, just the thing for a whip-in-training, and for the smallest sum imaginable. All Edward had to do was convey said man from the low district club where they'd met to his home north of London. There, the transaction was to take place. But for this Edward was forced to borrow his brother's curricle, which meant waiting until the small hours of the night to do it undetected.

To Edward's chagrin, when he was presented with the supposed prize, he'd never seen a sorrier looking equipage. Outdated, outmoded, its sides peeling with strips of languishing wood, and the wheels uneven. The man was not eager to lose the sale and harped on most unpleasantly about a gentleman's word being his honour and other such drivel. By the time Edward got away (and only after pressing a few shillings into the man's hand) it was well past morning light. He pushed the team hard to make time and was cracking along nicely—until Miss Fanshawe stepped into his path.

Looking at her now, he wished he'd been less hasty in bringing her to the house, for it began to be borne in on him that it would be an uphill climb convincing Sebastian to take her case. He'd best learn all he could before facing him. The next half hour in the morning room was spent in earnest conversation as Frannie laid out her case for Edward. Many emphatic sighs with outstretched arms were heard and noted. Edward listened with a growing frown, rubbing his chin, nodding now and again. By the time he'd heard the whole sorry tale, he knew one thing.

Sebastian wasn't going to like it.

Frannie and Edward had removed to the parlour by the time Sebastian appeared in the morning room for coffee and toast, his usual fare. Mrs. Arundell stayed abed with the headache, but her eldest son, in fitted trousers, dark shoes, a white shirt with a lightly pointed collar and unremarkable, though spotless cravat, sat down content to have the room to himself. Over his shirt was a hunter green waistcoat patterned in black thread. It brought out the green in his eyes, though Sebastian would never have chosen it for such a frivolous purpose. Light sideburns and a sensible hair cut showed him to be more conscious of propriety than fashion.

His cutaway tailcoat in dark brown he began to remove, for he was alone, but he stopped at Syke's report of Edward's having brought a young woman home. Scowling, he allowed the servant to help him back into the coat. Edward, that fool pup, was an endless pest. The additional information, that said woman's portmanteau had been placed into a guest bedchamber—chosen by Sykes himself, in order not to wake the mistress during one of her attacks—only deepened the scowl.

He'd just opened his book to the page where he'd left off and taken one sip of coffee when Edward entered. "Beau, eat quickly! I've got a horrid scramble for you to untangle."

Sebastian eyed his brother dispassionately above a pair of

narrow-rimmed spectacles, took a bite of toast, and chewing, returned to his book. "You *will* have a horrid scramble when I turn you out on the street for a thief."

"Oh, come, Beau! My entire object was to ensure that I never have to borrow your gig again!"

"Don't call me Beau," was the sole answer.

"It's what Mama calls you, and I own it puts you in a better mood!"

Sebastian lowered his book. "Nothing *you* say can alter my mood for the better. Stop blathering and explain to me why you stole my carriage, exhausted my horses, and brought home with you a street wench!"

"I don't associate with street wenches," Edward replied haughtily, with his nose in the air. "And Miss Fanshawe's genteel. She's an heiress!"

Sebastian's look lost some of its fierceness, though his eyes betrayed stark doubt. "Do go on," he said, wiping his mouth with a napkin. "Let us know the reason, for there must be some extraordinary circumstance, why this heiress is to be our guest?" He returned his eyes to the book.

"She's in a tangle, that's all."

Sebastian looked up with narrowed eyes. "How do you know her?"

"Let me tell you the trouble, then we'll get to that."

"What sort of tangle?"

Edward stared at his brother. "On second thought, I'll let her tell you."

Now hardness gleamed in his eyes. "You'll do no such thing. I've no idea how you stumble upon odd, low characters in your jaunts about town, rag-tag creatures from your gaming dens, no doubt—"

"Not at all!" interjected Edward hotly. "I've not been gaming, upon my word!"

But a gasp and a sob was heard in the corridor. Edward's eyes widened. Had he forgot to ask Miss Fanshawe to remain in the parlour?

Sebastian glared at his brother. "Is that her?"

Edward nodded guiltily. "Must be."

"You brought her? Without informing me!" He threw down his napkin, stood, and with a grim look on his face, still glaring at Edward, said, "I will make quick work of your heiress!" He intended upon doing it too, turning her out before she could say Jack Robinson. But only seconds after he'd left the room, he was back, preceded by Miss Fanshawe, who held a handkerchief to one eye and was sniffling. Edward gave her a weak smile, hoping it was bracing.

Sebastian had taken one look at her, instantly recognized a genteel looking creature, stifled the rebuke upon his lips, and, after a nodding short bow, said, "Please," and motioned for her to enter. Having expected to see a doxy (whom he would have unhesitatingly sent from the house) he instead was treated to the sight of a respectable, handsome, well dressed young woman. And when his eyes clasped her ridiculously large, intelligent but tear-rimmed orbs, a jolt of surprise ran through him. Without a word, she'd disarmed him. One sight of her was all it took. Was he a gudgeon? He'd almost offered his arm, by Jove, but checked himself.

"I beg your pardon," he said in the morning room, as he held out a chair, which she accepted. "I'm afraid I spoke rashly."

Edward breathed a sigh of relief. Sebastian was deuced particular, but never lacked manners in company, especially with the muslin set. It drove society belles near mad, as he never followed up his exquisite manners and courtesies with an offer. Edward wondered if his brother was waiting to come into the title before he'd wed. That would be Sebastian in a nutshell—doing everything strictly proper and in its time.

Sebastian cleared his throat as he resumed his seat. "Have you had breakfast, Miss—er—?"

"Miss Fanshawe," put in Edward, who hurriedly went on to complete the introductions.

"I have, thank you," she replied, watching Sebastian tragically. "I am very sorry to interrupt yours, sir."

To her sweet, expressive countenance of sheer misery, Sebastian visibly softened. The hard lines of his jaw relaxed, and his eyes, behind the round spectacles, looked almost large as he surveyed her with something approaching kindness. He had not quite decided whether to trust this young woman's account, whatever it might be, but he had lost the greater part of his suspicions.

He looked at Edward. "I'll deal with you and the matter of my curricle later." Turning his full attention to Frannie, he said, "Tell me your trouble, Miss Fanshawe."

Frannie's heart was in a tumble, for she was sure Mr. Sebastian Arundell was predisposed against her. Had he not referred to her as a street wench? And how alarmed she'd felt at his countenance when he'd rounded the bend. With spectacles and a book in hand, he was studious looking but with the fierce mien of a stern schoolmaster. The look soon changed, becoming less formidable, but his was a cynical soul, she was certain. Behind those spectacles she sensed the strict, proper countenance of a barrister or a cold clergyman, one that would stand upon the letter of the law and be anything but helpful to a woman in her circumstances. Yet what recourse did she have? The younger Mr. Arundell had promised this man would help. With little hope of success, she breathed a silent prayer that God would grant her favour as she spoke.

"You will scarcely credit my history, sir," she began, "for 'tis most unusual. I was raised by my mama, who died, I am sad to say, a year and six months ago; and Mrs. Baxter, a wealthy widow—er, *at one time wealthy*, that is—the dearest friend of my mother's."

"Your father?" Sebastian asked.

Frannie blushed and swallowed. "Well, my father, sir, is a nobleman—."

"Who is he?"

The blush deepened. "As I said, I was raised by my mama, and given the assurance that my father guaranteed a trust fund for my use upon my majority."

"And what is his name?" Sebastian persisted.

Frannie looked apologetic and now the blush ran to the roots of her hair. She clasped her hands uncertainly. "My mother and father had a great falling out of some kind. She— refused to speak of him. She never so much as gave me his name, his full name, that is. She said my future was secure only so long as I stayed wide of his family. I assume his name was Fanshawe."

Only with careful control did Sebastian's face not reveal his instant appraisal of this admission. Miss Fanshawe was a blow by!

She continued on, having little choice but to lay out her circumstances as best she could. "I was given the name of Mr. Charles Fanshawe, of Cheapside. His identity was only just furnished to me by Mrs. Baxter."

"A nobleman? In Cheapside? By name of *mister*?"

Frannie shifted in her seat. "Mrs. Baxter said he must be my uncle; the case is puzzling, I own, but that the trust fund exists there can be no doubt. We received annual sums all my life, and they came, I was told, from the interest of the trust."

"Did you never ask to meet your father?"

She shifted again, her fingers gripping the edges of the seat. "My mother gave me to believe he had died, and so of course that is what I accepted as true. I never thought to question what I was told. But—a fortnight ago—Mrs. Baxter revealed that my father *lives!* Yet she had only the name of Mr. Fanshawe of Cheapside, which made me wonder whether it was he. Mrs.Baxter was inclined to think he must know all the particulars of my case. And if this is true, he will know the identity of my father."

She blinked back tears. "I—I know how irregular this must seem to you, sir. I assure you, I had rather not pursue the matter, for 'tis mortifying! Only Mrs. Baxter left debts, you see. Apparently, while Mama and Mrs. Baxter allowed me to dress fashionably and for us all to live in comfort, debts were accruing all along. Mama should have given all of our income to Mrs. Baxter, whatever was sent on my behalf. But instead they chose to allow me to believe we suffered no want. I am afraid I—I gave all my means to cover the debts." Frannie swallowed, valiantly not letting the lump in her throat that assailed her at every thought of her *dearest* Mama and Mrs.

Baxter, get the better of her. Nor would she think about those horrible shopkeepers who descended upon the house and hounded her until she parted with nearly all she possessed.

"She left debts, you say. Has she absconded?"

"D-died, sir, a fortnight ago. Everything I've told you, she gave me to understand upon her deathbed." Frannie hated the waver in her voice. But she added, "She's in heaven now, God rest her soul."

His eyes pierced hers. "I am sorry for your loss. But you paid her debts? From your own means?"

"I paid all I could. I gave almost all I had, but it wasn't enough!"

"Great Scot!" he said. "You gave all you had?"

She stifled back a sob. "It wasn't enough. They have taken the house and all we owned. I had to dismiss cook, and our manservant and laundrymaid; and then last night—as if my troubles were too small—my purse was snatched! I now have only what is contained in my portmanteau and a single trunk!" She dabbed at her eyes.

"Had you no advisor? No one to counsel that you could not be held responsible for this Mrs. Baxter's debts?"

To his frowning look, she said, "Mrs. Baxter was ever, only, all kindness to me and my mother. How could I not endeavour to settle her accounts?"

To himself, he thought, *kind enough to leave you in debt!* But all he said was, "Was she a relation?"

"No, sir, a dear friend, the dearest of friends!" Again she blinked away wetness on her lashes and held a handkerchief to her nose until she'd conquered the moment.

To Sebastian, the case was now utterly clear. Miss Fanshawe was, in plain terms, an illegitimate brat that had managed to grow up in genteel circumstances. But wishing to know as much from curiosity as from necessity, he asked, "And how old are you?"

"I am but nineteen, sir."

"So, if there is a trust, you have no legal access to it yet." Gently he added, "No way to ascertain, even, that it exists, or that your father, if he lives, will acknowledge you."

Frannie's large eyes revealed the tumult in her heart. How foolish of her to suppose she could find help from a respectable gentleman of means! He had the disinterested mien of a magistrate and would of course find her case to be shocking. With a despairing heart, she said, eyes lowered, "Mr.—Mr. Fanshawe must be my connexion to the funds. That is what Mrs. Baxter tried to tell me. But sir, when I attempted to see him—as I told the younger Mr. Arundell—" here she gave a tearful glance to Edward, sitting silently in his seat; she swallowed, and finally conquering the urge to cry, finished, "This is the capstone of my misfortunes thus far— his wife turned me away! She—she said I was out to *grabble* what was not rightfully mine! So now it is quite impossible for me to discover more particulars of the case!"

He folded his hands upon the table, listening keenly. "So you are in dire straits, with no funds until this, er, trust is opened?"

Frannie nodded unhappily, her chocolate eyes pleading with him from their hopeless, troubled depths.

A sudden doubt crossed Sebastian's mind: that the whole presentation was a fabrication, a means of soliciting sympathy with an eye for financial gain. Everything about Miss Fanshawe *appeared* utterly earnest, herself a blend of innocence and sensibility, her grief for recent losses seemingly of the gravest nature; but he seemed to recall hearing of similar elaborate ruses done by such innocent looking actors as this woman, and perpetrated on those foolish enough to believe the lies.

Miss Fanshawe leaned forward earnestly, looking quite pretty with cheeks rosy with emotion, and her large eyes appearing larger than ever.

"Sir—despite the unhappy mystery of my heritage, which I *know* you can only despise—" she looked away. "Indeed, I despise it myself," she said, looking down at her hands. She looked up. "I beg of you: only point me to the proper authorities, someone who might help me gain an audience with Mr. Fanshawe, and I will trouble you no more. Believe me, sir, when I say I take no pleasure in asking! I am beyond mortification! I am painfully aware that I am, at this moment, very little different from a common—street urchin!" She bit her lip, blinked back tears, and refused to meet his eyes.

Sebastian, feeling his heart strings reluctantly moving toward this creature, said gently, "Normally such a dilemma could be easily resolved by applying to the benefactor of the trust; for he is the man, and the only man, with power to change the terms and relieve your current distress." His look hardened as he added, "But for that you must know his identity." He did not say the words that had flown to his mind, *if he indeed exists.*

Frannie's lips tightened as she fought to control a sense of panic or the urge to give way to tears. It was too, too, vexing! She didn't use to cry easily; it must be because of Mrs. Baxter's sudden death, and then, on its heels, the discovery that the inheritance she claimed to be leaving Frannie— enough to last until her trust could be obtained—was sadly dried up, according to the barrister who settled her affairs. It had all gone to long-standing debts that Frannie had known nothing about, the same debts that had swallowed up Frannie's funds. And now even their home had been taken from her on account of the arrears! She'd end up in the poor house, no doubt! How glad she was now that neither her mama nor Mrs. Baxter had lived to see this day. Mrs. Baxter's barrister had refused to take on Frannie's case, to try and locate her trust monies. She should have known then that it was hopeless.

Haltingly, she tried to explain this to Sebastian. Bits and pieces leaked out until he knew as much as she did regarding the trust. By the time she had done, he was certain he was dealing with an illegitimate pauper, but not a deceptive trickster. She was as genteel and well-spoken as any lady of his acquaintance, and still had not requested a shilling. The trust fund, sadly, was no doubt an invention of her mother's, a flight of fancy.

She went on to relate the details of how her reticule—her last remaining funds in it—had been napped the day before as she was jostled by a crowd on the street after she left the Fanshawes' house, reeling from the injustice of being turned away.

As he listened to Frannie, Sebastian found himself wishing her case was not so bedeviled. It was with something surprisingly close to regret that he had to accept his first deductions as true. Miss Fanshawe was a well-dressed, well-bred, blow-by orphan without a half-pence to her name. As such, she was the lowest of the low on the scale of gentility. He'd kept his countenance carefully neutral as he heard the sorry tale. But he took a breath now and asked, "Have you no other relations?"

"None I know of, sir," she said, hardly above a whisper, and with a sinking in her breast. *Why should he espouse her cause? Why would anyone?* "I have one friend, Mrs. Baxter's brother. But he is not a man of means. I did not wish to be a burden to him." In another second she hurriedly added, "Nor do I wish to burden you with my case, sir! Only I am come to such a pass—I know not what to do!"

Sebastian nodded, unsurprised. Only desperation would bring such a creature to this scene. "I understand you, Miss Fanshawe."

Edward had remained conspicuously silent until now, but at these words gave his brother a look of vast relief. "Well done, sir! I knew how it would be," he added, looking at Frannie. "When my brother isn't up to his nose in business or one of his books, he can be a vastly reasonable fellow."

Sebastian returned this dubious praise with a dour look. "Escort our guest to the parlour while I think upon what we can do for her."

Frannie's expressive eyes filled with hope. "Oh, Mr. Arundell! Sir! I hardly know how to thank you," she said in her earnest voice, coming to her feet.

"Don't thank me yet," Sebastian replied honestly. "I am in truth not at all certain that I can in any way relieve your distress." As Edward led the young woman out of the room, he turned back to give Sebastian a disapproving glare. He ought to have sounded more hopeful, Edward thought. At the very least he was sure his brother would never consign this lovely creature to the street! There must be *something* they could do for her.

The thought plagued him so much that he left Miss

Fanshawe seated in the parlour by herself, begging to be excused, and with the assurance that he should return in a minute. He met Sebastian just leaving the morning room.

"You're a Job's comforter, an't you?" he cried, at sight of him. "You could have said something more kindly to her!"

"And you could have done me the honour of not bringing a penniless orphan to my door!"

Edward grimaced. "She's an heiress."

"If she's an heiress, I'm the Prince Regent," he returned smoothly. "You never did tell me how you know her."

Edward sighed. "I nearly ran 'er down."

Sebastian's eyes flared. "With *my* curricle, which you stole—again! We'd not have this young woman on our hands if you'd kept your paws off my property. I'm withholding your stipend."

A hearty argument ensued, and only because they were still on the ground floor did Frannie, in the first floor parlour, not hear a word of it. All of Edward's arguments fell upon deaf ears, that he'd be forced to take vowels at cards, he'd have the duns at his heels, he'd not be welcome at his favorite coffee house, nor able to obtain a newly bespoken jacket; but finally Sebastian cried, "No more of this!"

"That's fine for you, you're all flush in the pocket!"

"We have that unfortunate creature to deal with."

Edward paused, and then said slyly, "She's an amiable, attractive unfortunate, you must grant her that." Sebastian always displayed impeccable manners to the softer sex, and he hoped to play upon his brother's gallantry.

"That is not to the point," Sebastian replied without offering a syllable of disagreement. He was aware of Miss Fanshawe's feminine virtues, but determined, with the usual air of disinterest, to ignore them. "It won't answer. My suggestion is that you give her £10 and be done with her."

"I!" cried Edward.

"I shall provide the blunt. You may give it to her, though, with our best wishes for her future happiness."

Edward's jaw dropped. "You hen-hearted, cowardly cove! You won't face 'er yourself?"

Sebastian's features hardened. "*You* took her case the moment she entered the curricle. You must deal with her."

In a careless tone Edward said, "Well, then, as you're letting me deal with her as I see fit; haply I've already welcomed her as our guest."

"Which was a grave error and shall be immediately redressed." In case there was any remaining doubt as to his meaning, he added in a severe tone, "She *cannot* stay."

"That's your judgment, is it? The best you can do for a helpless female in distress?"

Sebastian scowled. "Even you, cork-brained as you are, should know there is nothing more I can do. We are not an alms-house."

"You can look into her claim. Locate the father. Interview the relation who turned her aside."

"Which may all but prove impossible and/or pointless and/or both!" he returned hotly.

"But it must be tried," insisted Edward, "Before we turn her out!"

Sebastian, looking grim, accompanied his brother to the staircase. He didn't wish to distress Miss Fanshawe further, but he must keep his wits about him. Had she been a young man, or a woman reeking of the street, he would have had no qualms about throwing her out. It wasn't right, was it, that a pretty face and gentility of manners should influence the case? With compressed lips, he resigned himself to facing the muslin threat that, to his mind, was most unwelcome and must be got rid of.

C H A P T E R   T H R E E

Before the brothers had climbed the top step, Mrs. Arundell met them with a delighted smile. She was a lithe figure though in her late forties, and exuded an air of surprising youthfulness.

"I've seen her," she said, with sparkling eyes.

The brothers exchanged a surprised glance. Sebastian quickly interjected, "Good morning to you, too, Mama, and may I assume you're recovered from the headache?"

"Oh, yes," she said airily. "Binnie gave me a tonic last night. I woke up with the headache, but now 'tis completely gone! Binnie is worth a hundred servants." With hardly a pause, she went on, "I must thank you, Beau, for heeding me for once and finding this girl upon so short notice! I own it is a great relief, for now I may attend the ball this Thursday evening. You know I do not like to go out without a companion, not with my woeful deformity."

"Dearest, tisn't a deformity, for the thousandth time!" Sebastian exclaimed.

"Oh, a defect, then. Ever since I took that horrid fall—you know what it did to my hearing." Her face took on a tragic look as she added, "As if being an *ace of spades* wasn't enough!"

"Mama, there is no shame in widowhood! I've said it before—"

"Oh, but everyone knows my income isn't what it was

when your father was alive. In any case, I particularly do not want to miss this ball, not with Her Royal Highness attending. Mornay, too, you know, with his pretty new lady."

But Sebastian's face was a picture of concern. "Mama, a companion? Miss Fanshawe is—"

"Quite young, yes! I see that. Have no fear, Beau! I think, indeed, she is just the thing, I am sure we will suit. And the younger ones aren't nearly as particular as older dames, you know, who don't want to interpret conversations for me, because they cannot *remember* them! Which is the precise reason I need their service!"

Sebastian and Edward exchanged another glance, while she continued, "I was only just ready to decline the invitation—for this is not a public ball, as you know—so imagine my delight when I poked my head into the parlour to remind you, in case you were in that room because I didn't find you in the library or study, to find me a new companion. And there she was! A very genteel looking girl," she said, nodding with satisfaction.

"Did you approach her, Mama?"

"No. She didn't see me." Her features fell into a look of concern. "I'm sure she'll come around when she grows accustomed to it—being a companion, you know."

"Come around?" asked Sebastian, giving Edward a cautious look.

"Well, she looked rather blue-devilled. I believe she must be under some financial duress that forces her to take a situation? It is lowering, to be sure, but I've no doubt that once she is comfortable here, she will come around. I'm not such a drab that I'll keep her under lock and key! We'll go about town just as I used to. Perhaps, if she is truly as genteel as her appearance, and if she comes from good family, I may even introduce her as an acquaintance. Perhaps I can offer a lower wage if I promise this advantage!" Mama was always seeking ways to economize—at Sebastian's urging—though she wasn't usually successful in her attempts.

But at the words, "If she comes from good family," Sebastian made a sound in his throat. She had waved him to silence with a hand, but now he said, "Dearest," turning her so that they could complete their ascension of the stairs. "That is Miss Fanshawe in the parlour. And she is not at all suitable to your purpose."

Mrs. Arundell's face fell. "But whyever not? She is the picture of gentility, and I always like a pretty face. I'm too old to have pretensions for my own appearance—"

"Nonsense!" cried Sebastian.

"Not a whit!" echoed Edward. "Why all the swells say of you—"

"Pray, spare us from what all the swells say!" Sebastian interjected hotly. "'Tis perfectly plain that you, Mama, are still a handsome woman, and let that be the end of it." All this while, the brothers spoke in extra loud tones.

She smiled. "Thank you, my dears. In any case, I do prefer a pleasant face, and I daresay when Miss Fanshawe has got used to her new situation, she will be quite the pleasantest face in this establishment."

"Mama—" began Sebastian, but Edward took his arm.

"She is the perfect candidate to be your companion," finished Edward, giving his brother a look as though he were a scatter brain. "Hush!" he cried, beneath his breath.

"This won't answer!" returned Sebastian in an equally low tone.

"Boys, boys, you must speak louder! You know my deformity!"

"Defect, mama!" pleaded Edward.

"Affliction," said Sebastian. "For goodness' sake, just call it an affliction," he begged.

"Call it what you like, I loathe it," she replied. "I am quite deaf and you must speak louder."

Nevertheless the brothers continued their conversation in hushed tones. "Don't you see?" hissed Edward. "This answers perfectly! She can stay as Mama's companion, no impropriety, no questions asked, while you look into her claims. If she is an heiress, you'll save her fortune, and in the meantime, Mama will have her social life back."

"I do not like it."

"Don't be a loggerhead!"

"Don't be a gudgeon!" Sebastian replied, in a heated whisper.

"Oh, I see how 'tis," said their mama. "You don't wish me to hear. Well, take me into your Miss Fanshawe and let us have our introduction. I shall see what her terms are."

"Mama," said Edward. "Don't trouble your head. Sebastian will take care of all that."

"Will I?" Sebastian intoned. "Am I the housekeeper now?"

Mrs. Spencer was of course the usual personage to interview and secure new help, but Edward merely shrugged. "You've always been the tactful one in the family. Miss Fanshawe didn't come on a recommendation or with papers. You'll have to secure her; and we'll inform Spence that she needn't take the trouble of any further interviews." Edward's ears had been boxed as a youngster for dubbing the nickname on their housekeeper, but over time it had stuck. He fancied the stout woman employed for two decades as their housekeeper had even grown to enjoy the designation.

All this time Mrs. Arundell had been watching them with perplexity, for her skill at lip reading left much to be desired, and all efforts at it failed her now. "What are you boys disagreeing on?" she asked.

"Nothing of import, Mama," Edward said. "Go and have an early nuncheon, and we'll see to getting your new companion settled." After kissing her hand and bowing her off, they approached the parlour. Sebastian had one more objection. "If Miss Fanshawe is very genteel, she will shrink from hiring herself out."

Edward said, "When her alternative is poverty and the street? I think not!"

Sebastian ground out between tight lips, "You had ought to have brought her to a clergyman!"

"To send her to the poorhouse? I didn't even think of it, if you must know. I heard of her fortune and thought my elder brother, an intelligent and enterprising man—for even I can acknowledge you are considered as decent a buck as anyone—would do the pretties by her. Take care of the tangle."

"That's what solicitors and barristers are for," Sebastian replied.

But Edward turned to look behind him at his brother and said, "She can little afford either! And you are more than capable of untangling this hobble, I've no doubt."

Sebastian eyed him with his usual dispassion. "She will refuse. No properly bred young woman will accept a servant's situation."

"A companion ain't like a servant!" hissed Edward. "All

the old cathedrals these days have companions, they don't attend a ball or rout without 'em, and they're as respectable as you please."

"Are you referring to our mother as an old cathedral? She'd swoon if she heard!"

"O' course not," cried Edward. "I only meant that a companion is just the thing, these days. Miss Fanshawe won't be insulted."

"I suspect she will," said Sebastian. "And then I'll send her packing."

It took only a few minutes for the gentlemen to ascertain that Miss Fanshawe was more than equal to serving as a companion for Mrs. Arundell. It had never occurred to Frannie that she might be of some service to the household, but the thought filled her with relief and gratitude. She wasn't merely a pauper relying on their charity; now she would be of use to them. At the first mention of the situation, she closed her eyes and exclaimed, "Oh, thank God! I can be useful to you!" She looked up with eyes alight. "My prayer was, if you would be a blessing to me in my distress, that I would also bless this family in turn!"

Sebastian seemed at a loss by this reaction, for he hadn't expected anything of the sort. He explained her duties, expecting objections to erupt, but she remained calm, eager to please, nodding sagely. Chief among her responsibilities, she was assured, was to listen to conversations and help their mama understand the gist so that she might participate, answer questions correctly, and hopefully without appearing as deaf as she was. They explained the terrible fall on the stairs six months prior which had resulted in utter unconsciousness and such injury that they feared the worst. Mrs. Arundell had finally come awake and seemed no worse for the episode, save that her hearing suffered lasting harm.

Frannie felt uncommonly suited for the role of companion. Indeed, it filled her heart with oddly familiar warmth, for Mrs. Baxter had been much older than she, and their relationship was almost the same. For most of her life, Mrs. Baxter had been the superior and Frannie, younger, the inferior. Both understood that upon her majority Frannie would assume the superior rank on account of her wealth, but as she was not in possession of that wealth at present, it seemed entirely fitting that she ought to be in subservience to Mrs. Arundell.

By the end of the interview, Sebastian felt almost satisfied with the day's events. Miss Fanshawe's presence, which at first seemed a vexation, did indeed answer the purpose for Mama, and saved the household the trouble of finding a better applicant. Whether or not he would exert himself to study her affairs was another matter. He'd never let a pretty face sway his better judgment. In truth, he might have succumbed to the charms of countless ineligible young women and found himself ill-married but for a determination never to allow a female to turn his head for frivolous reasons. When he needed a wife, he would of course approach the softer sex in that light, searching for a possible future mate. But he wasn't looking for just a pretty face. If and when he became the next baronet of Bartlett Hall, he would want a sensible, intelligent woman by his side. Until then, he wouldn't think of displacing his mother as mistress of their home. There was no need for it. It was not to be thought of.

But Edward was a concern. Miss Fanshawe, with her ridiculously large, chocolate eyes, was just the sort of female his younger brother would be smitten by. That she was utterly without consequence would mean nothing to the pup. Had she known the name of her supposed noble father, it might have helped her case. But without his identity, the idea of a trust could only appear as a desperate hope, a wish, a longing, a prayer. She'd referred to her parents "tragic marriage," but he doubted there had been a marriage. Miss Fanshawe might be an orphan or her natural father might be alive; but either way, she was a blow-by. Exactly the sort of woman no Arundell could possibly align themselves with. He'd have to keep a weather eye upon Edward, to be sure.

CHAPTER FOUR

Despite her determination to embrace life as a companion and all it must entail, Frannie was abashed at how much energy was required to make herself heard by her new mistress. She realized now why it was that Mrs. Arundell had a difficult time keeping a companion. Because of this, she was not enraptured later that day when the lady instructed that she must take meals with the family. She would almost have preferred to be consigned to the servants' hall, shrinking at the thought of raising her voice at table. Too, she was conscious of her new status. Ladies' companions weren't always welcome at upper class tables. What if either of the Arundell men did not think her worthy of sitting with them?

She took courage when the younger Mr. Arundell gave her a bracing smile as she settled in her seat. She hardly glanced at Sebastian, for his stern countenance could easily unsettle her, but one chance peek made her stare. She had never seen Sebastian without his spectacles before. His entire demeanor underwent a transformation. The studious looking bookworm was a Byron! Mama called such men 'handsome devils' Frannie thought, though she saw nothing devilish about Sebastian. A strong nose and noble brow revealed keen, clear eyes that made you want to hold their attention just to look into their depths. He caught her startled gaze and she looked away, but with a sudden flutter in her stomach. What a handsome gentleman! Amazing how she had missed it, earlier.

A rich, three course meal followed, replete with lively conversation among the Arundells, to Frannie's surprise. She and Mrs. Baxter had been companionable dinner partners, but meals were mostly quiet. Here, it was quite the opposite. But both men were forced to speak every bit as loudly to their mama as she, however, so that any discomfort on that head soon dissipated.

Mrs. Arundell's favorite topic was town news, who was getting married, who had been declared a bankrupt, or who was moving into the apartments recently vacated by the French Ambassador. Edward's aim seemed to be to say as little as possible about his pursuits in the metropolis, while Sebastian plied him with questions about whether he'd been active at gaming dens, or laying bets at cock fights, or getting into fisticuff matches. About this last low pursuit he went on for some time, admonishing his brother that, if he wished seriously to comport himself as a gentleman, he must assiduously avoid street brawls. "Shows of physical strength are required only by the weak to prove themselves," he said. "Good men hunt, fish, or fence for a contest, but physical matches are repugnant to them." With a glimpse toward his mama and Frannie he added, "And even more so to ladies."

"I daresay you've forgot I'm studied in pugilism," Edward replied hotly.

"Keep your boxing to Gentleman Jim's establishment along with other young sprigs in training, and you'll do well. But I'll not hear of another street brawl. Striking a man for a provocation is the meanest sort of response I warrant a gentleman can display."

Frannie surmised that apparently Edward had been guilty

of participating in a fight that had not occurred within the bastion of Gentleman Jim's, that most famous of fisticuff instructors. Even she had read snippets about the famous boxer and his rooms on Bond Street, where he taught upper class males his art. Edward looked with supreme disinterest at his brother, as if further objections were not worth the effort. Sebastian finished his admonishments with a warning that Edward not fall into the duns again.

"I little see how I shall avoid *that,*" Edward replied, "if you withhold the blunt!"

"Dearest," said their mama to her elder son, "Are you indeed allowing dear Edward's pockets to be turned out? That looks shabby for an Arundell, my dear."

"He has only himself to thank," Sebastian returned. "I've warned him more times than I care to recall, not to conscript my carriage to carry out his cork-brained schemes without my consent."

"If I hadn't borrowed your curricle, Mama would lack a companion, for Miss Fanshawe wouldn't be here!"

"What was that?" asked the mama. "About Miss Fanshawe?"

"*I* brought her!" cried Edward gloatingly. "Not Sebastian. And for this, he persecutes me!" Sebastian eyed his brother with cool disdain. He wasn't about to attempt an explanation of the whole situation to their mama, and only nodded, with a congratulatory smirk at Edward when Mrs. Arundell went into a rapture of his defense, exclaiming that Sebastian was too hard on him and must not exact the slightest punishment, for she was *that* grateful to have Miss Fanshawe.

Frannie sat guiltily by, blushing, and would not meet Sebastian's eyes. But he declared he would come to a compromise with Edward, a settlement that seemed to satisfy Mrs. Arundell. Conversation then turned to the matter of a coming ball on Thursday evening.

"Since I will now accept the invitation, Beau, because I have a companion to help me,"—she stopped and smiled benignly upon Frannie—"you will, of course, accompany me."

Sebastian glanced at Frannie, who hurriedly looked away. She'd been admiring him furtively, still rather in awe of the high good looks that a simple pair of spectacles hid so well. His manner of dress was not meticulously fashionable like Edward's, but he exuded a far greater air of consequence and masculine presence, surprising for one she at first took for a bookish scholar.

He cleared his throat, returning his attention to his mother. "This reminds me. I've had a letter from Sir Hugo." He paused, giving his mama the opportunity to exclaim her utter astonishment that Sir Hugo had sent a communiqué of any sort to his heir, but she merely regarded him with curious expectation. Casting a keen look her way, he said, "He has accepted the invitation to that ball; he will shortly arrive in town; and begs the honour of giving *you* his escort."

Now Mrs. Arundell reacted as expected. Looking fairly amazed she cried, "Sir Hugo in London? What is that man about? He never comes to town!"

"The passing of his father must have something to do with it," offered Sebastian. "Perhaps Sir Malcolm required his presence until now; he would not be the first son to suffer an overbearing sire. Now that he's the Baronet of Bartlett Hall, and his own man—."

"Sir Malcolm was overbearing, indeed; and crotchety, to

be sure, or we might be more familiar with Bartlett Hall. He was severe upon poor Hugo, his only son; but he never cared a fig to know you boys. I daresay he thought of us as poor relations—"

"Mama! We are nothing of the sort!" replied Sebastian.

"No, of course not; but I never felt the slightest compulsion to encourage a better understanding between our families for I did not wish to subject you to his temperamental ways." She gave Sebastian a wide-eyed look. "It is all very well if Sir Hugo now wishes to become part of society. But to *presume* that I have not already accepted an escort! He is quite disagreeable in it!"

"He no doubt assumed what is most often true: that *I* would escort you. And he knows I should willingly allow him the honour in my place as he is rightly entitled to it, Mama. He is my elder in the family, my superior, not to mention, your cousin-in-law."

"How could he possibly know that *you* would accompany me!" she said scornfully.

Sebastian gave a little smile. "I am sure he reads the society columns."

But she shook her head dismissively. "In any case, really, Beau, you know better than to ask."

Sebastian placed his fork down and gave his mother a piercing look. "I am his heir; he is my uncle."

"He isn't your uncle really; he is your father's cousin, which makes him your first cousin once removed."

"True," said Sebastian, "But have we not always referred to him as my uncle?"

"Because he is older, dearest. And who wants to keep saying *your cousin once removed*?"

"There is no need for that," Sebastian said with a little smile, "but we are no children here, and for now on, I shall call him my cousin, and leave it at that."

"Call him whatever you like," his mama replied, waving a hand at him. "The important thing is, there are no other male heirs beside you and Edward."

Sebastian said, "Precisely, and for which case if he comes to town, by rights we ought to offer him hospitality. Isn't it time you let bygones be bygones—whatever it is that makes you refuse to see him? With Sir Malcolm gone, there is one less ogre for you to fear. In my past correspondence with Sir Hugo, he has always seemed very gentlemanlike and proper." He paused and gave her a penetrating look. "We had ought to be on good terms with the man who leaves his title and estate to me."

"He has no choice," replied his mama, delicately dabbing her mouth with a cloth.

She took a sip from her glass, but put it down decisively, her eyes widened. "So *that* is why he wrote to you!"

Sebastian's brows rose. "You knew?"

"Binnie saw the letter and told me of it," she explained, while moving aside just enough to allow a footman to give her a serving of cauliflower in sauce. "I daresay I thought it would be some such fiddle faddle."

Sebastian rubbed his chin, as though deliberating on what to reveal. "Actually, Mama, the biggest surprise in Sir Hugo's letter is that he wished to advise me of his intention to find a wife."

Mrs. Arundell froze. Her eyes widened. Quickly she put her fork down and sat there blinking.

"Have no fear, dearest," Sebastian hurried to say. "If he

sires an heir and disinherits me, we shall do well enough with my investments. We'd not suffer the slightest lowering in our current lifestyle, and you, I suppose, can grow accustomed to your son *not* being next in line to inherit. There is nothing you cannot countenance in it." Seeing her stricken face he added, "Perhaps I needn't have mentioned it. Perchance it may come to nothing."

"But—Hugo has ever been utterly *averse* to marriage, which I always thought nonsensical for a titled gentleman. But to change his mind now! So *that* is why he comes! He wishes to find a wife from the best circles, does he?" She stabbed her fork into a mound of boiled turnip. "Who would *wish* to marry that old clodpate!" Then, looking up as struck she said, "May I read his letter? I must hear his tone, the manner of his speech. I must determine if he is in earnest or if he seeks merely to vex me—"

"To vex *you*?" asked Sebastian. "I am sure my cousin has no wish to marry simply to vex you, dearest. 'Tis only natural a man wants an heir from his own loins, I daresay."

But Mrs. Arundell's face scrunched in distaste. "You don't know him as I do. He wishes to marry! Either his estate is out at the heels and he needs a wealthy bride, or 'tis *only* to vex me, I assure you!"

"If anyone has reason to be vexed, it is I; but I believe I can say with equal parts equanimity and honesty, that I wish him well. I wish him success. The few times I have met and spoken with my cousin—and I will continue to call him that, if it's all the same to you—I have found him nothing but amiable and good-natured. I never understood why you refused invitations from Bartlett Hall and denied us the society of our relations for most all our lives."

Mrs. Arundell hadn't heard this very well and looked to Frannie. She startled to attention, but then echoed loudly, "Mr. Arundell is *not* vexed by Sir Hugo, ma'am!"

"Yes, I caught that much," the lady said, nodding. "Refer to him as Beau for me, Frannie. That's what I call him, so you must also."

Frannie blushed, keeping her eyes on her plate.

"What else did he say?"

Frannie took a deep breath and replied with admirable volume, "He doesn't understand the difficulty between you and Sir—"

"Pray, Miss Fanshawe, do not trouble yourself," Sebastian interrupted. "My mother and I have trod this path before. She refuses to disclose the cause of their ancient argument. But more to the point, there is one other reason for his writing me, which I will inform her of." He turned to his mama and said vigorously, "Sir Hugo invites us to his home for the Christmas holidays; and I mean to accept!"

"For Christmas? So we may admire his new, simpering wife?" she said acidly.

"He hasn't found a wife yet, Mama. He wrote only to warn me that he is on the hunt." Sebastian could hardly repress a grin. "It does seem irregular for him to warn us."

Edward said, "You smile. Don't you feel the least sorry for it? To be disinherited when all your life you've been set up as the next baronet of Bartlett Hall after Sir Hugo? I daresay it disappoints *me*, and I'm not as close to it as you are."

"He's not married *yet*," replied Sebastian. "And baronetcies bring headaches and obligations as well as honours." But he returned his attention to his mother. "I shall reply by special messenger that you do not require his escort for Thursday night's ball; and that we will be happy to descend upon Bartlett Hall for the Christmas holidays."

"Wait, wait, sir!" cried his mama, as color rushed to her face. "I have not decided about Christmas! I must think on it."

Sebastian said, leaning forward gently, but speaking slowly so she might have the benefit of reading his lips, "As the head of the family, I have made the decision. I've supported your ancient grudge far too long by indulging your dislike of him; but I have no such aversion to the man; he is my elder relation. We will go, Mama."

Mrs. Arundell looked dejected. She swallowed. "If he has a new wife, I shall *not* go, no, by no means. You cannot force me, Beau."

Sebastian's mouth twisted, stifling a grin. "Mama, if I did not know better, I should say you were jealous!"

Edward too regarded his mother with a face that looked mildly embarrassed. "Indeed, Mama," he said gently—and thereby went wholly unheard.

Frannie shifted in her seat, feeling as though she were eavesdropping on private family affairs. She wished she could excuse herself. But if Mrs. Arundell didn't send her from the room, she was not at liberty to take leave. She looked imploringly at Sebastian.

Receptive green-grey eyes surveyed her and seemed to instantly comprehend her discomfort. "You must excuse our conversation, Miss Fanshawe. I'm afraid that as Mama's companion, you are fated to be included in all the familial, eh, *niceties,* otherwise known as dirt."

The matriarch apparently heard that. "Do not exaggerate, Beau! You'll give the poor girl frights! We aren't ogres; and as for being jealous, don't be absurd! I am not in the least jealous except on your account, for you are the rightful heir to the title!"

"Only if Sir Hugo has no son of his own, dearest!"

Mrs. Arundell pursed her lips, and nodding at Frannie to follow, rose from the table. The men instantly came to their feet and bowed. But their mother stopped, her head turned in thought. She leveled a defiant stare upon Sebastian. "You may reply to his letter," she said imperiously, her small nose in the air, "with the information that I will *accept* Sir Hugo's escort!"

While her sons stared in amazement, she turned on her heel and took a step but then turned back and added forcefully, "But I will not put him up, for there are inns and posting houses all over London where he may stay, or he can let rooms anywhere he likes!"

"Very *good*, Mama," said Sebastian approvingly and with no small surprise. He might have wished to open their home, but he knew a concession when he saw it and accepted it graciously. "I may count myself excused then, from the ball?"

"I suppose you may," she said, "though everyone shall ask why you aren't in attendance. You are talked of as almost a recluse, Beau." She paused, frowning. "Do you not care to see the princess?"

He gave her a patient look. "I am not averse to it, but I had my fill of balls during the season. Why there should be one now, when all the best families are at their country estates, I cannot fathom."

"Word was put out long ago," she returned. "Many of those 'best families' have harkened back to town for this event. There may be some special announcement from Her Royal Highness, I daresay."

She glanced at Frannie, whose face was frozen in amazement. Imagine it, passing up a chance to meet Princess Charlotte! Frannie had often daydreamed of meeting the Regent's daughter, who seemed to genuinely care for her subjects. She'd never known anyone who could enjoy that opportunity and now this family, the Arundells, her only benefactors in the world, had the social standing to meet her—and Sebastian wasn't interested!

Seeing Frannie's countenance, Mrs. Arundell cried, "Oh, dear, I have it! You must come, Beau, and take Frannie upon your arm. We can style her a long-lost cousin or some such thing."

Frannie's heart swelled at the thought, both of meeting the princess *and* of being upon Mr. Arundell's arm! But Sebastian's countenance darkened. "Mama, that is quite impossible. Be sure there will be some who go home and search Debrett's, or otherwise discover the falsehood. The Arundell name has never been associated with a scandal, and I wish it to remain so." Frannie's hope plummeted as quickly as it had risen. Shame brought a blush to her features. Sebastian feared her dubious background would provide fodder for gossips, occasion scandal-broth gatherings to the detriment of the family name.

Mrs. Arundell gave him quite the oddest look.

"What, do you know of a scandal?" he asked, though in a tone that made his disbelief evident.

She merely said in a fallen voice, "If I have not Frannie, then I may not accept Sir Hugo's escort. For he will discover my deformity."

"*Defect*, Mama!" Sebastian and Edward cried together.

"I have a notion about that," ventured Frannie, getting

everyone's instant attention. She said the words with a sinking heart, for her only means of subsistence and best hope was to stay on with the Arundells. If Mrs. Arundell's hearing defect was redressed, she would be out of a situation. But her heart refused to remain silent. The poor woman was clearly tormented by the problem. Frannie knew of a solution and must speak. She looked at Sebastian. "If I may have use of a carriage to call upon Mrs. Baxter's brother—he resides in the warehouse district—I believe he has an instrument that will help your mother's affliction." With all eyes still upon her, Frannie felt a blush steal across her cheeks.

Mrs. Arundell said, "Thank you, Frannie dear, but I could never use that monstrous hearing trumpet, such as the one Earl Brent goes about with. I have a horror of such a device!"

Frannie said, "No, ma'am, the one I have in mind is quite small."

"You know of a small instrument that can help a hearing defect?" Sebastian inquired.

She nodded. "I do, sir. I have seen it work for someone who is similarly afflicted with the impairment. Mrs. Baxter's brother, one Mr. Withers, is something of an inventor, sir. If he is still making the devices, your mama can safely keep her engagement...." In a low tone, she added, "without me."

Sebastian eyed her keenly, but Edward cried, "Impairment! I daresay, that answers better than *defect*! We must only call it only an impairment, Mama!"

But Sebastian's attention was still on Frannie. "You know where to find Mr. Withers?"

She nodded. "I know the street name."

He surveyed her with cautious optimism. "Very well. I think we must acquire this marvel."

"Mama," put in Edward, "you could allow *me* the honour of taking you to the ball. I can translate conversation for you. Sebastian cares nothing for society, for it always welcomes him. He can rub shoulders with anyone he likes, all the *ton*, any blue blood, whilst I am completely ignored and overlooked. A younger son must have *some* right to society, and if you will go upon my arm it will raise my consequence."

"You have no consequence," said Sebastian, with an arched brow, "None to begin with, and you will not prevent my mother from extending this olive leaf to Sir Hugo. It hasn't come betimes!"

Frannie's brows rose. The lack of accord between the brothers surprised her, though she had no experience of siblings other than in the families of her acquaintance from the village where she'd grown up.

Mrs. Arundell smiled fondly at Edward. "Do not take it to heart, dear. Your brother is to inherit a baronetcy. He is of course good *ton* on that account." All this while the four adults had been standing at the table, ever since Mrs. Arundell had risen to leave. She now turned once more to go but stopped and said to Frannie, "In the morning, Beau will take you to town." To Sebastian's knit brows, she added, "Your curricle is open, my love; there's no need for a chaperon. And if Miss Fanshawe knows of anything that can ameliorate this dreadful deformity"—Sebastian ground his teeth—"then we must have it!" she finished, smiling upon first Frannie and then her son.

"I could take her," muttered Edward, giving his brother a look of some resentment.

"I wouldn't dream of putting Miss Fanshawe's life in such danger as that," returned Sebastian instantly. Frannie's heart went out for the younger brother, but she said nothing. It was not her place; and she could not dislike the thought of Mr. Sebastian Arundell accompanying her.

CHAPTER FIVE

The following morning found Frannie with an unsettled stomach. She was acutely conscious that she was to spend time in Sebastian's company. She'd prayed thoroughly that morning for the success of the mission, but hadn't thought to pray for her own poor nerves. When she was seated on the board beside him, she could not help but notice the understated elegance of his figure and dress; or his manners, which were so fine as to make her think he had forgot that she was not perfectly respectable. Was it mere condescension? He'd handed her up to the seat with gentle assiduity. He'd checked to be sure she was ready before giving the reins a slap. He'd inquired if her redingote was sufficiently warm, or would she like a carriage blanket?

En route to the shopping district and the particular street she remembered, she took the opportunity to inquire why the house was kept conspicuously dim in the evenings, for it seemed so to her the prior evening when she had sat in the parlour with Mrs. Arundell. The lady busily worked a tapestry with thread by the barest candlelight, though she chatted companionably about the running of the household, telling Frannie about the usual coming and going of its inhabitants.

"My mother has a dread of fires," Sebastian explained with a little smile. "When she was a child, a tragical blaze broke out on Upper Grosvenor Street and burned itself, you might say, into her brain. Lady Molesworth and much of her family, besides servants, perished in it. My mother cannot forget the horror."

He turned a corner onto a wide avenue and said, "But let me inquire of you; what evidence do you have, or can you recall, that proves the existence of your noble benefactor?"

Frannie's face scrunched into thought. "Besides my mother's assurances?" She reflected on it a moment. "Mrs. Baxter revealed to me, sir, as she lay dying—" here she had to stop and conquer the now familiar streak of sorrow that rose in her breast for the losses of both her dearest mama and dear Mrs. Baxter—"that what sustained us all my life were interest payments from a trust set aside by my father. She said there was a family feud of some kind; that he was alive but my mother insisted upon the separation." She turned to him with earnest eyes. "This was the first I ever heard of his being alive, I assure you; my history as my mama gave it, was that my papa died at sea when I was an infant. I had always believed the trust provided only for the smallest part of our upkeep, and that Mrs. Baxter was to be thanked for the better part of it. Indeed, I considered myself so deeply obliged to her that I felt duty-bound to cover her debts when they were presented to me."

He nodded, listening as he handled the team. "What precisely did she say of your father?"

Frannie shook her head. "All that she knew. But unfortunately my mother, for reasons known only to herself, never disclosed the details of her marriage or separation. All Mrs. Baxter could tell me for certain is that my father is very much alive; and has a title. This much she had from my mother, but no more." Her face crumpled. "But she assured me, oh, in the strongest terms!" She gave him a look of utmost earnestness "That just as my mother said, there was a trust in my name, guaranteed upon my majority! Mrs. Baxter was exceedingly devout, a strict adherent of our faith, I assure you, and would never have invented such things!"

"Sebastian had fallen silent, but now he said, "His supporting you all your life speaks well of his character, but there is no nobleman with the name of Fanshawe, and your mother, I presume, did not style herself Lady Fanshawe, or Lady something or other?"

"She did not," Frannie admitted, shaking her head.

"Why would a woman not use every honour her marriage afforded?"

Frannie thought hard and remembered something. "Mrs. Baxter said there must exist between my parents an agreement; one that guaranteed our income only so long as she waived the use of her title and all other marital rights."

"Would she agree so far as to keep secret the very name of the father of her child, when to do so must surely give an appearance of a disrespectable nature?"

"As for that, Mrs. Baxter said my mother feared I should take it into my head to seek out my father. She—she must have had a dread of him! Mrs. Baxter said I ought to follow my mother's example, for we know not what manner of man he is, except that his generosity was most uncharacteristic, as many men separated from a wife give no such support or notice."

"You are certain they were legally wed?" asked Sebastian.

Frannie stared at him, momentarily bereft of speech. "Thunder!" she said lightly. "If they were not—God forbid, sir! But—but—of course they were!" she cried, finally. The idea of their not being married had not occurred to Frannie.

But suddenly she had a thought and undid the top frog fastener of her redingote. She felt beneath the ruff of her gown and presently pulled out a chain bearing a gold ring. "What a goose I am!" she said, greatly relieved. "This was my mother's wedding ring." She held it out for Sebastian to see, though he could take only a passing look, as he was driving. It appeared to be of gold.

"But if they were married," Sebastian said, endeavouring to sound merely sensible and not judgmental, "would you not know, at the very least, your father's name? And why did they live apart?"

Flustered, she gripped the seat, staring ahead. "My mother did not wish me to know him—I think we must surmise this much—though I have not the slightest knowledge why." A worse suspicion suddenly interposed itself onto her brain. What if it was her father who did not wish to be known? What if, for some unsavoury reason, he was willing to send support, but required absolute anonymity? She felt an awful horror as the implications played in her mind. Her father might be furious if she found him out. Perhaps he would somehow rescind the trust.

And what if the direction of Mr. Arundell's thoughts, that she was illegitimate, had any bearing in truth? He doubted the marriage had taken place. Suddenly it seemed reasonable to doubt it. Dread and confusion filled her breast as she realized that the implication was not his, but embedded in her circumstances. Why *didn't* she know the name of her father? Why, if he and her mother *were* married, had they not lived as man and wife? Suddenly it seemed absurdly obvious that Mr. Arundell's thought must be correct. Oh, thunder! Was it *true*? Why hadn't she realized it? Why hadn't Mama or Mrs. Baxter told her?

Frannie swallowed as a hollow thud resounded in her being. Sebastian was right. Her mother would surely have kept the title of 'lady,' even separated from her husband. What Englishwoman would not? Agreeing to keep wide of the man was one thing; but to dispense with every right of marriage—that seemed too fantastic a possibility.

Sebastian gave her a sideways, dubious look. "If there was a marriage and a subsequent separation, your father could not legally marry again and sire an heir." Frannie nodded, miserably aware that he was perfectly right. A nobleman would sooner pursue a divorce, no matter how difficult to obtain, than support a wife secretly when the estrangement left him without an heir. Suddenly a remarkable thought filled her breast. "Sir!" she cried, turning to Sebastian, her face alight.

He looked over and almost smiled at the lovely vision.

"I wonder if I have a brother!" she cried. "Perhaps my parents' falling out occurred after his birth. Or perhaps we are—twins! Separated when they parted ways. My mother took me, and he got his heir! It would answer as to why he would not seek a divorce!"

Sebastian's brow creased. "I'll make some inquiries," he said. Secretly he thought the idea too fantastical to hold any real merit, but somehow he was not averse to investigating the matter for this lovely, gentle creature. She was earnest and hopeful and young. She was already a blessing to his mama. He must help her if he could.

He said, "If interest payments are still forthcoming, and the agreement was for you to keep yourself scarce, it may not be advantageous to seek out this man."

"But recall, sir, that I used all I had to pay Mrs. Baxter's debts, and it is just December. The interest will not come until the end of March, if I am not mistaken. And now, when the duns have taken everything from me, I have no choice but to find my father!"

Frannie remembered nearly word for word the terrible bills of indictment she'd been served, saying "the penalties and forfeitures of the departed are to be recovered by the distress and sale of the offender's goods and chattels..." She swallowed and continued, "They would not heed my assurance that I would, as soon as I had it in my power, pay all. *Dear* Mrs. Baxter assured me so vehemently that I am to inherit a fortune that I could in good conscience promise repayment. But they heeded me not. So you see I *must* seek him out. I find myself quite homeless—except for the kindness of your family, sir."

Sebastian considered it propitiously fortunate for Miss Fanshawe's sake, that Edward had championed her cause. He had saved her, perhaps, from starvation, for she was an absolute pauper! And on his hands. They drove without speaking for some minutes while he thought it over. The fortune, he was certain, could not exist; to attempt to track it would mean following a vale of tears. It could only bring heartache to his young companion and put him in the unenviable position of making delicate inquiries among the *ton* about a blow-by child no nobleman of his acquaintance would desire to have known.

"How do you receive the annual payment?"

"That is precisely the dilemma, sir. Mrs. Baxter knew only that my mother received it by post. I have no means of receiving it now that our home is lost to me. I left word with the postmaster, of course, that I would furnish a new direction at the soonest possible time, for it must come." She paused and added with a determined nod of her head, "Anything that comes my way, I will of course turn over to you."

Sebastian looked faintly horrified and hurriedly said, "That will *not* be necessary, Miss Fanshawe."

She swallowed and added, "That does relieve my mind, I own, sir; for I still consider Mrs. Baxter's debts to be mine; they are debts of—of honour!" she said, nobly. "I must repay them and redeem what's been lost."

Sebastian could not help but smile at that. But he said, "If they've taken possession of the house and furnishings, you might honourably and in good conscience consider her debts paid."

"But I *want* to buy it back!" Frannie said earnestly. "I grew up in that house; all my memories are there." She clung to those of her mama, which to her seemed inextricable from the house.

"I find it difficult to fathom that your Mrs. Baxter never extricated the name of your father from your mama. You lived with her for years, you said."

"All my life," nodded Frannie. After a moment she said, "Perhaps she believed he was dead, too. I wonder if my mother told her when she died—that was a year ago August— that he was alive."

"I wonder she didn't pass on the information to you at that time."

Frannie sighed. "I wish she had. But it was only as Mrs. Baxter lay dying and could hardly speak at all that she told me, and then she gave only the name of Charles Fanshawe. She was quite sure he was not my father, but an uncle. This must be true, for as you pointed out, there is no title." Again she sighed, this time deeply. "When I found his home, I had hoped to explain my predicament, and—foolishly, you will say!—thought he might look favourably upon me and welcome me as a relation; at least until the trust is secured. But as I told young Mr. Arundell your brother, his wife took an instant horror when I appeared, and told me I was—an—an *impostor*!" Here Frannie's voice broke and she continued only with some difficulty. "She said the only Miss Fanshawe they would acknowledge was her d—dear child, and I should never receive aught at their hands!"

Sebastian stared at her strangely for a moment at this revelation. Unthinkingly, he took the reins in one gloved hand so he could pat hers, which were folded upon her lap. "Is that what she said?" he asked, mildly.

"Yes, sir. I know it seems a muddle! And perhaps too deep for you to unravel…!" Sebastian frowned, but kept his eyes upon the road. Frannie continued, "She also said that if I had the cheek—the p-pluck—to return, she would summon a magistrate or Charley to haul me to King's Bench!" She blinked back tears. "It is a terrible thing, sir, to find yourself friendless on the streets of London." She turned her large, chocolate eyes up to his, and Sebastian found himself saying, "Poor child." But something in her account had given him second thoughts. "Did you say anything at all about a trust fund to Mrs. Fanshawe?"

Frannie thought for a moment. "No. Only that I was a relation and hoped to know them. I asked if I might have an audience with Mr. Fanshawe."

Sebastian's eyes narrowed. "In that case, methinks the lady doth protest too much." He turned to Frannie's puzzled eyes.

"She knew what you were after, or supposed she did. That is, she must be aware of some prize, the trust, let us say; and hopes her own daughter will receive it."

Frannie gasped. Suddenly Mrs. Fanshawe's cold antipathy made sense. "Thunder! I fear you are right. She said the *only Miss Fanshawe* they would *acknowledge* was her own child."

"Precisely. But acknowledge to *whom*?" Sebastian asked. "If this Charles Fanshawe is your father, he would know of a certainty that *their* daughter is not meant to be the recipient of a fund he put aside for the *illegitimate* child." He glanced over. "Begging your pardon, Miss Fanshawe."

She nodded, lips pursed, at the odious words. *Illegitimate child.* Since her mother's death she had believed herself to be an orphan, but the truth, this reminded her, might be far, far worse! She might be the result of a union outside of marriage! Her face coloured rosily.

But now it seemed to Sebastian that Miss Fanshawe's case might have merit. She was still illegitimate, to be sure, but that she might indeed be entitled to a fortune of some substantial amount seemed probable. Why else would Mrs. Fanshawe have been so hostile? Unless she hoped to secure it for her own daughter? There were cases where men had treated their illegitimate offspring with largesse, sometimes granting them lesser titles, even. If Frannie's sire was extremely wealthy, he might in fact be liberal enough to grant her some fortune of her own.

He turned to his companion with fresh energy. "I suspect this man, as you yourself surmised, must have full knowledge of the trust and is involved in the business, though I have yet to ascertain what his role is, or has been."

As they turned a busy corner, he said, "Tell me again what

you said to Mrs. Fanshawe when you arrived at her doorstep. Word for word, if you please." He listened closely, as they had reached the bustling warehouse district and had to speak above the din of street vendors, besides much traffic of other carriages, wagons and carts.

Frannie thought back to the horrible encounter. She took a shuddering breath. "I told her my name, Frances Fanshawe, and claimed to be a relation. I trusted that when my name was given to Mr. Fanshawe, he would grant me an audience so I could plead my case. At the very least I hoped to ascertain, with his help, temporary lodging whose direction I could furnish to the postmaster."

"And the lady flew into the boughs immediately?" he asked, his eyes keenly stealing glances at her while he maneuvered the equipage along the busy street. It wasn't the highbrow shopping district of the upper class, and Sebastian wished they'd come in a closed carriage, for their presence was being noted by many on the street.

Frannie nodded unhappily. "No sooner than I claimed the connexion. She seemed astonished and demanded to know how I'd found them; and then went on to insult and threaten me in the most horrifying manner!" She turned to him. "I cannot say I was *entirely* surprised, for I had no great hopes of being welcomed wholeheartedly by Mr. Fanshawe, were he my father, after he took such pains to remain aloof. And I can hardly blame the woman for not taking kindly to the knowledge of my existence—."

But here Sebastian interrupted her. "But it wasn't that. She resented your appearing, which suggests she *already knew* of your existence. More, that you are in pursuit of something she hopes you will not acquire. Something, I begin to believe, she covets for her own daughter." As he directed the team past a standing wagon, he added, "I daresay she has a cloven foot in the business."

Frannie looked admiringly at Sebastian. "Thunder! I warrant, sir, if you wanted employment, that Bow Street could do no better than to have you! To think, that you could see so much into the situation, when I, who experienced it, missed it entirely!"

Sebastian smiled, pleased with the approbation given with shining eyes, though of course the thought of employment was absurd. He was a gentleman. Gentlemen did not work.

"Is this the street you remember?" he asked as they turned a corner onto a bustling lane teeming even more with pedestrians and merchants of all descriptions. Carriages, berlins, calashes, wagons and carts were everywhere. Frannie scanned the scene, smiling faintly. "Yes. There's the confectioners, and fan makers; there, the glass sellers and stationers, near the printer's shop. I do not recall the soap and basket makers," she said reflectively, "but the clock maker, yes, I remember, and there, a glove makers."

"You remember it well," said Sebastian, wonderingly.

"Mrs. Baxter's sister lived…." She pointed at an apartment above the glovers. "There." She turned to him. "Before she passed away. We called upon her once a month with…" she hesitated. "A few necessaries. She had so little. We brought vegetables from the garden, cloth, when it went on sale, for she was a seamstress, and other such things we could easily spare."

Sebastian swallowed. The actions were kind, but furnished more proof of Miss Fanshawe's humble situation. This widow, Mrs. Baxter, had even humbler relations. He said hastily, "I see." And then, "Where is this Mr. Withers we seek?"

Frannie nodded and pointed. "Over there."

He pulled the curricle to a stop in front of a singularly unpromising establishment, an old Elizabethan style structure with a second storey protruding out over the first, leaning toward the street like the famed tower of Pisa. A sign, creaking from rusty hinges and badly in need of paint, proclaimed, "Peddler of All Good Things." Inwardly shaking his head with a sudden conviction that he was on a fool's errand, he motioned to Will, his boy perched on the rear of the vehicle, to take the ribbons and stand guard while he and Miss Fanshawe entered this strange mercantile.

Upon entry, his first impression was confirmed. In the sudden darkness, he could just make out murky shelves loaded with baskets piled high with wares of a dubious nature. He wrinkled his nose as a mild odor he could not identify but which was instantly abhorrent accosted him. The floor, he noted, sported a gloomy layer of dust. He expected Miss Fanshawe to draw back in disgust or exclaim that it was no longer the place she remembered, but to his surprise she sailed along, crossing the main aisle and heading determinedly toward a back room. Moving aside a curtain that separated this apartment from the rest, she stuck her head in. "Mr. Withers?" she called loudly.

Sebastian stood by, torn between perplexity and amusement. He wouldn't have believed it possible that a gently bred young woman—even one of questionable pedigree—could be at ease in such a place. But Miss Fanshawe evidently wasn't a typical squeamish miss. "Did you say Mr. Withers was also a relation of your Mrs. Baxter?"

he said in a low tone, trying not to laugh.

"He is her younger brother!"

"This gets better and better," he murmured sardonically, following her inside the room, where a little man was bent over a table at work. This apartment was brighter than the outer room, and fortunately better smelling. The man was examining something tiny with a magnifying glass and was so intent that he hadn't heard them approach.

"Mr.Withers!" Frannie exclaimed again at his elbow. He almost dropped the magnifier, but his face lit with delight when he recognized her.

"Frannie, me dear! I've been *that* worried about ye!" he exclaimed, jumping to his feet, taking her hands in his, and bowing over them. He was a small, wiry man, with a thin layer of gray curly hair, small eyes, but a beaming smile. His joyous visage turned into a frown. "When I 'eard they'd possessed me sister's 'ouse—I tried to get word to ye. But ye was gone already!" His eyes were pained. "I—I 'ave a small spare room," he began, awkwardly.

"There is no need of that," she assured him smilingly, with a squeeze to his hand. "At least not yet," she added, trying to sound light-hearted. She looked at Sebastian. "Mr. Arundell has provided a situation for me. I am companion to a very fine lady!"

Mr. Withers' face crumpled. "Ye, a companion?"

She smiled. "'Tis only temporary."

"Me sister always said ye was raised to *be* a fine laidy," he said sadly, trying not to look too resentfully at Sebastian.

Frannie shook her head. "And I may soon very well be, I daresay!" she cried with false bravery. She couldn't bear to let him know that her future was uncertain.

"Yer father was a right honor'ble gen'leman."

Frannie's eyes widened and she gave Sebastian a look of undisguised hope. Turning back to Mr. Withers she asked breathlessly, "Do you know my father?"

"Nay, me darlin', but yer mother did." Seeing this was not meant as a joke, she said, "Go on."

"'E was a man of means. Married her agin' 'is father's will; that much is certain."

Sebastian's brows knit as he listened keenly. He cleared his throat.

Flustered, Frannie cried, "I beg your pardon. Sir, may I introduce Mr. Withers to you? He is almost like family to me."

"By all means," said Sebastian graciously, though under most circumstances an introduction to Mr. Withers, or anyone of his sort, would seem quite curious if not repugnant. Before Frannie could say another word, however, the man quickly grabbed a small object from his worktable which ended in a miniature horn and placed it in his ear.

Frannie turned to Sebastian with a knowing smile. "The little instrument I told you about. Now he'll hear the introduction better." The little man bowed respectfully to Sebastian as his name was given, but couldn't help immediately volunteering the information afterward that surely when Mr. Arundell recognized Frannie's worth, for she was a "real laidy," this business of being a companion would no longer suit.

Blushing, Frannie ignored this and told the little man why they were come.

"Ah!" he said, smiling. "I've just perfected it with a little adjustment." He pulled the gadget from his ear. "See, there's the smallest device ye'll find anywhere, now."

Sebastian peered curiously at it. He saw a metal object that looked almost like a miniature French horn with the minutest coils imaginable.

"It's wonderful!" breathed Frannie.

Mr. Withers said, turning to rummage in a pile of gadgets on one side of the table, "I've got a few 'ere like it." He chose one, a pewter instrument, and handed it to Frannie. She admired it momentarily and passed it to Sebastian, who examined it closely. Mr. Withers gave him a lesson on how to adjust it in the ear, pointing out that the tiny coils, if necessary, could be compressed yet further, but warned that, if done too often or too hard, the device might cease to work.

"What do you call this?" Sebastian asked.

"'Tis an ear trumpet, sir."

"Like its larger counterpart," Sebastian murmured. He turned to Frannie. "My mother will be in raptures if it works."

"Oh, it will, sir!" Mr. Withers assured him.

Sebastian dug in his pocket for payment. The little man seemed embarrassed by that, but Frannie insisted he take it. After a tender goodbye, and many entreaties to come to him if she needed aught, they left, Sebastian commenting that if the ear trumpet worked, he would be back to buy another and give the man more for it than he asked.

"Do not return without me," she said. "I *adore* the chance to see Mr. Withers."

Sebastian regarded her with a little smile. She certainly had no pretensions about the society she kept. When they were seated again in the curricle, he said, "Before we take this to my mother, I think I must speak to Mrs. Fanshawe. May as well face the business and get on with it."

Frannie looked at him with undisguised hope. "*Would* you? I am certain she must behave more civilly to you than she did, me."

He nodded. "Let us hope."

CHAPTER SIX

They progressed a mere two streets before traffic brought them to a standstill. Frannie took the opportunity to study the busy street with its stalls, carts and shops. She looked past the woollen drapers, patten makers, a pewterer, a stall of ribbands, and a fishmonger, before looking fixedly at a street vendor. "If I may, sir. That baker's wares are superb! Mrs. Baxter and I always filled a basket from his stall before returning home."

Sebastian's mouth twisted as he suppressed a smile. "I noticed you failed to eat this morning." Frannie pursed her lips but said nothing of the fact that she had not been able to eat on account of their expected outing, as it meant spending time with him. She had awoken with a healthy fear of Sebastian, who seemed stern to her yesterday. But now she felt more at ease; especially since he seemed to have espoused her cause. He dug in a pocket, turned to Will and gave him a coin along with a motion of his head at the vendor's stall. "Get whatever this buys," he said, "and keep one for yourself."

"Thankee, sir!" Will cried. He hopped off the equipage and ran to the stall.

Frannie continued to look around, bright-eyed, and suddenly gasped. "Oh, there's the chestnut man!" Smiling, she added, "We roasted our own at home many a time; there's nothing like a hot chestnut in winter, is there, sir?"

Sebastian surveyed his young charge benignly. Her innocent chocolate eyes sparkled with light when she smiled. Her cheeks and nose were tipped with rose-red from the cold, and altogether she made an appealingly pretty sight. Her artlessness surprised him. He could scarcely imagine another young woman in society who would exclaim innocently upon the delights of roasted chestnuts. Too, he could little explain why this young woman should delight him with such raptures. He felt an uncustomary sensation of protectiveness, as though he was with a younger sister.

When Will returned, he was sent immediately to the chestnut man. After that, they acquired apples from an apple cart, a needle from a needle maker (for Sebastian's mama, he was assured, had broken a needle just the previous evening), and hot buns from another baker's cart. Frannie held the paper-wrapped parcels upon her lap gingerly, guarding the treasures. The aroma of hot bread and chestnuts was unmistakable. At another traffic impasse, Sebastian looked over and sniffed. "A shame those buns will turn cold before we are back to the house."

Frannie looked at him with a question in her eyes. She looked down at the small bundle. "Indeed." Her fingers were itching to unwrap the buns—just one taste would be heavenly. But well-bred people did not eat on the street. She peeked at him again, and he nodded toward the buns. "Let's just have a taste, shall we?" He grinned mischievously.

She almost gaped in surprise. Smiling, she removed her gloves and undid the paper enough to extract one bun. It was still warm in her hands. Taking a furtive glance around, she broke off a piece and offered it to him. He held reins in both hands, however, and so opened his mouth, to her surprise. She popped it in, but blushed. She broke off another piece for herself. While chewing quietly, both their lips were turned up in smiles. Frannie felt absurdly delighted that he had allowed her to feed him by hand. It felt like an intimate gesture, a privilege. And on the street!

Edward was wrong, utterly, in calling his elder brother a starched shirt. While she reminded herself that the action could hold no meaning to Sebastian, he said, "You were quite right. Excellent texture, and just the right hint of sweetness." He turned to her with a little smile. "Thank you. We must have Spence send a man for these buns in future." Frannie nodded, very pleased.

Just before leaving that crowded thoroughfare, as they waited in line behind a farmer's dray, Frannie's hand grasped Sebastian's arm. "Oh, the unfortunate creature!" Before he could reply or inquire, she scurried from her seat to a child at the kerb, a youngster who could be no more than seven or eight years old. She held out her hands to the ragged street urchin. "God bless you!" she said to the large, hopeful eyes upturned from soot-covered features, eyes holding a world of pain it seemed to Frannie. They glanced from Frannie's face to her hands, and then the buns and paper sleeve of roasted chestnuts were torn from her palms. With a last wondering look at her, the imp turned and ran off as though a demon was at her heels.

Frannie returned to the curricle and Will assisted her up. With rosy cheeks, she realized she hadn't thought to inquire whether Mr. Arundell would approve of her feeding his newly bought nourishment to a vagabond child. But in truth she had scarcely thought at all. The sight of the large-eyed imp, gaunt cheeks and clothes coated in soot, had thoroughly silenced her brain to any thought except to aid that poor soul.

As they rounded the bend of a corner, she turned to Sebastian. "I—I hope you don't mind," she said awkwardly. "I apologize for not asking your permission."

He gave her a mild look. "What I bought for you is entirely at your disposal, Miss Fanshawe."

"Thank you," she said meekly. She could not tell whether he approved of her action, but at least he was not cross about it.

After a circuitous route, they turned onto the bustling Cheapside. As they pulled up, the tower of St. Mary le Bow Church was visible, perched like a lookout over the busy thoroughfare. At Frannie's motioning to a modest brick building of three storeys, Sebastian pulled up to it and slowed the carriage to a stop. In a moment, a curtain was pulled aside from the first floor window, though no face or figure could be seen.

Handing the reins to Will, Sebastian said to Frannie, "I think it best you remain here. I'll come for you if necessary." She nodded, her face no longer merry. Sebastian said, "Chin up. I believe we'll get to the bottom of this."

She gave him a grateful smile from within her bonnet. "Thank you, sir."

To Will he said, "Do not allow anyone to plague Miss Fanshawe while I am gone; no street hawkers or anyone else who may come along." With a twinkle in his eye, he handed Frannie a half crown. "Unless, of course, you see something else which you know to be superb and must have!" Frannie saw he was teasing her and blushed.

Sebastian approached the door and rang, taking a little silver card case from his waistcoat pocket. He drew out a card to have at the ready.

Watching from the curricle, Frannie saw a butler appear, to whom Sebastian spoke. She wished she could hear what was being said.

"If neither your master or mistress is home," Sebastian offered nonchalantly, "I will wait."

The butler hesitated, and swallowed. "That will not do, sir."

"When are they expected?"

"I cannot say, sir."

"In that case, you must convey a message for your master." He hesitated impressively. "If I must return at another time, inform your employer that I will come in company with an officer of the King's Bench. I have reason to believe that some mischief is taking place on his part. And I intend to have justice in it." Suddenly a woman came storming out of a side room, plump, with a starched mobcap, her face a picture of ill-usage.

"What do you mean, threatening the King's Bench on us? I am sure I have no notion of any mischief taking place! Who are you to accuse a body of mischief?"

Sebastian observed her placidly. "May I assume you are the lady of the house? Mrs. Fanshawe?

She glared at him and merely demanded, "And who might you be?"

"If you will grant me an audience, madam, and five minutes of your time, I will explain everything to your satisfaction."

She eyed him angrily, received his card from her butler, and read it. She looked past Sebastian to the curricle on the street. Seeing Frannie, her eyes widened, but seemingly satisfied that Miss Fanshawe was not approaching, she gave a stiff nod, so that Sebastian entered.

Frannie saw the angry countenance of the lady, and then watched as Sebastian disappeared behind the closed door. Her heart was a mixture of hope and despair. The more she thought on her position, the more she was forced to acknowledge there was little evidence to support her claims. What did she have but hearsay? If the Fanshawes pleaded ignorance of her existence, ignorance of anything having to do with her or a trust fund, what evidence did she have to prove it otherwise? With Mrs. Baxter's possessions gone, she didn't even have access to a single receipt or postal notice that funds had ever arrived for her. She had nothing.

She felt numb at the prospect of having nothing, indeed, of being a nobody. All her hopes, she realized, now depended upon the integrity of Mr. Fanshawe, a man she had never seen and who had never, to her knowledge, seen her. And to think, she might be worse than an orphan, a mere blow-by, illegitimate!

Surely the Arundells would despise her. Mr. Arundell, as pleasant as he seemed today, would come to his senses and renounce their acquaintance. Mrs. Arundell, a most amiable woman, would spurn her as a companion. What would become of her?

While these dreadful thoughts filled her breast, suddenly Sebastian was back. He climbed into the seat before her with an enigmatic look. Frannie hardly dared meet his eyes.

"Mrs. Fanshawe was not cooperative," he said, turning to her. His mouth turned upwards into a little smile. "But she is rattled. I've given her to understand that you have powerful friends, a solicitor who will contact them shortly, and that we know about the trust fund and will not suffer its loss."

She was almost breathless with relief. "Thank you!"

"She did not claim ignorance of the fund," he said, "which is strongly indicative that your mama was right about its existence." He looked about before slapping the reins to start the team. "I left my card. I expect Mr. Fanshawe will call upon me in King Street very soon; and then we shall untangle this hobble."

Frannie nodded gratefully, but fear nibbled at her heart. If Mrs. Baxter and Mama were correct about the trust belonging to Frannie, why was it all shrouded in mystery? Surely a simple letter from a solicitor could prove everything to everyone's satisfaction. What if it was all a mistake and it was in truth Charles Fanshawe's daughter who held the proper claim to the fund? But why should her mama fill her with false hope? Why invent such a thing? No, it *must* be true.

There *was* a trust fund just as she had always been told. Elsewise, Mrs. Fanshawe would have claimed ignorance of it in the strongest terms. And it must follow then, that Mr. Fanshawe was concerned in the business. *But how? Could it be he was her father?* This is what Frannie most wished to know. And, if not he, who? Would she ever meet him? Would he desire to know her? She had so many questions! Oh, why had Mama not revealed her father's name? How much vexation would thus have been spared her!

Mr. Withers said her father was a right honorable gentleman—and that he'd married her mother against his father's wishes. This was news to Frannie. Defying one's father was dire, indeed. But at least he had pronounced them to be married! Better a frowned upon union than an unholy one. And if they had truly married, she had no fear of being branded as illegitimate. Her heart rose and sank as these succeeding thoughts made their way through her mind.

The rest of the drive she spent in a sad reverie, imagining herself quite without friends or hope in the world. Despite Sebastian's efforts, it all might come to naught. He told Mrs. Fanshawe that she had powerful friends, but aside from his family, there were none. He had said she had a solicitor, but this was not true. And now, with Mrs. Arundell's hearing problem solved (for she was certain it would be; she had that much faith in Mr. Withers' device), her services would no longer be necessary. Had she been respectable, she might have hoped to be kept on. But if Mr. Withers was mistaken! A blow-by child! She did not expect they would consider keeping her.

As they neared the corner of King Street, Frannie said haltingly, "Sir—as your mother will no longer need me for a companion—and if Mr. Fanshawe does not call upon you shortly—may I ask? What is your best advice? Would Mrs. Arundell recommend me to another lady for a situation? I am sure I cannot apply without a recommendation—"

Sebastian glanced at her warmly. "If that little gadget cures her defect, my mother will not repay your kindness by throwing you to the street." Keeping his eyes ahead, he added, "And neither will I."

That gave Frannie a small lift to her spirits, but the stark reality of her situation in life still weighed heavily upon her, and once more her spirits sank accordingly. Oh, why hadn't Mama made the situation plain! Why hadn't Mrs. Baxter? Her birth was no doubt a *mistake*! They had shrouded her situation in mystery because she was not by rights a member of the gentry, as she'd always thought. Illegitimate children were a disgrace. That meant *she* was a disgrace.

She thought back to her first meeting with Edward, how she'd told him she was an heiress! He'd have reacted mighty differently, she was sure, had she realized then the truth about herself and presented herself differently. Her thought of someday meeting Princess Charlotte now seemed like the utmost presumption! It astonished her, in fact, that Sebastian hadn't sent her packing the moment he heard her tale of woe. He, surely, had understood it at once, better than she. He knew her to be completely without consequence, without honour, without a shred of merit in society. That he was championing her cause seemed nothing short of a miracle.

Looking at the profile beside her she was filled with sudden admiration. Indeed, it bordered upon affection. As he handled the team, she had a full minute to watch him and decided that Sebastian had not the sort of face that appeared beautiful upon first inspection, but that it was a noble, pleasant face upon closer examination. How had she found him frightful at first? His sober expression wasn't sternness, but thoughtfulness. His quiet manner of dress was not without elegance, and in truth made Edward's exuberant modishness appear ostentatious. Overall, there was something decidedly tasteful about Mr. Arundell's appearance. And vastly reassuring.

If only she weren't so wholly without merit to recommend her to such a man! But now that she knew her place, she would never plague him with the slightest indication that she admired him. She would adhere to her station, such as it was. If, in time, her fortune were found and proved to be substantial, perhaps then…but no! What had he said? *The Arundell name has never been attached to a scandal, and I wish to keep it that way.* Sebastian Arundell would no more look at a hired companion than a scullery maid. To do otherwise would be scandalous. She must not forget it.

Mrs. Arundell received her new device eagerly, exclaiming, "Upon my word, how small 'tis! Nothing at all like Earl Brest's ponderous monstrosity. And he must hold it continually to his ear, at great inconvenience. Nobody can overlook it. And it did not remove the necessity of raising one's voice to be heard by him. I own, I had a *dread* of using such a thing. I had rather give up society—which, you know," she added, looking earnestly at Frannie—"I nearly did. I daresay I haven't been out in an age!" Placing the little metal piece in one ear, she said, "Now say something, Beau, in your usual tone."

Sebastian said, "How do you do, ma'am?"

She responded with a shriek of excitement. "I hear you! I hear you perfectly well!" She turned to Frannie and grasped both her hands. "My dear, God bless you! This answers all my prayers!" Turning to Beau, though keeping Frannie's hands in her own, she said, "Beau, darling, I *must* bring Frannie to the ball. She has done me such a service!"

But he said firmly, "No, ma'am, you must not. Until we know for a certainty how to introduce her, she would be grilled mercilessly by the ape leaders. They never fail to plague a new face if it be pretty. One glimpse of Miss Fanshawe will have them arrayed for battle, and we have not the defense at present to rout it. You must not subject her to it."

Frannie's cheeks flushed rosily. Sebastian was telling his mama in the kindest words possible that Frannie wasn't acceptable for the upper class. Though she knew it to be true, it stung. A week ago, no, a *day* ago, she had thought herself respectable. A fatherless girl was not without honour. But a child of sin—a child who knew not her father's name—that was a different story.

Mrs. Arundell nodded with reluctant agreement. "Well, I hope you shall sort out the muddle then, dearest; for if Frannie indeed possesses a fortune, all else can be forgiven, even by the ape leaders." Frannie comprehended instantly that her mistress must have possession of the details of her dilemma. Edward no doubt, had laid it out for her, how the winds blew, what a sinking ship was Frannie's life unless the treasure were found. Oh, how she hoped Sebastian could decisively sort it out! The money was hardly important; only inasmuch as she could repay Mrs. Baxter's remaining debts, buy back the house, and live independently. But even these worthy aims now paled in comparison with one that surmounted all else: to be respectable. Not so she could meet Princess Charlotte, but to be on equal footing with Sebastian—that is what her heart most desired.

That is what her heart told her she would never, ever, possess.

The following morning only the brothers appeared at breakfast. Mrs. Arundell preferred a late meal, and Frannie must accompany her mistress. Edward soon learned that Sebastian had reasonable assurance of Miss Fanshawe's claim to a fortune, a morsel of knowledge that sent him into a silent reverie. He wore a look of contemplating most earnestly a weighty matter for a young mind. Finally he exclaimed, in a challenging tone, "I daresay, if she is an heiress, a second son might do very well by her!" His face scrunched in thought. He got as far as saying, "But we had ought to do away with this companion business. My mother can hear perfectly well with the help of that little device, and Miss Fanshawe is thoroughly genteel—"

But here he was punctiliously cut off. "Don't be a gudgeon. Miss Fanshawe must be my mother's companion, unless you prefer to put her up at an inn."

"No need for that. We can say she's a distant cousin," Edward rejoined. "I warrant it's been done before!"

"Miss Fanshawe is *not* a distant cousin," countered Sebastian with meticulous precision. "And if she is entitled to a fortune, it does not remove the fact that she may well be a blow by! The natural child of nobody knows whom. That is hardly the type of woman an Arundell can align himself to. And even were she perfectly legitimate, which I doubt, you are a puppy, and not in a position to align yourself with any self-respecting female."

Edward's face flushed. "Are you not to be a baronet? A second son is next in line. Not every pup can make *that* claim."

"Your brother *may* inherit a baronetcy if your cousin does not remarry and have his own son; and your being next in line answers nothing unless said brother is so amiable as to fail with regard to having his own son, or does you the service of dropping dead."

"Which you seem intent on doing!" Edward shot in.

"Eh? What's that?" Sebastian asked, scowling.

"Not dying, but I mean, the matter of an heir—you haven't made a single offer to any of the eager young women, the eligible ones that is, who harken well enough to your side! How often my mother tells me that Miss So-and So has set her cap at you." With a look of disdain, he added, "You seem quite impervious, sir, to marriage."

Sebastian shook out his newspaper. "We are discussing *your* marriage prospects, not mine. And as things stand, you have precious little. Your stipend is hardly enough to live upon in style, as you are a slave to being modish; you must allow that."

Edward longed to rebuff this assertion, but as he was wearing a yellow cravat in the latest style, and had only just bespoken, the day before, new breeches of white satin, and got his hair trimmed and curled into the Brutus style, he said nothing.

"I offered you a commission many times—" began Sebastian.

"I'm not cut for the military!" Edward cried. "I'm only fit to be a gentleman, and you well know it."

"Then you must needs learn to invest—or you will indeed be forced to seek a wealthy bride."

"Which is precisely my point!" exclaimed Edward, slamming a hand upon the table. "Miss Fanshawe!" He stared triumphantly at his brother.

Sebastian's face hardened. He lay his paper down with careful, measured movements. Looking into Edward's eyes he said in an even tone laced with ice, "You will not marry my mother's companion."

"If she owns a fortune, she won't be any lady's companion. She'll be hiring servants of her own."

But this only caused a flash of ire in Sebastian's eyes. "You worthless whelp! Keep your eyes off that child. We don't know anything for certain, least of all what constitutes her fortune, whether it be small or great. In any case until we find out, stay wide of her."

Edward shrank into his seat with a sigh. "As you wish, big brother. But when we find out, *then* I'll make my move."

"You'll do no such thing without my permission," Sebastian spat out.

Edward eyed him sullenly. "She ain't a child, you know. She's nineteen. A year older than I."

"As I said," Sebastian returned, rather severely. "A child. As are you."

Sir Hugo sent notice from the Royal Crown Inn of his arrival in London on Wednesday. On Thursday evening, he appeared for Mrs. Arundell promptly at eight-thirty to escort her to Lady Merrillton's ball. A rotund sort of person, he was dressed in meticulous evening wear which had the effect of making him look exceedingly uncomfortable. His neckcloth and collar were neat but tight, judging by the redness of his face, giving it a mildly strangled look. His wide girth seemed severely restricted by a tight coat; the breeches skintight and stretched; even his black shoes looked tight.

Sebastian received him in the parlour while they awaited Mrs. Arundell's appearance and thanked him again for his kind invitation for the family to spend the Christmas holidays at Bartlett Hall. His words were no sooner heard than met with equally gracious thanks on Sir Hugo's part, who was "deeply obliged, and humbly gratified." Small talk, polite chit chat, followed.

Sir Hugo was all graciousness but Sebastian could not help but notice he seemed ill at ease, his manners bordering upon timid. The nephew attributed this to the man's penchant for solitude, as he eschewed society more often than not. But perhaps it was due to the long-standing feud which existed between Sir Hugo and his mother. Or that he had scarcely laid eyes upon Mrs. Arundell for most of Sebastian's life. With a hand upon his chin, Sebastian said, "You must allow me to express how grateful I am that you are come to escort my mother; this will heal the family breach. I have never understood, sir—I'll be frank with you," he said, extending a hand. "What the discord was, between you."

Sir Hugo shifted uneasily in his chair, but his eyes held a gleam of interest that hadn't been there earlier. He cleared his throat. "It seems, my boy, that your mother has finally seen fit to lay aside her complaint, which, I assure you, no one can be more gratified at, than I."

"Do you mind my asking—what was her complaint, sir?

You'll pardon my curiosity, but you must allow that an ancient grudge which has been guarded and kept secret for all my life must hold some fascination." He smiled wryly. "'Twas on account of it that we hardly know you."

Sir Hugo seemed surprised. "I was not aware, sir, that your mama would grant me enough notice to constitute an ancient grudge; do you indeed call it that?"

Sebastian shook his head. "It has been my impression; I beg your pardon if I am mistaken. My mother has ever been reticent on that head, but I did have the understanding there was ill will on some account between you, to be sure." Sir Hugo frowned and lapsed into silent thoughts but offered no further comment on the matter. Sebastian understood he was not to be enlightened. He rubbed his hands together. "No matter; as she has accepted your escort this evening, I have every hope that bygones are now bygones, and our two families can enjoy as much felicitous accord and mutual society as any who are related."

Sir Hugo said, "Hear, hear! My hope exactly, sir."

Sebastian wondered if he might broach the matter of Sir Hugo's wife seeking, but just then the door opened to reveal his mother. The men came to their feet while she stopped in the doorway so that Frannie, moving in front of her with her back to the room, adjusted something in the region of Mrs. Arundell's turban. "There you are, ma'am, I've fixed it into place," Frannie said in a low tone.

"Thank you," said Mrs. Arundell. Beneath her breath she added, "I hear you perfectly!" Then, gently, "Perhaps next time you will accompany us." Frannie nodded, gave a small curtsey and then, after turning her head just enough to steal a glance at Sebastian, she turned away and disappeared from sight. Her face had been visible for no more than a second, her profile for another. Sebastian was about to greet his mother but the words, "Good evening Mama, here is Sir Hugo," froze on his tongue. Sir Hugo was staring in consternation toward the doorway, the color wholly drained from his face. Sebastian did not know what to make of it. His mother, surely, was not *so* changed as to cause such a reaction in the man. Indeed, she had a remarkable youthfulness about her.

As Mrs. Arundell entered with a light step and a smile, Sir Hugo recovered himself and made a deep bow. Sebastian said with real pride after making his own bow, "You look splendid, Mama!"

"Thank you, dearest," she murmured, still moving towards the estranged cousin-in-law with an outstretched hand, the smile still upon her lips. And she did look exquisite in deep blue cotton velvet with short, puffed sleeves, and a contrasting gold-embroidered sash with gold tassels circling the high waist. A bejeweled hem with a design in rich gold thread, and a gold brooch centered upon the bodice were striking. The matching turban not only set off light, feminine curls about her face, but served ingeniously to keep her hearing device securely in place.

"My word!" said Sir Hugo, deeply impressed. He extended a hand to take one of hers. "My word, Penelope! You don't look changed at all!" His eyes beamed approval.

Sebastian noted with relief that he no longer seemed flummoxed.

Mrs. Arundell blushed faintly, but smiling, said, "Nonsense, Hugo! You know we are both quite ancient now."

"Ancient?" he asked, amused. "Not yet, Penelope. Not quite yet." Keeping his eyes steadily upon hers, he added, with quiet emphasis, "'Tis good indeed to see you, my dear."

Mrs. Arundell met his eyes. "And you, sir," she said in an equally sober tone. Watching the pair, Sebastian's mind did a cartwheel. *Of course!* Why had he never guessed it? There was something of a tragic romance in their past, he'd swear upon it! While the two still surveyed each other, he said heartily, "Neither of you are Methuselahs. Now go and enjoy the ball."

His mother turned to him. "We shall, dearest, but do not forget to ensure that the servants snuff out all the candle lamps in this room as soon as you vacate it. Last week I came home well after midnight and found *two* burning in the first parlour! We must not leave them unattended!"

"Am I to play butler tonight?" he asked, with a wan smile. Seeing her face fall, he hurriedly said, "Depend upon it, dearest, not a single candle will remain lit a moment longer than absolutely necessary. Now be off!" When they'd gone, he thought back to Sir Hugo's reaction upon spying his mother. Something had drained the man's colour. He did not think it likely that Sir Hugo could be in love with her, for they'd barely crossed paths in more than two decades. No doubt a romance was part of the history between them, a tragic romance to be sure, but that was long in the past. It could hardly account for the look of shock on Sir Hugo's face. Thinking back on it, he remembered that Frannie had been in the doorway with Mama. But she, certainly, could have nothing to do with the baronet.

He had never sufficiently pressed his mother to explain the long-standing grudge that until now, had kept their family aloof from Sir Hugo. Sir Malcolm's recalcitrant nature seemed a mere excuse, an easy thing to fall back on as her reason, but Sebastian knew it had more to do with the son than the father. Unfortunately, if he pressed his mama, she became petulant, and so he'd let the matter lie. But the time had come. He must unearth the past.

Frannie hurried down the corridor after leaving Mrs. Arundell at the door of the blue saloon. Her quick glance into the room had taken in Sebastian, tall and elegant looking without his spectacles. She could not prevent the rush of color she felt infusing her cheeks simply at sight of him. She was glad to escape to the library where she knew he would leave her in peace. She thought wistfully of the ball and wondered if she would ever meet Princess Charlotte. But if she were to go to some great affair upon Sebastian's arm, she feared she would never stop gazing at him, so noble he looked in evening wear. In any case, it was better this way, for her to remain out of society. Until she learned precisely who she was—who her father was, and whether she was legitimate—she had no wish to make new acquaintances that might later be denied her. She ought not make any attachments who might spurn her later, nor deepen those with the Arundells.

Especially not Sebastian.

CHAPTER EIGHT

Frannie waited anxiously that evening for Mrs. Arundell's return, despite Sebastian's coaxing her not to miss her rest. At length, he'd come to the library, found her with no fire, clucked his tongue and told her she'd catch an ague if she wasn't careful. He went to summon a servant to build a fire, but she wouldn't hear of it, asking only for the usual one in her bedchamber. She thanked him and curtseyed, and would have fled to her room, there to continue reading by candlelight far from his unsettling presence. But Sebastian, after giving the bell pull a yank, leaned back against the mantel easily and asked her what she was reading.

A very happy hour ensued. A maid started a fire, while Sebastian took from a shelf his favorite book of verse, recommending it to her. He bade the servant remain in the room, no doubt to ensure Frannie's comfort. She went off to one side and sat watching as Frannie and Sebastian went on to discuss the poetry.

Spying the prayer book beside her, a discussion of its cadences followed, the rise and fall of the words when read aloud. Soon they were discussing the Book of Psalms as poetry, which delighted Frannie for she hadn't taken Sebastian for the type of man who added private devotion to his church-going. And yet it was not a complete surprise, for though Frannie had supposed that most of the upper class did not attend church or care for religion, to her joy the Arundells were an exception. They went faithfully to church upon a Sunday—even Edward—since her arrival. The only lapse was the first week when Mrs. Arundell claimed she could not hear the rector's sermon, and moreover, hadn't been attending church since her "deformity" had occurred.

As minutes ticked by, Frannie forgot to be shy of Sebastian, who welcomed her opinion on the Psalms and promised to read her favorites the following night aloud to the family as they sat in the parlour. She knew she must be ignorant of real scholarship in countless ways, but if he thought so, he hid it. As it grew late, he asked if he might escort her to her bedchamber.

Frannie hid a little yawn behind one hand, but then said, "I am determined to wait for your mama. I must know if Mr. Withers's device was a success for her." What she did not say, but what was of even greater concern was if it meant her days with the Arundells were numbered. Indeed, after this lovely evening of easy companionship with Sebastian, she feared it more than ever. She'd been careful, of course, in all she did or said, to keep her growing affection for him out of sight. *He* mustn't be made uncomfortable.

After he left, she continued reading but dozed off. It was near four o'clock in the morning when she awoke with a start upon hearing stirrings in the house. Surely it signified Mrs. Arundell's return. She picked up the candle sconce that was still lit, though burning low, and hurried to greet her.

Mrs. Arundell was astonished to find her up, told her not to *think* of waiting up for her again, and then fell into her manner of easy chatting. She had a delightful evening and claimed her "odious deformity" was cured. In fact, she was filled with raptures, for she was able to curtsey to Her Royal Highness

Princess Charlotte and exchange a word even with the Prince Regent! "Of course we all know the prince would hardly be respectable were he not royalty, but he is royalty, you know, and that makes it exciting, doesn't it?" she asked, as if Frannie might have had exciting opportunities to curtsey to the prince any number of times. To Frannie's question about whether she would still be wanted as a companion, Mrs. Arundell reacted with raised brows and momentary silence. Finally she replied in the sweetest terms that she had no wish, no wish at all, to lose Frannie, and she must not even think of such a thing.

Frannie was filled with relief and gratitude. Sebastian was right, thank heavens. She accompanied the lady to her bedchamber as she continued to glowingly describe the evening. About Sir Hugo, she said only that she had seen no evidence of his exerting himself with the opposite sex. "Indeed, he failed to put himself forward at all," she said, shaking her head, "though many eligible ladies were present. Miss Latham, with her ten thousand, and others, many others." She paused while Betsey, her maid, lifted off her gown, leaving her in a chemise, stockings, and stays. "If he truly wishes to find a wife," she continued, as all but the chemise was removed, "he is not going about it properly, he is all at sixes and sevens."

A frilly mobcap replaced the turban and Mrs. Arundell climbed into bed. As her maid settled the blankets about her, she turned to Frannie. "My word! I'm keeping you from your rest!" She removed the little hearing device from her ear and placed it lovingly upon her night table. "We'll talk in the morning, for the boys will wish to hear about the ladies with their fortunes who were utterly ignored by their cousin." She sighed and looked up at Frannie, blinking. Suddenly her eyes filled with a thought. "Why, my dear, *you* would make Sir Hugo an excellent wife! Your fortune merely caps it!"

"Oh, ma'am!" Frannie exclaimed, blushing. "A poor orphan?" she said, forgetting for a moment that her father might be alive, and falling back into her long-standing belief that he had died while she was an infant. As soon as she spoke she remembered he was said to be alive, but she merely added, "I think Sir Hugo must set his sights higher."

Upon hearing that, Betsey gave Frannie a dark look before curtseying to her mistress to leave. Imagine it! A *poor orphan*, she thought. In the Arundell household!

But Mrs. Arundell would have none of it. "My dear, Edward told me all about the mishmash, but you are not a *poor* orphan! First, there's nothing disrespectable about losing your parents. And second, your fortune is far above that of Miss Latham. Indeed, I daresay she has little else to recommend her, possessing nothing in the way of looks or bearing except what is in the common way." She glanced appraisingly at Frannie. "Fortune aside, your looks are *uncommonly* fine, your large eyes alone quite striking. Any gentleman must see that."

Frannie winced inwardly, for she knew the truth about herself now. "But ma'am," she said, at which Mrs. Arundell quickly reclaimed her hearing aid and held it to her ear, listening.

"I am not, perhaps, a poor orphan, but as to that, my parentage is yet—"

Here she was cut off. "My dear, your family history needs only the smallest embellishment to pass muster, and £30,000, I maintain, is the greatest embellishment a body can have among the *haut ton*. Even to a baronet, 'tis no small sum. In point of fact, such a dowry makes you a good deal more respectable than many who move in the highest circles. Certainly, 'tis enough for Sir Hugo! And, do you know," she said, putting a hand to her cap and patting it, "I nearly forgot—Sir Hugo inquired about you. You see you cannot hide a genteel upbringing." She let out a titter of laughter. "I said you were 'my dear cousin Frannie.' He wanted your full name, and that made me tease him, so that he changed the subject. But now that I think on it, you must be introduced."

"Ma'am, I daresay he is old enough to be my father, and the fortune is *not* secured yet." Frannie spoke patiently but was hoping to snuff this idea of her being suitable for Sir Hugo. Moreover, she needed to be perfectly honest with her mistress.

"Oh, but Beau will see to that! And really, Frannie dear, though I hate to say it, if you are in any doubt of your fortune, an arranged marriage with a baronet would be the best thing that could happen for you. Sir Hugo is a bumbler, I grant, but he is kind-hearted." And to the look of downcast confusion upon Frannie's face, she waved a hand and said, "To your bedchamber! Sleep, sleep, my dear. Nothing helps low spirits like sleep." She covered her mouth for a small yawn. "And Frannie dear; you must no longer consider yourself a companion, not in the way of a servant, at any rate. You are my guest! I need a lady friend nearby, for I have only the boys, you know. And so for the next ball, wherever it is, you will accompany me."

They said their goodnights, and Frannie picked up her candle to make her way back to her bedchamber. As she left, she heard Mrs. Arundell's plaintive call. "Frannie, dear, *do* have a care with your light! *Do* blow it out before you sleep!"

Frannie's heart was in a jumble. She could hardly sort her feelings, so tumbled they were. Relief that she was not to be dismissed; joy at the thought of staying on in the house (which seemed primarily to have to do with Sebastian Arundell's inhabiting it); amazement that she was not to be considered a paid companion; and yet a foreboding she could not dismiss. Mrs. Arundell and the family treated her as though she were respectable, but Frannie knew only too well that her claim to respectability had shattered the moment she learned she might be illegitimate. Sebastian would soon enlighten his mama on that point. The younger Mr. Arundell did not realize what Sebastian knew and therefore had not told his mother: that Frannie had no proof her parents had married other than a simple ring. She had no proof that she was entitled to a trust fund. And she had no one to name, moreover, as the benefactor of that trust.

The next morning, Frannie wished to speak to Sebastian as soon as possible. Despite getting few hours' sleep, therefore, she made it a point to take breakfast by 10:00 o'clock, hoping to catch him. She needed to make him understand that his mother had a misconception about her (alas, that it was so!) but that she must be instructed as soon as possible, so that no more notions of Frannie making a good wife for any baronets would be put forth. She could not live a lie. But she met

Edward in the corridor, who, upon spying her, bowed most politely.

"Miss Fanshawe," he said. "My compliments, I'm sure." His eyes were fixed on her in a curiously thoughtful way, an admiring way, and Frannie wasn't certain what to make of it. He even offered his arm, which she smiled at, but shook her head. "No such formality is necessary, if you please, Mr. Arundell," she said.

"Oh, you must call me Edward," he said with large eyes. "Or even dear Edward, as Mama does, if you like."

Frannie blushed. To accept such an invitation would mean that Edward would, in turn, be free to use her Christian name. Frannie was not sure she wished to have Edward calling her by her first name, but when she hesitated, he added, leaning in conspiratorially, "No formalities *are* necessary, eh? Not between us."

She stared at him strangely, and then reluctantly said, "I— I suppose not. Very well, thank you, Edward."

"My pleasure, Frannie." He leaned in again. "That is what I may call you, isn't it?"

She nodded, while lengthening the space between them and keeping her eyes ahead. Why was Edward cosing up to her? Then she remembered that he, like his mama, had the wrong idea about her. Was he actually thinking—oh, what direction were his thoughts? She must disabuse him of any false notions.

When they were seated at table with no servants about, she said, "You must understand, Mr. Arundell—that is, Edward. My fortune is most uncertain, much more so than I knew when we first became acquainted."

Edward made a dismissive sound. "No worries at all! Sebastian'll secure it. He said you are entitled to it, and he's seldom wrong in matters of blunt, you know."

"He said that?" Hope dawned in her breast. Somehow it was reassuring if Sebastian believed in her cause enough to have stated it thus. Edward nodded vigorously, taking in a spoonful of egg and sausage pie. In truth, Sebastian only said he had "reasonable cause" to think she *might* be entitled to a trust fund, but for Edward, it was all the same.

Nevertheless, Frannie's dejected spirits remained. Edward had yet to understand she was not respectable, with or without a trust fund. Mrs. Arundell's words were meant kindly, but pedigree was of utmost importance to the upper class—even provincial Frannie understood that. Yet she had not the heart or the courage at the moment to enlighten Edward, to warn him about her shocking illegitimacy and make him know she was not at all the sort of woman he should admire. He would learn it soon enough.

When Sebastian appeared and greetings were exchanged, Edward was suddenly anxious to depart. He mumbled a hurried explanation of having business which "by heavens cannot wait," with an acquaintance he had arranged to meet in Haymarket.

"Haymarket?" repeated Sebastian with a sardonic glance. "There's no theatre at this time of year. I hope you're not taking part in a boxing match. I had your word you'd refrain from boxing, and from wagering upon it."

"I'm merely a spectator," Edward assured him haughtily. He bowed deeply to Frannie. "Good day, *Frannie,*" he said with a parting, triumphant glance at his brother. Frannie blushed and pursed her lips as he left.

Now she was alone with Sebastian but knew not what to say. Sebastian's look at the departing sibling was not one of approval, but when his gaze fell upon Frannie, the look softened. Something inside her joyfully noted the softened gaze, indeed, wrapped itself around it, wishing desperately to keep it. But she must remember herself. She was not worthy of an Arundell. "Sir, your mother has a mistaken notion about me." The green-grey eyes pierced her soul. How clear and penetrating they were! They were arresting, long lashed, nothing short of beautiful. It struck her every time she met their scrutiny.

"How is that?" he asked.

Frannie shifted in her seat and glanced at her plate. Looking up again she said, "She thinks I am…respectable." In a small voice, she continued, "You must tell her what you know. What *I* now know. That I am uncertain about my parentage." Her voice grew jittery, for it filled her with shame to have to say the things she had to say. Sebastian leaned forward in concern as she continued, "That my fortune is uncertain… That I am, in short, utterly un-unworthy of th-that term, 'respectable.'" She swallowed a sob, and dabbed her eyes with a napkin. Sebastian hastily drew a handkerchief from a pocket of his waistcoat and proffered it across the table, but his eyes clouded. Was he annoyed?

"Do not fret over what Mama thinks," he answered. "And do let us wait to draw conclusions until we hear from Mr. Fanshawe. You must not torture yourself with such notions."

She blinked at him, surprised to find him so affable on the matter. "What if he does not call?"

"If he does not, I shall turn up at his doorstep."

She gave him a little, watery smile. "I am *greatly* obliged," was all she could say. He nodded and then asked how long she'd waited up for his mother the night before, listening with amusement while Frannie told him of the lady's triumphant experience. She left out entirely his mother's ridiculous notion of Frannie being a suitable wife for the baronet, and hadn't quite done with other details when Mrs. Arundell appeared.

Standing to bow, Sebastian exclaimed, "Mama, I should have thought you'd take a tray in your bed this morning. I understand you came in shockingly late."

She smiled and shooed a hand at him. "Nonsense. I've come home with the dawn in the past, as have you, sir. You know how 'tis with society." She allowed a footman to pour a cup of coffee and then said, "Your absence was noted, Beau. Miss Compton particularly asked about you. As did the Misses Beaufort, and two gentlemen, let me see…their names were…"

"No matter, Mama. I am eager to hear of only one gentleman."

"The Regent?" she inquired, looking over her cup at him.

"Sir Hugo. How went it with him?"

She looked down at once, and said carefully, after swallowing, "He is very gentlemanly, though in his bumbling way, just as I remember him. He didn't neglect me for a moment." She looked up again and met his eyes. "But if he is in town to find a wife, I saw it not. He failed to put himself forward, not even to the most eligible ladies!" She took a sip of tea and then continued, saying with a laugh that bordered on a bitter note, "I own, if he hopes to marry, the lady will needs must make the offer!" She glanced at Frannie and said,

"Which, by the by, should perhaps be made by you, on Frannie's behalf, for she has no one else to speak for her."

Frannie and Sebastian stared at her. Even Sebastian seemed momentarily bereft of words.

"Dearest," he said, "do you mean to say, you wish me to arrange a wedding for the man who may very well disinherit me if he has his own child?"

A frown crossed his mother's face. "Well, of course—I wasn't thinking of that. I suppose Frannie, being so young, would of course—" She giggled.

"What were you thinking?" Sebastian asked, smiling. "Of Miss Fanshawe's future?"

She swallowed a sip of coffee. "I thought only of Hugo— that big, bumbling *oaf*!" she finished, vehemently. "He needs a sweet tempered girl, an amiable creature; Frannie is just the thing. And with her fortune, I thought her most suitable."

Sebastian thought it now more and more evident that something of significance had occurred between his mama and his cousin. A broken heart was his thought. But Sir Hugo hardly seemed the type to bestow broken hearts on lovely young women, which his mother, still lovely now, had surely been in her youth. A portrait of her shortly after marrying his father hung in the library, a testament to that beauty. His cousin, while not a fright of a man, was paunchy and heavily fleshed in the face, which was often reddened, either by nature or self-effacement. He had bushy brows, and moved timidly, light on his feet as though trying to be unnoticed.

Frannie interrupted his musings when she cleared her throat, giving him a look imbued with meaning, her brows raised at him in expectation.

"Oh, er," he said, leaning forward to his mama, "You should know that Miss Fanshawe's fortune is far from certain."

Mrs. Arundell gave him an impatient look. "Well, Beau, dearest, in that case, you must leave no stone unturned on her account! Put Mr. Harley on the case, you have my permission."

"Our solicitor may be of some use," he acceded, "in future. After I've finished inquiries of my own." While his mother buttered a piece of toast, he added, "As it stands, I await a call from Frannie's relation, Charles Fanshawe. We shall see where that interview leads."

"I didn't know you had family!" cried the lady. "Is this a close relation?" she asked curiously.

Frannie squirmed in her seat. Now it would come out. That she didn't know for certain how he was her relation, or what the name of her father was, or whether there was even a fortune. She had wanted to clear up this very thing with Mrs. Arundell, but now they were come to it, her toes curled.

But Sebastian cleared his throat and said, "Mama, I am much more interested this morning in why you feel it incumbent upon you to marry off my cousin to anyone. Particularly when said marriage is more than likely to result in your son's being disinherited."

Again Mrs. Arundell frowned, but she waved a hand dismissively. "Oh, I was addle brained, I suppose! I thought only of the poor man being alone all these years, and as he has expressed his wish, according to you, to find a wife, though he said nothing to me about it—"

Sebastian leaned forward and steepled his hands upon the table. "Do you know, dearest, I have an idea about that?"

His mother was just lifting a cup to her lips but stopped to hear it, her small features framed prettily in a frilly mob. Frannie also looked curiously at him.

"I think," he said, with a little smile, "that *you* ought to marry my cousin."

CHAPTER NINE

Sebastian's suggestion was bold but impulsive, more a test to gauge his mother's reaction than a genuine wish. Mrs. Arundell nearly dropped her cup.

"Heavens! You couldn't have shocked me more!" she cried. She dabbed an eye with a handkerchief. "But you mistake the matter," she said, composing herself. "There was, at one time," she added, carefully weighing each word, "an *expectation* that Sir Hugo would offer for me." She paused, her eyes roaming the room and settling upon the far wall, lost in memories.

Sebastian silently congratulated himself for having correctly divined that much.

"But as you know," his mother continued, "and fortunately for you, I married your father, his cousin."

Sebastian's brows furrowed. "Why did you never tell us he was to offer for you? And do you mean to say, that Sir Hugo failed you, dearest?"

Mrs. Arundell's head popped to attention, and she said, archly, "He did, indeed." But her face softened. "I daresay it was the dearest wish of Sir Malcolm, who considered my father his nearest friend; but it was not enough to Hugo's liking to bring it to pass."

Sebastian added astutely, "And it is this for which you never forgave him. Until now."

She blinked at him. "I met your father at Bartlett Hall. And even my mother, who longed to see me become the wife of a future baronet, encouraged that courtship. We had all considered Hugo was quite, quite decided against marriage and would never come round." She shook her head. "It matters not. All is ancient history now. I have you and Edward because of how it turned out, and I assure you, I am eternally grateful for that."

There was no call from Mr. Fanshawe that day, or the following two. Frannie despaired again for the coming inevitable disappointment, though Mrs. Arundell maintained an enormous optimism regarding the fortune. In two weeks they'd be arriving at Bartlett Hall for Christmas—Frannie was assured that she must accompany the family, for Mrs. Arundell had grown inordinately fond of her. Indeed, Frannie wondered at it. Why should the lady regard her kindly? Why did she not wish, rather, to banish her from the house with two handsome, perfectly eligible young men living in it? Young men were known to choose wives poorly just as often as young women. Yet Mrs. Arundell treated Frannie with affection, like a social equal, though Frannie did her best to make herself useful in as many ways as possible.

Mr. Arundell was another mystery. She knew that, had he wished, he could change his mother's view of her situation merely by portraying the truth of it in cold, hard facts. Mrs. Arundell did not bother herself with cold, hard facts in most things, such as how she regularly overspent her jointure and would be in debt if not for Sebastian. But he never made it plain to her in a way that would condemn or shame her, and he never enlightened her on Frannie's circumstances in a way that would cast doubt upon Frannie's respectability. He seemed determined to treat her kindly, though she did not know why.

In her nightly prayers, Frannie gave thanks and held her breath, wondering how long it could last. She also wondered how much time Sebastian would wait before going again to Cheapside to confront the Fanshawes. In the meantime, she went on drives and errands with Mrs. Arundell, and in the evenings joined her in knitting caps and socks for the poor box while Sebastian read from one of his treasured tomes. Then one morning, he announced, "Tomorrow we shall call again in Cheapside. I have written to my solicitor, as it seemed best to have the law on our side."

Our side. Frannie's heart skipped a beat. Mr. Arundell might have said, "your side," but he spoke of the matter as if it were as much his concern as hers.

"After Harley has an audience with Mr. Fanshawe we will know how the case stands."

Frannie hardly heard the last sentence, for her heart was still beating strangely, and not only because Sebastian had taken ownership of her wrangle, but because of the way his eyes spoke to her as he did. She swallowed, reminded herself strongly that she had no guarantee of a happy settlement, and no right, no right at all, to set her heart on a future baronet. He meant only to be kind. Perhaps the look in his eyes was given to all young women. Did not Edward say that his brother caused hopes to rise in many a female breast without the least intention of making them do so? She must not forget it; nor that despite his kindness, indeed the kindness of all the

Arundells, Frannie might end up being an outcast to society. Or, at best, companion to a less fine lady.

"Mr. Harley will call tomorrow morning," Sebastian continued. "And has sent word to Cheapside of our coming, using the strongest terms to adjure their compliance in the matter of an audience." He gave her a questioning look. "My mother is with Mrs. Spencer, the housekeeper, planning, I believe, our menu for the next week to take to cook. I propose an outing, Miss Fanshawe. Mr. Harley expresses a desire to meet you before confronting your relations. Can you suffer it? You must know, he will examine you, I have no doubt, minutely. The facts of your case may distress you when presented in the manner of a barrister. If you prefer, he will make do with my account of the matter, which I've written to him in as much detail as you afforded me."

Frannie said, "Sir, if you think it is beneficial to—she hesitated here, not being able to say "our cause"—to my cause, then I am all willingness. I wonder, however, at his learning anything useful or new from my testimony, as I've told you all that I know."

"He wishes, nonetheless, to hear it from your own lips." His clear eyes pierced hers.

"I am at your service," she said.

When they arrived at the offices of the solicitors on Mount Street, Sebastian entering first to hold the door for Frannie, Mr. Harley stood to bow a greeting, but with a troubled look. Upon being presented to Miss Fanshawe, his look became yet more befuddled. "Do you mean to say, sir, this is the young woman you wrote of?" He glanced at open papers on his desk. "Miss Fanshawe?"

"Of course," Sebastian replied, put off by the man's countenance.

He cleared his throat, motioning them to take a seat, if they pleased. When they were seated, he said, "Sir. You must know that a woman by name of Mrs. Charles Fanshawe was here only an hour since."

Frannie and Sebastian shared a look of surprise. "What was her mission?" asked Sebastian.

"She wished to assure me that a grave hoax is underfoot. She gave me to understand, sir, that Miss Fanshawe resides beneath her roof; that she is, in fact, their only daughter, and that a trust fund awaits her upon her majority." He paused and looked sadly at Frannie. "She claims this young woman is trying to wrest the trust from her daughter on a false pretense."

A gasp escaped Frannie. Sebastian placed a hand upon one of hers, which now gripped the arm of her chair.

But his face hardened as he faced the man. "I put it to you, sir, that the case is exactly opposite. Here before you is the Miss Fanshawe entitled to that trust. You must give your assurance that you will do everything in your power to prove her case."

The man relaxed. "Sir, as my firm has served your mother's family since long before her marriage to your father, I am predisposed to take your side in the matter."

Frannie had felt ready to sink, but these words gave her heart. She took a deep breath.

"Perhaps Miss Fanshawe can start from the beginning." He

looked at Frannie. "Allow me to summon my clerk. Then you must give me your full history, everything you know of it, every detail you can recall, beginning with the parish where we may find record of your birth."

"Certainly, sir," she replied. Sebastian gave her an approving nod, and she straightened in her seat. She would need to face the man's disapproval of her circumstances, no doubt, but if she had the least hope of ever meeting Sebastian on grounds as anything near an equal, it was paramount that her case be examined in its entirety. When the clerk had come in and drew up a seat and had a pen and ink at the ready, she began. "I was born, sir, on 4th June 1796. All my life I have lived with my mother, until her passing a year ago, and Mrs. Flora Baxter in …"

A letter from Mr. Harley arrived by messenger the next morning. Tipps paid the rider and conveyed the note to Sebastian, who sat at breakfast with Mrs. Arundell and Frannie. Edward was out.

Sebastian read the note and laid it on the table. "Mr. Harley asks us to postpone our call to Cheapside until he's had time to further investigate your case."

Frannie nodded. "I see." She had a little sinking of heart at his words, for she interpreted the solicitor's meaning to be that he had suspicions about her claims.

Mrs. Arundell opined that Mr. Harley was known to be meticulous; and what good hands Frannie's case was in.

Sebastian too, nodded with satisfaction. "I am glad for this.

He'll root out whatever evidence exists, I am certain."

Frannie leaned forward, the sole hearer of the tidings who was left troubled. "What sort of evidence might he find, sir?"

Sebastian gazed at her. "He'll start with the parish record of your birth; the name of your father should be found there. If not, he'll look elsewhere for a record of your mother's marriage. All marriages are recorded, even many of the Covent Garden sort."

Frannie winced inwardly. Did Sebastian think her mother's marriage might have been one of those spurious unions made by fly-by-night hucksters posing as clergymen? They offered their services to perform hasty weddings, no questions asked. While such a wedding might be recorded somewhere, it would likely not stand legal scrutiny. She shuddered at the thought.

As if reading the direction of her thoughts, Sebastian said, "Have no fear, Miss Fanshawe. The more I think on your situation, the more certain I am that you are indeed in expectation of some reward; else the Fanshawes would hardly contest the matter."

Mrs. Arundell's head popped up. "Are they contesting it? Oh, poor Frannie!"

Frannie acknowledged the sympathy with a small smile and nod of her head. Sebastian said, "It only adds weight to her claim, ma'am. Where a fortune is at stake, the greedy will assemble."

Mrs. Arundell cried, "Indeed!" Sighing, she looked upon Frannie and exclaimed, "I have it, my dears! Let us cast aside all of this for now; let us not give it another thought until we hear from Mr. Harley on the matter. Take us somewhere diverting, Beau, dearest. Perhaps a drive through the park…"

Sebastian looked at Frannie. "Is there somewhere

diverting, Miss Fanshawe," he asked, smiling, "in early December, that you might wish to see?"

Frannie gazed at him with surprise and gratitude. Would he truly cater to her preference? And how propitious that she had one! "I confess," she said, looking meekly at her companions, "I have longed to see Vauxhall. I know 'tis past its heyday; they say 'tisn't fashionable any longer, but I understand 'tis nevertheless a pleasant place and well worth a visit."

Mrs. Arundell said, "The gardens are best in spring, my dear. But no matter! We'll bundle up with bricks for our feet in the carriage and come home to hot negus. I daresay we shall have a cose together. Beau can read to us as he likes to do, while we warm ourselves by the fire." She strained her head to see, from the window, beyond the neighboring buildings to the sliver of sky that was visible. "The skies are middling blue; I think we must brave the weather and show Frannie the place, even though it is nothing now to what it is in summer."

Sebastian was secretly pleased at her choice. While it was hare-brained, in his opinion, to visit Vauxhall in winter, he expected to see no acquaintances equally pigeon-headed and braving the elements. There would be no awkward introductions for Frannie to suffer. Society was uncommonly hungry for details about anyone who approached the circles of the upper class. Until her story was bolstered by legal evidence, he could not, of course, even hint at a fortune; and the possibility that she was in fact hardly respectable still presented itself as an unfortunate reality. If it came to it, he'd introduce her simply as a family friend and hope the matter ended there. But far better to keep Frannie from prying eyes until they heard back from Harley.

"Why do we not call upon my cousin, Mama, and see if he will accompany us?" Sebastian asked, as he rose to help himself to more coffee.

"Sir Hugo?" she asked, amazed. "He is no doubt in Gloucestershire by now."

"He is not," Sebastian said calmly, returning to his seat. "He stops in town."

Mrs. Arundell let out a breath. "Wife hunting, no doubt!" She took a determined sip from her cup.

Sebastian smiled. "You could save him the trouble, dearest."

She looked at him warily, her sweet countenance shaded with suspicion. "Do not say you are clinging to that nonsensical notion of *my* marrying him!"

"Very well, I shan't say it." He winked at Frannie, who felt a frisson of pleasure run through her at the unexpectedly playful gesture. Sebastian was normally staid and proper.

"However," he went on, raising a finger to press his point to his mama, "you did almost marry him once. There must be something of that old affection lurking somewhere—for both of you."

Mrs. Arundell stared at him for a moment. "You mistake the matter. I grant, it was the wish of both our parents. And I own, I did think Hugo amiable and pleasing—though no more an Adonis then, than now—but let us just say he had no ambition for marriage, and really, now I look back, I see we did not suit. Let us just say we did not suit." She stopped and stirred her coffee slowly—"And it all proved fortunate for me, as I have said." She gave him a bright smile. "I lived happily with your father, God rest his soul. And I got you boys as a result."

"Did he ever tell you outright that he had no ambition for marriage?"

Flustered, she said, "There was an extenuating circumstance. I—I don't wish to talk about it!"

Sebastian finished chewing a bite of toast and said, very calmly, "Dearest, you know I've no wish to distress you, but none of us are children here. I think it long past time we unlocked this buried conundrum. My cousin's sudden appearance in our lives has dug it up—he evidently has ambition for marriage now—and we've only to look at what happened then in the light of day. Afterward, you can toss it into the past for good, never to be opened again. This circumstance you speak of—it cannot be so very dastardly in nature to be beyond mention now. I know my cousin at least well enough to be sure of that."

Mrs. Arundell's face clouded while he spoke, and she took to stirring her coffee with more vigor. Frannie's heart went out for her. "Sir, you are too severe on your poor mama."

Mrs. Arundell cried, "He is abominable, indeed! Thank you, Frannie! Is this not monstrous?"

Sebastian could only smile and shake his head. To Frannie he said, "The difficulty is that I've been far too easy on my mother. She is accustomed to not having to explain the matter, and so it rankles her when I ask for it."

Mrs. Arundell stared at him. Lifting her cup to her lips, she hesitated and said, "Plague or tease me all you like; you shan't get another word from me on the subject."

Sebastian removed his spectacles and smiled. His eyes never looked weak without the glasses, and Frannie admired his still surprisingly noble features while he said, "But why the deep, dark, secret, ma'am? Surely you see how your silence must lead only to speculation and imaginings, the likes of which are no doubt ten times more full of devilry and dishonour than the account could ever be." He spread his hands to her. "Do you not see that if you force us to solve the riddle ourselves, we can only contrive situations that cast either my cousin, or you, or the both of you, into villainous roles, infamous actions!"

"Dishonour might be appropriate, but devilry! In truth, Beau, you needn't imagine anything of the sort. What happened between us, your cousin and me, was a long time ago, and as we have now put the past behind us, I see no reason to dredge it up. No reason at all."

When he saw how firm she was on the matter, he said, "So be it."

Mrs. Arundell's face softened.

But he added, "I shall apply to my cousin for an explanation. I'll ask him as we stroll the grounds at Vauxhall."

Mrs. Arundell came abruptly to her feet. "No, Beau, you must not! You will oblige me not to invite him. I am resigned to Christmas at Bartlett Hall, but until that time, I do not wish to see your cousin's face!"

She turned to leave and Frannie rose hurriedly to join her. But Sebastian said, "Miss Fanshawe, pray you, spare me a minute." She stopped and gave him an expectant look. He waited until his affronted parent had quite gone from the room, then turned mild eyes upon her. "My mother confides in you, I think. Could I perhaps call upon you to tease the story from her? To worm it out?"

Frannie's eyes widened and then grew troubled. She wished to oblige Mr. Arundell, but she felt equal loyalty to his mama. "I could not, sir!" she cried, though her eyes spoke regret. "Your mother trusts me as a—a friend. She has been all kindness to me, as you yourself must appreciate more than anyone, for you know—indeed, you alone of this household know best—that I have little but my word to recommend me as a proper houseguest. Yet she keeps me on, and not as a companion but an equal." The colour in Frannie's cheeks grew warm.

Sebastian's heart swelled with surprising approval at the picture of lovely distress. He had expected she would do anything he asked, but her noble refusal was more pleasing than compliance, her sense of honour, refreshing. Somehow though, he felt compelled to test her further. Call it the devil in him, call it pride or flat out mischief, but he said, "You are aware, of course, that she approves of you because I allow her to. I could disabuse her of the notion that you are respectable with merely the right word."

Frannie looked bereft. Speechless for a moment, she fought within herself how to proceed. She knew of course how precarious her situation was. Why Sebastian had mysteriously refrained thus far from disabusing Mrs. Arundell of the notion of Frannie's respectability, was a mystery. She wished very much to please him, but coming to a resolve, she shook her head, blinking. "You must do as you see fit, sir. I am sorry; but I cannot betray Mrs. Arundell!" With that, she turned and strode with more emotion than dignity from the room.

CHAPTER TEN

In half an hour Frannie ventured from her chamber in walking-out dress, but wondered if her refusal to do Sebastian's bidding would have repercussions. Would he now disavow any further help for her dilemma? Worse, would he wish to send her from the house?

As she approached the staircase, she was smoothing out her gown when he stepped into her path. She hadn't noticed his presence until now and looked up with trepidation. Sebastian flashed a smile at her. He wasn't miffed! Offering his arm, he said, "I've sent for the carriage. Mama waits in the hall. Come." Frannie gladly took his arm.

Soon the threesome were en route for Vauxhall in the Arundell carriage. If Sebastian eyed Frannie with something more than the usual benign expression—for he admired her mettle—she did not see it. She was too busy taking in the sights of town, especially the hustle and bustle along the Strand. So many shops! Mrs. Arundell pointed out those she favoured, and then Scotland Yard, the Admiralty, and the Horse Guards along Whitehall. Progress was slow, and now and then Frannie's eyes would stray to Sebastian, sitting across from her and his mama. He wore his spectacles only at home, she now knew, meaning that the whole world saw him at his noble best. That so handsome a man hadn't taken a wife seemed marvellous.

When forced to sit for minutes on end in traffic after

turning onto New Vauxhall Road, Sebastian peered impatiently out the window. "I believe this crush extends all the way to the bridge! I should have told Sykes to cross at Westminster."

Mrs. Arundell said, "Gilley would have known."

Frannie knew that Mr. Gilley was the usual coachman called upon by the Arundells, but he hadn't been available.

"Why is there such traffic?" the lady continued. "Only a soiree at one of our town mansions usually causes such a muddle."

"A carriage accident, I fear. They are all too common."

"Perhaps, Frannie dear," Mrs. Arundell ventured, peering at the line of carriages ahead, "we should tour the quieter sections of Mayfair today, show you our mansions, instead of waiting for this frightful crush to clear. I do not think we will cross the river for an age at this rate."

Frannie said, "That's a lovely alternative. May we go by Carlton House? I've never seen it except in newspaper illustrations."

"The regent's home isn't the imposing palace you might expect," said Sebastian, "on its exterior. But inside—"

"Oh, every extravagance known to man!" put in Mrs. Arundell. "I was there only once, but 'twas unforgettable in its brilliance and richness, everything in satin and gilt, tapestries and paintings of enormous sizes, architecture you've never seen the likes of!" She looked earnestly at Frannie, her eyes alight. "One could hardly take it in!" Then, to Sebastian, "Let us go past, by all means."

Sebastian hit the wall of the carriage. When a footman soon appeared, he was told to inform Sykes of the change in plans. They continued to crawl ahead for an interminable period, as there were few intersections at this edge of town between them and Vauxhall Bridge. At length, they achieved a left onto Rochester Row. A number of circuitous turns brought them to James Street, a wide avenue, but it came to an end and they were forced to turn left again onto Stafford. Sebastian cried, "Good heavens! He'll have us traversing every side lane and dubious inch of this town before finding his way to the mansion!" They turned onto a street called Arabella, then onto the scenic Grosvenor Place, finally passing St. George's Hospital and Hyde Park Corner onto Piccadilly.

"Now it won't be long," said Sebastian, looking chiefly to Frannie.

"I assure you, no drive in town is unwelcome to me," she said. "Every scene, every street, whether mean and narrow or spacious, holds its own fascination. I never saw the like except when we visited Mr. Withers." Soon town mansions brought all due effusions of praise from both ladies. St. James's Palace, and Marlborough House , only seen from a distance, were duly admired. One side of Carlton House was passed, but they continued along St. James's Street—while Sebastian swore beneath his breath—only to turn and traverse the beautiful tree-lined St. James's Square. Frannie craned her neck for a better view. They then admired the impressive rows of town homes of light-coloured Portman Brick along Jermyn and Mount Street. It was as if Sykes knew to travel every surrounding back street just for Frannie's benefit before coming back to Pall Mall and Carlton House.

Finally, there it was, a wide, handsome residence of cut stone and understated dignity that ran the length of the street. Surely Mrs. Arundell had said rightly that it housed untold opulence, Frannie thought. A portico of Greek columns with corresponding arched entrances faced the street, appropriately imposing for a prince. How she wished she could see inside! And then they were past it. Despite her admiration, she told Sebastian she agreed with him that the royal residence wasn't nearly as magnificent as European palaces and castles she had seen in illustrations.

From Pall Mall, they turned left onto Market Street. Minutes later, when they were just crossing Old Bond Street, they were stopped again. A noisy crowd was massed in front of a nondescript shop in such numbers that the street was partially blocked. While a few carriages moving in the opposite direction crawled past, they had no choice but to wait until a lane cleared. But Sebastian suddenly came sharply to attention, raising both brows. With a hardened jaw he exclaimed, "By Jove! I've caught him!"

Mrs. Arundell and Frannie exchanged mystified glances, and then sat forward so all three faces peered out the left-side window. From what glimpses they could catch through openings in the crowd, it seemed a street brawl was afoot. Sebastian rose, but Mrs. Arundell grasped his arm. "Do not go, Beau! What do you hope to accomplish? I daresay 'tis mischief for the constable or sheriff! This mob seems unruly, dearest."

"Dear heart, the crowd is no threat. I warrant the excitement is due to placing wagers on the fight. I'll only be a minute."

"But, but—" She wished to object further, but he jumped out of the coach. After speaking a word to Sykes, Sebastian quickly joined the hobble of bodies pressing in to watch the contest.

"My word," murmured Mrs. Arundell, shaking her head. "I knew Edward enjoys a rousing match of boxing, but I would not have thought it of Sebastian. He has ever spoken against displays of brute strength."

"Might he have gone to lay a wager?" suggested Frannie, who also believed Sebastian's abhorrence of brawling to be too strong for him to have mere entertainment in mind. She reflected that although he did not enjoy the spectacle of a fight—indeed, he disapproved of it—he might nevertheless take advantage of an opportunity to multiply a crown or a pound. Gentlemen seemed prone to enjoy these opportunities. She tore her eyes from where he'd disappeared into the crowd to look at his mother. Mrs. Arundell's pretty face was creased in concern. "Beau isn't a betting man! What could have possessed him?"

Suddenly a roar from the crowd went up, followed by groans of disappointment and then raucous laughter. Sebastian emerged, leading Edward along by an ear. Edward, bleeding from the brow and lip, his fashionable hair gone flat, coat grasped in his hands, shirt sleeves rolled up, and his cravat and leather gloves nowhere in sight.

Mrs. Arundell gasped.

Frannie's amazement was equal to the mother's, for she recalled how vehemently Edward decried having anything more to do with street boxing. Mrs. Arundell swiftly produced a handkerchief from a reticule and motioned Frannie away from the window. As the men approached, they heard Edward. "You have no notion of what you've done!" he complained. "They'll call me a white-livered milksop now! Not to mention you've lost me a fortune! I was on top of it. Ready to darken his daylights, sir!"

"You were getting thrashed. I merely saved you from further humiliation."

"A man's not beaten until he's down! I was upon my feet! *Saved* me!" he grumbled, as a footman opened the vehicle's door. "Ruined me, more like!"

As he stepped into the coach, Edward spied his mother and Frannie and froze, momentarily, in horror. Sebastian nudged him from behind. He finished his entrance, sitting down across from the women in sudden meekness. Spying his wounds, Mrs. Arundell cried, "Oh, my dear boy! Poor, poor Edward!" She rushed to his side to nurse him, dabbing her handkerchief across his brow and then his mouth tenderly. "Did you have a disagreement with someone, dearest?"

"Not at all, Mama," he replied. "'Twas merely a diversion, a contest of skill, winner take the prize. Gentlemen often compete in such sport."

With his mother beside Edward, Sebastian had no choice but to sit beside Frannie. This put him directly in Edward's line of sight, however, so that the injured young man cast belligerent eyes his way whenever he could see past his mother's ministrations.

"You might have driven past and taken no notice. Leave it to you to distress my mother!" With a glance at Frannie he added, "And Miss Fanshawe. Boxing isn't fit for ladies' eyes."

"Do you call that boxing?" Sebastian returned calmly. "Brawling like tomcats, more like."

"Pugilism, sir! Have you forgot I took lessons on Bond Street with Jackson? He called me quite the fancy, if you must know!"

"Of course I know. I paid for those lessons and studied

with him myself—strictly as an exercise for optimal health. But I didn't afford you lessons to make you a street brawler. This was no sponsored fight with the Pugilistic Club. That sort of boxing is permissible, but for us, street fights are strictly for self-defence when or if the need arises."

"A challenge was issued, sir! I had no choice but to accept, or where's our family honour? And I employed Jackson's scientific style."

"I saw you scrapping—you butted your head at him. Did not Jackson instruct that a well-aimed fist was of more effect than all the brawn and bulk in the world?"

Edward's armour cracked. "I did what the case needed. I have an exceedingly hard head."

Mrs. Arundell clucked her tongue. "Not hard enough, my dear, to prevent injury!"

Sebastian said, "You realize where you might have ended up if we hadn't chanced by? In city college, no doubt, for disturbing the peace. The magistrates frown upon these brawls."

"Gaol? Good heavens!" cried Mrs. Arundell, looking to Sebastian. "Do you indeed think that likely? Edward, dearest, you must oblige me and promise never to engage in such a contest again!"

"Gaol's for criminals," he responded haughtily to his brother. "Boxing's no crime." To his mother he added, "Ma'am, if my brother hadn't interrupted, I might have made off with more blunt than six months' stipends! Instead, I'm ruined."

"How, ruined?" she asked, perplexed.

"Who will take me on, when they know my brother is like to come along and put an end to the business before 'tis settled?”

"But it *was* settled," put in Sebastian comfortably. "You lost."

"You forced me to run like a coward!"

"I saved your skin. And unless I'm mistaken, I should think you will be sought out more than ever for such contests." A gleam of humour in his eyes accompanied his next words. "Who will avoid the man who abandons the fight before damaging his opponent?"

Edward's jaw hardened. "I gave him damage, by Jove, and would've done worse if you hadn't interfered!" He said this whilst rubbing his sore right fist.

Meanwhile, the carriage lumbered up to King Street.

The following day Sebastian's coach stopped in Mount Street to collect Mr. Harley, who joined him and Frannie to call upon the Fanshawes in Cheapside. Along the way, Mr. Harley expressed surprise that Frannie had come with them, adding, "You must expect opposition, Miss Fanshawe, and I'm afraid, some unpleasantness."

She nodded. "Indeed, sir, I understand."

He nodded and gave her an appraising look, as if he'd thought her constitution too weak for the challenge but now had to reconsider. After a moment, however, he said to Sebastian, "I wonder if Miss Fanshawe would be more comfortable waiting in the carriage while you and I speak to the family."

Frannie said, "Sir, I assure you, I am perfectly capable of

facing my relation." She gave Sebastian an imploring look, so that he too assured the solicitor that all would be well. For some reason Frannie felt it of paramount importance that she witness firsthand whatever would befall. Too, she had committed the matter earnestly to the Lord only that morning in her prayers. Mr. Harley eyed her in his businesslike fashion and added, "So be it. But allow me to speak for you, ma'am."

At the door, the butler took cards from Mr. Harley and Sebastian. To Mr. Harley he said, after perusing the card, "Ah, sir, you are expected." To Sebastian and Frannie, however, he gave only a doubtful look and hesitated. Mr. Harley said with a touch of asperity, "We are all one party. Show us in, man."

They proceeded up a flight of steps and down a narrow corridor. Frannie suddenly felt the anxiety and distress that a now familiar train of dismal thoughts elicited in her. It would all end badly. She wasn't entitled to a farthing; or, if she were, she would never gain access to it. She would be a cast out, her future nothing but the workhouse. She'd live with Mr. Withers before letting it come to that, she thought. She could be useful to him in his shop and a comfort in his old age. Sebastian must have read her thoughts or at least the morbid direction of them, for he said with a bracing look, "Chin up."

And then, no sooner had they taken their seats, Mrs. Fanshawe entered the room. A stout matron with a serviceably fashionable gown but a tight, stiff cap, she looked imperiously at the threesome. Mr. Harley had situated himself in a wing chair but now came heavily to his feet, as if the effort was cumbersome. He bowed lightly and sat back down. Sebastian rose with no hesitation from the sofa and bowed most gracefully before reclaiming his seat. In return, Mrs.

Fanshawe glared at him. She gave Frannie an equally scathing glance, and said to Mr. Harley, still from the doorway of the room, "What is the meaning of this? Did I not warn you about this young woman trying to impose upon what is rightfully my child's?"

Mr. Harley cleared his throat. "I must warn you about making false statements, ma'am. If it is found you are attempting to take possession of what is rightfully *this* Miss Fanshawe's, you will be guilty of attempted felonious theft."

Mrs. Fanshawe stiffened. She stalked into the room, lips pursed. "I know naught of another Miss Fanshawe, sir, besides my only and dearest child! I tell you, there is no other! My husband is the only male in his line, and he is not this— this—*imposter's* father!"

"When do you expect the return of your husband, ma'am?" he asked now in his strangely calm tone. He'd told Frannie and Sebastian earlier that Mr. Fanshawe was first mate on a commercial vessel. His tone was reassuring to Frannie, whose consternation rose considerably when she heard there were no other Fanshawe males. If that were true, would it not mean that this Mr. Fanshawe must be her father? But he held no title; how would such a man of middling means have a fortune set by for her in a trust? Despite this perplexity, and the venomous looks of the lady, still there arose in Frannie's breast a faint hope. If he was indeed her father, nobleman or not, her paternity would at least be settled. More, she would know her father!

"My husband's ship is not expected for a month, sir. But I assure you, I await his arrival anxiously, as he will settle this matter." She tossed her head and added, "I warrant you, he has no child other than ours. This one here," she motioned derisively at Frannie, "is none of his get, I tell you."

"What do you know about the trust?" Mr. Harley asked.

Mrs. Fanshawe's face blanched as if she'd little expected to have the question thrust upon her. Hesitantly she said, "I know only that it awaits my daughter upon her majority."

"How much is it worth, ma'am?"

She gave him an alarmed look. "If you do not know, sir, I shan't enlighten you."

Mr. Harley's countenance darkened. "Do not trifle with me, madam. If I find your claim has merit, I will be your advocate. I seek only the truth. I will defend the rightful claimant, whoever it is. Now, unless you are prepared to admit your daughter is *not* the heiress of this trust, then I suggest you cooperate fully."

All of this was spoken in decided tones. Frannie's anxiety returned, for it seemed as though Mr. Harley might yet be convinced that Mrs. Fanshawe's child was the rightful claimant. She happened to glance at Sebastian, but his gaze was upon the woman of the house. He turned his head, as though he felt her eyes upon him, and, when he saw the look of trepidation on her face, gave another bracing look, with a slight nod. "Do not fear," it seemed to say. She swallowed and returned her attention to the others.

Mrs. Fanshawe said, almost meekly now, "I don't rightly know the value. It's an investment of some sort. All I know is that there is a trust, and it belongs to my daughter."

"Who is the benefactor?" he asked, with his peculiarly officious, detached tone.

Uncertainty flickered in her eyes momentarily, but was replaced by a hard glint. "My husband! He wins prizes at sea, you know—all kinds of cargo and chattel. He alone has the particulars. If you must know, he never wished to tell me of it, but I overheard it, I did. There's a fund, alright, and 'tis a fortune by now. It belongs to my daughter, and there's an end of it." Raising her voice and with a finger pointed at Frannie she added, "We shan't be fobbed off by this upstart! How she knows aught of it, I cannot say, but 'tis our business only."

Mr. Harley rose and paced the room, staring at the lady. "Do you mean to say, you have never inquired about it?" He turned to share with Frannie and Sebastian a look of stark incredulity before turning it in full force upon the lady. She seemed to shrink beneath his gaze. Mr. Harley raised a finger and pointed it at her. "You are aware of a trust fund, and you say it belongs to your daughter—" he waved an arm as though he were giving a summary in a court of law to a jury—"but you never asked the amount? It's value?" His voice filled more and more with doubt.

Mrs. Fanshawe's face grew rosy. "As I said, sir, my husband has the full particulars of the case. He never wished to speak of it. I daresay he thought I'd put an anchor on it, make him spend the hard-earned prizes." She glowered at them. "Or perhaps he won it at gaming and didn't wish me to know. I own, all men succumb to gaming at one time or other. I did *not* inquire—to spare his feelings—and because I *wanted* the money for my daughter." With pride in her voice she added, "She is to marry Lord Whitby, you know."

Mr. Harley had been watching her keenly and now said, "The fact is, if a family man wins a fortune, whether by gaming or other means, he uses it to better himself and for the good of his family. You reside in middling circumstances, I perceive." He made a pointed glance at worn carpet. "Not exactly living in clover now, are we? It makes little sense that your husband—or anyone in such a case—would start a trust fund rather than enjoy the full benefits of the prize for himself and his wife. Miss Fanshawe here," he turned and gestured at Frannie, "has subsisted all her life upon the interest of that trust." He raised a brow and settled an icy stare upon the woman. "Men of ordinary means would do their utmost to keep their *current* family in the best possible situation, rather than economizing for the sake of an earlier *mésalliance*. Surely you see the unlikelihood of it."

Mrs. Fanshawe for the first time looked unsure of herself. She cried, "I know not his reasons! But I do know there is only one Miss Fanshawe, and she lives beneath *this* roof!" She turned to Frannie with blazing eyes and pointed. "This young woman is a tufthunter! Brazen hussy!"

Frannie gasped. A gold digger she was not!

"Remember yourself, madam," said Sebastian coldly.

She gave him only a cursory glance and sniffed in an injured fashion before turning back to Mr. Harley. "Only Mr. Fanshawe can supply you with the particulars of the trust, including its value. But this is monstrous! You, sir, have offered no proof that this—*impostor*—has any business in our affairs! Why should we divulge to you any of our concerns?"

With a sinking heart, Frannie swallowed her indignation. No words came in which she could defend herself. All she could manage was to falter out, "My name is Frances Fanshawe, ma'am."

Suddenly the door opened. A young woman walked in and looked about curiously at the various faces, all of whom stared back at her. She had hair every bit as dark as Frannie's, and a mild resemblance in features. But where Frannie's chin was narrow, this young woman's was wide, much like Mrs.

Fanshawe's. She shared the lady's broader nose and prominent brow as well. She had hazel eyes, intelligent but mild. Her gaze flicked from one face to another, then hovered upon Frannie's pretty countenance with apparent interest, offering an uncertain little smile. Frannie returned a relieved nod and smile of her own.

"This!" cried Mrs. Fanshawe majestically, sweeping an arm in the direction of the young woman, "is my daughter, Miss Catherine Fanshawe—the *only* Miss Fanshawe in England, I daresay!" The young lady coloured rosily. "Mama, you—you didn't tell me we had guests."

"They are not guests," said Mrs. Fanshawe coldly. Glaring at the company she added, "In fact, they are just leaving." She went and stood by the door, opening it triumphantly so they could exit.

Mr. Harley stood first. "Inform your husband that I await his call. If I do not hear from him, I will take Miss Fanshawe's claim to King's Bench."

Mrs. Fanshawe let out a snort of a breath. "You have no case against us!"

"We shall see, madam," he replied. "The law will be the judge. You will incur legal fees, whatever the outcome. If you wish to avoid them, Mr. Fanshawe must call upon me at his earliest convenience." The others had risen and now were heading behind the solicitor to the doorway. Catherine stood by surveying them with perplexity. The two young women met eyes. Like Frannie's, Catherine's clear, thoughtful gaze was troubled, but there was no incrimination in them. Frannie felt certain she did not share her mother's hostility. Perhaps she did not know about Frannie yet, or what her claims were. Perhaps she, too, would despise Frannie when she learned of them.

Sebastian stopped before Mrs. Fanshawe. "What is the name of your husband's ship?"

The lady glared, her mouth twitching. "The Golden Sovereign," she said coldly. He bowed politely to both women.

When they were outside again, Mr. Harley said, "Good of you to get the name of the ship. We'll watch the papers for news of when it docks." Turning to Frannie, he added, "If Fanshawe doesn't come to me directly, we may have a long fight ahead. Despite what I said inside, I'll need more evidence before putting a barrister on it to bring it to court."

While he and Sebastian continued to discuss the matter, Frannie sat by, her heart sadly flummoxed. She hadn't considered that she might be bringing such ruckus into the Fanshawe home. Clearly, Mrs. Fanshawe hadn't known of her existence, any more than Frannie had known about Catherine's. It now seemed likely that she, Frannie, must be the illegitimate daughter of her husband! If Mr. Fanshawe had never told his wife about her, it could only follow that he must be ashamed of her. Catherine Fanshawe looked to be about the same age as Frannie. If it turned out they were of the same age, surely only one could be legitimate. And only the legitimate daughter, she was certain, could have claim to sums owned by the father.

But it all came back to the central perplexity: would a man of Mr. Fanshawe's means have a large sum set aside at all, much less in a trust for someone outside his legal family? The Fanshawes lived respectably, but not affluently. The contrast of their home to the Arundells' smartly appointed furnishings and rich artwork was noticeable. The more she thought on her case, the bleaker and more hopeless it appeared. She wondered if she ought to drop the enquiry. Leave the Fanshawes in peace. Let Catherine have the inheritance that surely she deserved more than Frannie. Her mother and Mrs. Baxter had never rightly understood how things were. If only her mother had told her that she was a baseborn child! Had she known it from the outset, she could have saved all of them, the Fanshawes, Mr. Arundell, Mr. Harley, a great deal of bother and vexation.

CHAPTER ELEVEN

After the strangers had gone, Catherine Fanshawe turned to her mother with a questioning look. "Mama, one of those men said he would take 'Miss Fanshawe's case' to court. I am aware of no dispute. Why would he call it my case?"

Mrs. Fanshawe's eyes sparked daggers. "That young woman you saw just now; she claims to be Miss Fanshawe!"

Catherine cried, "She claims to be *me*?"

"She claims your rightful due! The trust fund. Says her name is Frances Fanshawe."

"Is that why they wish to speak to papa? To verify her claim?"

Mrs. Fanshawe nodded.

"Is papa in trouble?" she asked, her eyes filling with worry.

"If that girl is his, you can be certain he is!" She paused, stopping to meet her daughter's worried visage. "The law may acquit him of guilt, but I'll give him grief like he's never met with!" She stalked from the room, leaving Catherine blinking, her face a picture of deep concern.

An only child, Catherine tried to imagine what it would mean if she had a sister, a half-sister, that is. She remembered the troubled countenance of the young woman who had been in the parlour earlier. She looked like an amiable, well-bred creature, just the sort of young woman Catherine would most like to associate with. She said the name in her mind, slowly.

Frances Fanshawe. It was a nice name. And suddenly she remembered something she had witnessed, though it had taken place many years before.

She'd been playing in her father's study, the only room in the house aside from the servants' quarters that she wasn't supposed to enter. She looked around curiously at the forbidden sanctum, an ordinary study. Shelves of books, dark wainscot, and a simple desk with a globe, barometer, and an issue of "The Maritime Report" upon it met her eyes. Hearing people approaching, she ducked quickly into the recess beneath the desk. She feared no one in the house, but a child's sense that she ought not be in the room gave her enough fright to stay huddled with knees pulled up against her chest, determined not to make a sound. Soon she heard voices, one belonging to Papa, but another that of an unknown woman. They entered the room, talking in low voices.

Childish curiosity made her hazard a peek by looking around the edge of the desk. Across the room she saw Papa and the lady standing by an inlaid bookcase. She was a pretty woman, dark-haired and large-eyed. She looked faintly familiar, and yet Catherine knew she'd never seen her before. The woman drew some folded papers from a purse and handed them to papa.

Frowning, he read them. Afterward, he gave her a very disturbed look and glanced at the papers again. Certain words jumped out at Catherine's curious ears, words she still remembered. *Trust fund...a tidy sum...guaranteed.* Only an extraordinary brain could have recalled the entire conversation, but Catherine had always excelled at her lessons due to a memory that was sharp to a turn. Clearly she recalled her father's voice: "Why should you accept this agreement?"

And then the woman's tight-lipped reply: "'Tis the only way. He'll disinherit him, otherwise. We'd all be penniless! He's a blackguard, as heartless as they come!"

"We'll get a solicitor," her papa said.

"No! He forbade it. The conditions are clear, and I must abide by them…or forfeit all." She drew in a shuddering breath.

Other phrases floated across Catherine's memory. The woman's voice, *I will not be the cause of his ruin... aristocratic pauper...stripped of his rights... at least 'twill provide for my child.* The lady was crying now. Her last desperate words rang in Catherine's brain to this day: *I revert all rights and must never contact him or the agreement's null and void. Give me your word that I may depend upon you, Charles, to keep my secret!*

He nodded sadly. "Of course." His final words then were so ominous that they too lingered in Catherine's brain. *If the old devil passes on, then all will set to rights.*

Papa searched among the books and pulled one out. Opening it, he inserted the folded papers, closed the book, and returned it to its place. Watching him, the woman's face relaxed. She sighed. *I'm obliged, Charles...*

Her father nodded again, took her hand and squeezed it hard. *Blessings go with thee, Meg.*

At this point, Catherine unfortunately had to sneeze—she could not contain it, and the adults heard the sound. Mr. Fanshawe strode to the desk and peered beneath at her. "Come out."

Shame-faced, she scrambled out and to her feet. A quick peek told her the woman was staring at her, but her face showed mild amusement, an indulgent look. *She's nice!*

Catherine thought in surprise, which added to her shame for eavesdropping though she hadn't meant to, exactly.

"Whatever you heard, Cat, you will now forget; and say nothing of it to Mama."

"Yes, papa."

"Go, now."

She stole a final peek at the nice, pretty woman, who was now almost smiling at her. To her surprise, when she left the room, she found her mother beside the door against the wall, a finger to her lips. While Catherine watched, Mama bent over at the keyhole, listening.

Inside the study, after Catherine had gone, Frannie's mother looked again at Charles. "When he comes looking for me, tell him I've gone to America."

Mr. Fanshawe nodded sadly.

"He'd keep looking, otherwise," she said simply. "And nothing must nullify the agreement. The papers are in your hands for safekeeping—payable to *Miss Fanshawe* upon her majority."

When Catherine sat on her father's knee before the hearth that evening, she had asked who the pretty lady was that he'd spoken to earlier. Papa was usually soft-spoken, but his voice hardened. He told her again to put it from her mind and to say nothing to Mama. Ironically, his stern injunction to forget the incident seemed instead to have seared it into her brain.

"Do you have a fortune, Papa?" Catherine had asked. "Is that what a trust fund is?" She'd thought those words quite wonderful. Images of gleaming gold coins, stacks of them, spilling out of a pirate's treasure chest, ran through her child's brain.

"No, m'dear. And not another word about a fund. It's a great secret, do you understand? Or it may all be lost." He put a finger to his lips and gave her a conspiratorial look. "Not another word. Especially to your mother."

Now, all these years later, Catherine understood. Papa had a sister, but due to some mysterious circumstance (that neither parent would disclose) her name was never mentioned. The most she'd learned was from Mama, who once said Papa's sister had foolishly gone to America many years ago after a tragic affair of some kind; she was not to be thought of.

Now it all made sense. The woman she'd seen with Papa in his study must have been that sister. The child she mentioned, the one that would be "provided for" was her child, the other Miss Fanshawe. This explained the disgrace, for she must be a child out of wedlock! But it reassured her that Papa was not Miss Fanshawe's father.

What neither of them knew was that Mrs. Fanshawe had heard only enough to assure her there was a secret trust fund for 'Miss Fanshawe'—and who could that be but Catherine! Indignation that he had income not at her disposal was quickly followed by mollification, for would not her daughter be rich one day? A daughter who would surely take care of her mother? What woman could be cross over that?

Over the years Catherine had thought about the hushed meeting and the secret fund, but dutiful daughter she was, for she adored Papa, she'd never spoken of it. Only once had she tried to find the mysterious papers that had passed from her aunt's hand to her father's. After his ship had left port, she'd returned to the forbidden room, straight to the bookshelf where she'd seen him tuck the papers into a book. But which one? With the room to herself, she searched through one shelf of books but to no avail. At that point, Mama found her in the room and gave her a great combing, for was not Papa's study for himself alone, his privacy not to be intruded upon? Catherine never attempted to find them again.

Now, a decade later, she went again to Papa's study with fresh curiosity. Surely Papa wouldn't be angry now if she wished to investigate, not under the circumstances. That man earlier had threatened Mama with the law. Surely that was reason enough for her to get to the bottom of the matter. Whatever was on those folded sheets, the ones which had settled her aunt's mind, must be the answer. One by one she went through each shelf in the room.

But, after exhausting the books on each and every one, she found nothing. A few faded bookmarks gave her pause, but these she put back and continued the search. Finally, she concluded her father had hidden the mysterious papers elsewhere, papers that would explain the trust, and prove, alas, that Mama was *wrong*. The trust did not belong to her, Catherine. It belonged to the other Miss Fanshawe.

En route to King Street, Frannie worked up the courage to ask Sebastian what she had lacked courage to ask Mr. Harley. As he handed her down from the carriage, she said, "Sir, might I inquire? Did Mr. Harley find evidence to bolster my claim when he made inquiries on my behalf?" Her heart beat painfully, for she was well aware that the evidence was likely to be scarce, even non-existent.

Sebastian hesitated. "He found the parish record of your birth."

"Yes?" Her heart skipped a beat. Sebastian looked regretful.

"The entry was not complete, but appears to have been doctored. Your father's name was blotted out." He paused, met her eyes and added gently, "It does raise questions about the legitimacy of your birth, I'm afraid."

"Questions?" Dread filled her heart.

He looked away and then back at her. "The difficulty is that your mother's maiden name is Fanshawe, and you share that name. Charles Fanshawe of Cheapside had a sister Margaret, who must be your mother."

A wave of mortification washed over Frannie. Did this not indicate that she must be illegitimate? Had Mama hidden the truth from her all her life? Had Mrs. Baxter known? Her eyes brimmed with tears. Thoughts and fears filled her mind, but she stared at the ground as they walked. She would no doubt be sent packing now.

"Mr. Harley finds it curious that your father's name was crossed out. He said it may be indicative of possible foul play."

"Foul play?" she asked.

"It's a crime to alter a parish record," he explained. "But it was done. This raises the possibility of unusual circumstances surrounding your birth and situation in life." He paused. "Nothing can be concluded at present." Before she could reply, he motioned her to silence as they entered the house and handed their accoutrements to Tipps.

"Is Mrs. Arundell here?"

"Gone out, sir, with an acquaintance," Tipps replied.

Sebastian turned to Frannie, "Where shall I take you? To the library?" A smile curved his lips.

The Arundell library was Frannie's favourite room, stocked with more books than she'd ever seen in a home. It seemed no one else in the family frequented it, but apparently her habit of retiring there to read whenever she wasn't needed, had been noted. She often took one of Mrs. Arundell's magazines with her, such as *Le Belle Assemblée*, or, *The Ladies' Monthly Museum*. She did this not because she was enraptured by fashion plates or advice for young women on etiquette or beauty, but so that none would think her a bluestocking. Her real object was to read as many new titles from the shelves as she could manage. It was also a quiet place for morning devotions, to read the prayer book.

At this moment she thought of escaping to her bedchamber to throw herself upon the bed and have a good cry. Her birth record was shameful! Her father's name crossed out! But another part of her rose up. She would go to the library. Only God knew how much longer she'd have access to it. "I know my way, thank you," she said in a low voice. But he continued to walk with her to the stairs, and she felt his company like a comfort, a warm blanket on a cold day. He might have shunned her after learning about that birth record.

He suddenly turned to her. "You lived with your mother and Mrs. Baxter in Lincolnshire, did you not?"

She nodded. "Yes, at the edge of town."

"Well, you weren't born there. Mr. Harley's clerk found that record of your birth in Gloucestershire. Did you know?"

Frannie shook her head. "I had no notion."

"Bartlett Hall is in Gloucestershire. When we're there at

Christmas, we can ask to see the record, if you like." He paused, then continued, "The good news is, Harley traced the annual payment you spoke of, at least to the extent of confirming that your mother did indeed deposit a sum annually. The bank as yet hasn't come forward with the name or company name on the banknotes. Until they do, we cannot trace their origin. But it indicates that someone somewhere did assuredly provide for you and your mother."

She felt a wisp of hope and caught her breath. "Yes! I am sure it must be my father."

"We hope to find out." They had reached the library and he now motioned her in. Seeing no fire in the grate, he went to the bell pull.

Frannie waited, her heart torn between hope and discouragement. When he returned to her, he said, "We may hope that Charles Fanshawe is indeed your uncle and, since his name was furnished to you, that he understands the particulars of this business, both your birth and the trust. Your mother must have confided in him."

Frannie stared at the Oriental rug as he spoke, but nodded.

He continued, "Let us hope he is prepared to be forthcoming, and that they are not conspiring to take what belongs to you."

She slowly raised her large doe eyes to meet his. "My father—if he can be found—can sort this out properly."

"In the meantime, your uncle may be an honest man. We'll say nothing about the circumstances of your birth until we understand them better, and hope for his help in that regard." He hesitated. "If the other Miss Fanshawe was entitled to the trust, her family should also have been the recipient of the annual sums, the interest sent to your mother. Mr. Harley found no record of such, and their lifestyle indicates otherwise."

A deep unrest filled Frannie. How she longed to know the truth, no matter how damning! If only Mama were here to fill in all the gossamer threads of her past. Feeling full of shame, though she had no culpability in the circumstances of her birth, she could not meet his eyes.

A chambermaid entered with a coal scuttle and set to building a fire. Sebastian casually took a book from a shelf and paged through it, while Frannie sat there squirming beneath the gloomy foreboding that she must be illegitimate. Sebastian was doing his brown best to soften the blow, behaving as though it were only a possibility, but Frannie could sense the writing on the wall. How lowering! How sad! She would never be his social equal! Could anything be more impossible than for a respectable family to accept than an illegitimate daughter?

Even if she were not a blow-by child, her father had likely refused to allow his name on her parish record. She searched her mind for other possibilities. Might her parents have divorced before her birth? Or been unlawfully wed? She was grasping at straws.

When finally the maid left, and with a small flame already growing, Sebastian put the book away and approached the settee where Frannie sat. In a gentler tone he continued, "'Tis possible a baptismal record in Lincolnshire may yet be found which could contain the name of your father, though it is doubtful. Mr. Harley has men on it, searching as we speak. Take heart."

She looked up at him gratefully but could not hide tears that had pooled in her eyes. She said, "If there were such a record, would it not have been discovered first? Before a parish record in Gloucestershire? I daresay I must prepare myself for the workhouse!"

Sebastian frowned. "Nonsense. Well-bred young women have other...options." His gaze remained clouded as he surveyed her. "Indeed, Miss Fanshawe, do not despair. If the very worst is found to be true, that your father and mother never married, it is still remains that the man has been supporting you all your life and means to continue doing so. You are not in a hopeless condition. There will be no poor house for you." He hesitated. "And—you have friends," he added awkwardly.

His words were meant kindly, to remind her that the Arundells were on her side. He hoped to lighten her gloom. But Sebastian did not know, could not understand, that in addition to the crushing revelation of her low birth was the realization that she could not be considered proper wife material. She would not be respectable, making her forever unfit for *him*. No amount of money could ever make her acceptable to this very proper man who stood to inherit a title. She sat in frozen silence. All her worst fears—*true*!

Rubbing his chin, Sebastian added, "Mr. Harley remains cautiously optimistic. You must adopt his attitude."

She nodded disconsolately. But the thought of Mama, of her whole upbringing, how she'd been assured of a noble parent, and of the trust, made her cry indignantly, "It cannot be so black as it appears! If it were," she said, looking up at him with anguished eyes, "I am sure my mother would have told me!" She flung her mind to grasp at anything else that might support her claim. "She was a church-going woman! And there is the ring," she added, though in a weak tone.

"Indeed," he said, bracingly. Whether to soothe her spirits or because there was conviction, she could not tell. But he added, nodding, "And your father's name was recorded before being scratched out—this suggests a legitimate birth. Nor did the record say, 'Frances Fanshawe, *baseborn* child of X,' which is usual in cases of illegitimacy. Let us be encouraged."

Frannie's heart took a lift, for he'd said, Let *us* be encouraged. Another thought occurred. "Could we apply to the rector or curate for the name? One of them might recall it on account of the unusual circumstance of it being scratched out."

He shook his head. "There is a circulating rector who seldom visits, but he's a new man; same for the curate, who's been there only five years. The former churchmen are no longer living. In any case, the birth might have been recorded by a clerk. And no record of a marriage has turned up thus far. I'm afraid that without it, your father's name shall remain a mystery for the time being." He paused and approached the fire. Leaning over it to warm his hands, he added, "We'd have to put a Bow Street runner on the case to discover more, I think. But they don't like civil disputes. They prefer weightier matters, unsolved murders and the like." He turned and smiled. Frannie stared at him, savoring that smile—it seemed the sweetest in the world.

He turned back to the grate, but she continued gazing at him. In his pantaloons, boots, and jacket, Sebastian was a fine figure of a man. His features could often look stern, his eyes veiled, such as when he was quietly contemplating a matter, or looked up from the pages of a book. But when he smiled, every hard line vanished. In fact, it seemed only when he smiled that she saw his real nature, where his true feelings lay on a matter. Smiling as he was now, all was clear. He'd turned to her, his eyes infused with concern. *For her.*

It made her want to cry. For one miserable fact was seeping across her brain, trickling into every space in her heart. A miserable fact she had failed to suppress or prevent.

She *loved* him. She wasn't just attracted to Mr. Arundell, as she'd previously thought. Oh, to be on equal footing with him! To have the luxury of hoping for something more to come of their acquaintance than what it was. He took a fireiron and stirred the coals while she tried to get hold of herself. When he turned to her again, rubbing his hands of coal dust, he said, "There is hope of a happy outcome. When we learn your father's identity, there may yet be a perfectly respectable explanation, if unconventional. And if your parentage is *not* completely respectable, you may end up with a fortune nevertheless. You could live quietly anywhere you like. You needn't be concerned with what society thinks."

Frannie nodded reluctantly with a troubled countenance. Her heart told her she could never be unconcerned with what society thought. Dark images crossed her mind like turbulent ocean swells, breaking upon her heart and suddenly they bubbled up into speech as she cried, "But I am concerned! I fear the censure of man *and* God! I hardly dare raise my eyes to Him if—" She could not complete the sentence.

In a soft tone, Sebastian said, "You needn't fear divine judgment. You had nothing to do with the circumstances of your birth, and if our religion teaches us anything, it is that forgiveness in Christ is available to all." In a darker tone he added, "Society is the harsher judge; but let us hope for the best."

She sniffed and looked up gratefully, but still there

lingered doubt in her breast. She said disconsolately, "I am above fond of your mother, sir. I hate to consider what she will think of me—" She stopped, unable to say more without dissolving into tears, and certainly unwilling to say it wasn't the loss of Mrs. Arundell's good opinion only which she feared.

He took her hand. "My mother is a charitable woman. She shan't abandon you, though she values upper class society."

His unspoken words, *even though you are not upper class,* cut her heart. "Thank you," Frannie murmured, keeping her face turned down. Acutely conscious of her hand in his, she tried to memorize the feel of his large hand encompassing hers, strong, solid and reassuring, though his grasp was light. He seemed as if he didn't notice their hands—she dared not breathe too hard, lest it wake him and he recall himself and drop it.

He said, "Be certain that the first matter we will address with Mr. Fanshawe is your paternity. Mr. Harley assures me he has land agents on the prowl. As soon as *The Golden Sovereign* returns to this shore, we shall be upon him."

"Do we know when that is?" she asked, her face prettily scrunched in worry.

"We will know. The maritime columns in the paper supply the expected arrival. With any luck, I'll meet him at the dock myself."

Frannie's heart sang for a moment. Sebastian Arundell, the fastidious man with clean hands, would do that? Brave the noisy, dirty, sea-stained docks for her?" She smiled gratefully at him.

He said, "I consider it vital to reach him before his wife gets word to him." He released her hand, bowed politely, and started toward the double doors of the room. "I'll leave you now to your reading."

Frannie took a deep breath and tried to settle her mind. But just as the door almost closed behind him, she remembered something. "Oh, Mr. Arundell!" she called. Sebastian was back in an instant, his face a question.

"Though we do not believe Mr. Fanshawe is my father, I am afraid we left his wife with the impression that he must be. That I am, in fact, the *blow by* of her husband's!" She took a shuddering breath. "It is utterly horrifying to be thought of as such."

"I believe she knows you are her niece; but if not, Mr. Harley anticipated that a little suspicion of foul play on her husband's part would make her more cooperative with us. I apologize for the aspersion it appears to cast upon your character."

"Little wonder she loathes my existence!"

"She loathes it most, I believe, on account of the trust fund."

"Also, sir—" here she hesitated, for only an extraordinary circumstance could induce her to made this request. "When we go to Gloucestershire…would you mind very much if I do not use my mother's last name? The shame of it! I fear that something might arise from the past that cannot be pleasant."

"I don't suppose you have anything to fear," he said, with some surprise. "But what name would you prefer?" Frannie had somehow already decided upon this, though the idea of using an alias had seemed to form in her mind only a minute earlier. "Miss Baxter?" she asked.

He hesitated. A little smile formed at the edges of his mouth. "Under normal circumstances I should think such a request was impertinent at best, or possibly even wicked."

Frannie's breath caught in her throat. "I am trying to *avoid* the appearance of evil, sir," she said. "If questions should arise, as almost certainly they will—if I am known to share my mother's maiden name, I fear it will cast a shadow upon *your* family! Guilt by association is unfortunately an iron-clad tenet of society, would you not agree?"

He gazed at her with thoughtful eyes. "I have no fear for the reputation of my family, but I understand your hesitation. Considering the mystery of your past, and that no one at Bartlett Hall could possibly be concerned in the matter, I see no reason why we must call you Miss Fanshawe." Relief filled her heart. She thanked him.

When he'd gone, she opened her book but only stared at the words on the page uncomprehendingly. She must reconcile herself to what the circumstances suggested. That her father's name was scratched out was ominous to her mind, more supportive of the notion that she was born out of wedlock than in it. Further, it was nothing that would stand up in a court of law, if it came to that, to bolster her claim. All she knew was that the more she probed into the matter of the trust, the worse her situation looked.

If only she'd not had to pay Mrs. Baxter's debts! She'd be living as she was before, in relative comfort and gentility, with her dignity intact, respectable in everyone's eyes, and in full expectation of a yearly sum to keep her thus situated. But as she reflected upon it, she knew that those debts were hers too. Mrs. Baxter had accrued them while keeping Frannie and her mama beneath her roof. She was right to have paid what she could.

Then another thought came. Had she not been forced from

her home, she would not have met Sebastian. *And*, a dark voice reminded her, *neither would she have fallen in love with a man she could never have.*

CHAPTER TWELVE

Frannie retrieved her copy of *Hamlet*, determined not to reflect upon the darker possibilities of her situation. Sebastian had said Mr. Harley clung to optimism regarding her case despite her parish record, and that she must too. She opened her book. Nor would she think about Sebastian. She ought not to lose herself in foolish dreams just because he was everything she could want in a husband. His beautiful eyes, neatness, intelligence, manners, his concern for her—all qualities that blended to make one remarkable man. Especially his concern for her—he was beyond generous with his time and help. How many men would so willingly invest themselves in a cause that appeared dubious at best?

Also, he had no vile habits like gaming or much drinking—none she had seen, in any case. His temper was stirred only by Edward, for otherwise he displayed a steady polite restraint of manner. He was not gregarious or demonstrative, but quietly thoughtful in his way. She could enjoy such a man for a long, long time. *For the rest of her life.* Good thing she refused to think of him. She spent the next few minutes staring into the grate seeing only the face of Sebastian, hearing his kind words, savoring how he'd held her hand.

Suddenly she came to as from a reverie and focused her eyes on the page. Like some of the other tomes she'd browsed through, this one had notes penciled in the margins. A few books even had pages of notes tucked in at the back, though this one did not. She had meant to ask the family about their origin, assuming they'd been written by the late Mr. Arundell, for it had been his library.

But she turned a page and saw a date beside an entry. "1805." The late Mr. Arundell had died at the turn of the century when the boys were young, she'd learned that from their mama. With a start, she realized it was likely Sebastian's hand that had written the notes! Was he not often carrying books from one room to another? Even at breakfast he usually had a book beneath his morning paper. He was too polite to read when she or Mrs. Arundell joined him at table, but she realized he must often read while taking meals if he was alone. She thought of the many evenings while she and his mother sat at sewing in the dim light, how he'd read to them, often with great feeling, stopping for a sip of sherry or Madeira now and then. In daylight, on many a rainy afternoon, had he not also read to them, walking about the room as he did so? Further, Mrs. Arundell was no great reader, and neither had she seen Edward pick up a book since her arrival.

The notes took on more significance. That he had written them warmed her heart. And then she realized that her preference for curling up to read in the library might be an inconvenience to him. What if he used to spend more time in that room, but now acquiesced its use to her for her pleasure? He had his study, which was some comfort, but the library was a special retreat with its warm Chinoiserie yellow papered walls, dark wainscot, high ceiling, desks and cosy reading nooks. It would be just like Sebastian to say nothing of the loss. A quiet sacrifice that met with no complaint or cold air.

She slowly examined the notes in the book with fresh interest. She'd been relying heavily upon them all along as to the meaning of archaic words, for Shakespearean English was as puzzling as it was beautiful, tripping off her tongue as she read aloud to enjoy the sound. Now she read them with greater interest. There were notes about blank verse, the source material that had likely influenced the great bard, about functions of rhyme and couplets, and more. She'd never approached a book in such a studious way, and it fascinated her.

It was so fascinating that when the door burst open two hours later, she hadn't realized, between the terrible murder of Polonius in Act III and the sad fate of Ophelia in Act IV, the passage of time. Teary-eyed about Ophelia, she looked up to find Edward standing in the doorway. "Beau said I might find you here."

Frannie blinked and sniffed and put the book down. "Oh, dear! Were you looking for me?"

"Dinner's on hold until you join us," he said, with a gentle grin.

"Upon my word!" Frannie got hastily to her feet. "I won't trouble to dress, unless you think it would affront your brother or mother."

"I daresay they'd be more affronted to be kept waiting," he replied easily. "Besides," he added philosophically as they walked down the corridor, "My brother only sits upon points where *I* am concerned. Haven't you noticed?" he asked, eyeing her with a raised brow. "He's a cat's paw when it comes to women!"

Frannie wasn't quite sure what Edward meant. Her eyes

looked the question.

"A kitten!" he said derisively. "My mother always makes him amenable to doing anything she likes. Her spending exceeds her monthly jointure, but she carries few debts, and only until my brother discovers them. He keeps her from the duns." He snickered. "He is obliged to pay for jewellery and baubles and fur stoles and tippets, instead of putting the blunt where he'd most like."

"In horses or carriages?" she asked, understanding these to be common interests of gentlemen.

"Not him; he's got two equipages, enough for his needs, so he says. Nothing so fine as Lord Harry's, of course." Edward paused here to consider the matter of how fine this Lord Harry's equipage was in comparison to his brother's, but then continued in a matter of fact tone, "No, he cares only for investments—he's got a huge interest in East India—and adding to his collection."

"His collection?"

He gave her a surprised look. "The one you've been enjoying. The library! Books are all the rage with him."

Of course. It was just as she'd surmised. "I presumed your late father set up the library."

"He did, of course; but Sebastian adds to it, extravagantly, if you want my opinion. He could be far more 'the thing' if he took a care at his tailor's instead of fribbling his time for trifles in book shops."

Frannie bit her tongue to contain the instant rejoinder that to be well read could hardly be called fribbling one's time. She did not wish to argue with Edward, considering he would never come round to an agreement on the topic. But she thought again of how Sebastian read to them with animated zeal to amuse, entertain, or enlighten them. 'Twas not only for their own entertainment; he enjoyed his literary pursuits. There was nothing fribbling about it.

She realized she had ought to give up the library. Her occupation of it was likely a deterrent, keeping him from his favourite room in the house.

"Your continued presence here is further proof," Edward said with uncanny timing, "of Sebastian's weakness for the softer sex." Little did Edward know just how true that statement must be! With Frannie's legitimacy in question, many a proper man or woman would have barred her from the house. She had long wondered why Sebastian hadn't sent her packing the moment he'd heard her story. Edward's assertions seemed to answer.

He added, "Says you're the gentlest creature he's yet met with." He smiled. "A bruised reed, he called you. And far be it from Sebastian to break a bruised reed of the muslin set."

Frannie wasn't sure whether she liked being considered a bruised reed, but she said, "He doesn't always give way to our sex. Your mama does not wish to go to Bartlett Hall next month, but Sebastian will have his way in that."

"So he will," Edward acknowledged, rubbing his chin. "I daresay he's in the right. He ought to be on good terms with his inheritance. We Arundells aren't crawling with relations, I suppose you've noticed. The importance of the matter must have made him firm on it."

Frannie wished to think more on this, whether or not Sebastian was a cat's paw with women, as Edward said, or if he was indulgent only towards certain of them—such as herself and his mama. But they arrived at the dining room. She offered an awkward apology as she took her seat.

Mrs. Arundell said, "Do not give it a thought, Frannie dear. The only one truly put out, I daresay, is cook, who worries the roast mutton will grow tough, or the potatoes coarse."

"Oh, dear," Frannie said, and chancing to glance at Sebastian, saw that customary, veiled expression. Was he too worried about the roast mutton being tough, or whether the potatoes turned coarse?

"If we were famished we'd have eaten ahead of you," Sebastian said, as if to answer her unspoken question. Two footmen brought in the covers. "Only a savage cannot wait for his meal," he finished. These words relieved her mind, and his eyes, she saw gladly, were mild as ever when she raised contrite ones to meet them.

"Nevertheless, I do apologize," she repeated. "I'm afraid I lose track of time when I'm reading."

"Ah!" cried Mrs. Arundell. "Were you lost in a novel? I adored *Waverley*! I warrant I hardly left my couch for a week when I was in it." Before Frannie could agree that *Waverley* was a delight, Edward cried, "She jumped like a March hare when I entered. I warrant it was Byron; all the ladies sing his praises. They fuss and fret over him as if he was Wellington!"

Frannie blushed, but Sebastian said, "If she jumped, it was no doubt because you failed to knock, you brute." Turning to Frannie, he said, "I admire anyone who gets lost in a good book, be it novel, or poetry, or something else."

Frannie nodded gratefully, recalling Edward's words that *books are his thing*. But to end the speculation she said, while searching Sebastian's face for a sign of recognition, "*Hamlet* is what has me in its grips." She was certain, after her conversation with Edward that it must be Sebastian who had written the notes and she watched for his reaction. To her gratification, a look crossed his features, surprise, perhaps. Watching him she added, "I must admit that my enjoyment—and understanding—of it is much enhanced on account of notes I found in it."

"Are you reading those notes?" Sebastian asked in surprise. "Can you truly read that scrawl?"

"Scrawl? Did someone actually write in the pages of our books?" his mother asked in astonishment.

"Dearest, I did. I pencil notes in margins of certain works, such as Shakespeare's , that I particularly enjoy. They can be erased if anyone is scandalized."

Bright-eyed, Frannie exclaimed, "I am glad you did! They taught me quite a lot! I think…that is, I am sure I will now read additional plays with far more intelligence than I would have before." Edward smiled indulgently.

Frannie saw his pitying look and wondered if his amusement was on account of how un-schooled in literature she must seem in their eyes—a thing easily accounted for, since she'd had a governess only intermittently. Or perhaps he found it amusing to see a female interested in more than art and music. Blushing, she held her tongue from further effusions, but in Sebastian's eyes she saw no teasing look or smug indulgence. In his normally veiled expression she saw something else, and it sent colour to her cheeks. His eyes were upon her, but alight with what seemed like a new idea or thought, like a door opening to reveal a hitherto unknown room.

The sudden look of a shared understanding, the beauty of his expression, made her look away for fear that her admiration for him would be obvious. Their old cook had said

Frannie was "as easy to read as a whistlin' kettle." Thoughts of cook, Mrs. Baxter, Mama, indeed her old life, were plaguing her less of late. But worries about her future life were her new distractions. Reading books was a welcome escape from it all.

"I left notes in a number of books," Sebastian offered. "I must say, I never expected them to be appreciated by anyone else, and meant to discard them altogether. But I hope you continue to find them enlightening."

"I am certain I shall," she said, still appreciating the different way Sebastian regarded her.

"You should have been born a man, Frannie," put in Edward, while helping himself to a dish from his end of the table. "You'd have studied poets and books to your heart's content. Lord knows I had to slog through it all."

"But she may study them now," put in Sebastian. "Like Edward Waverley of the novel, she may have an 'unstructured education.'" Reprovingly he added, "And I must say, your idea is reprehensible. Miss Fanshawe is eminently suited to womanhood."

"O'course," said Edward, smiling at her as if he hadn't inferred that she was a bluestocking.

Mrs. Arundell looked from Sebastian to Frannie and back at her eldest son. She said nothing.

CHAPTER THIRTEEN

That night, Frannie tossed and turned. It amazed her to have discovered that strait-laced Sebastian was a romantic at heart! To think, he'd written all those notes. He might have done it as any student, dutifully, only of necessity. But he'd kept the notes. He'd put them in the books where they pertained. He must have intended upon reading them again. And how his eyes had suddenly burned with appreciation when she spoke of them! But it might have had nothing to do with her. He had been reminded of his enjoyment of Shakespeare, or perhaps the feeling of youthful days in academia. He might have been put in mind of visits home between terms when his father was alive.

His father. If only *she* had a father. One with a name, that is. She sighed. She thought of Mrs. Fanshawe who despised her, and hoped heartily she would not again see that lady; but what chance that, when speaking to her husband seemed of paramount importance to discover the truth of Frannie's past? When she fell asleep, she dreamt Mrs. Fanshawe was pushing her out of her house, pointing her to the street, to poverty, to infamy. Frannie's tears were to no avail. The young Miss Fanshawe appeared, but she too, coldly turned away. As Frannie pounded on the Arundells' front door in her dream, she awoke. She had forgotten about the Arundells earlier in the dream, but suddenly remembered. It wasn't Mrs. Arundell her dreaming self hoped fervently would open the door, and whose arms she would rush headlong into, however. Neither was it Edward.

Mrs. Arundell informed the family at breakfast that she planned a day of shopping, and that Frannie would accompany her. The idea was delightful to Frannie after the dream ordeal, and especially on account of the headache which assailed her from the moment of waking. Uneasiness in the pit of her stomach furthered her discomfort. But the prospect of browsing high-end shops from Piccadilly to Oxford Street (for Mrs. Arundell was *prodigiously* fond of examining all the new and modish merchandise, and knew where to find the *finest* Brussels lace for a bonnet, and every *fallall* a lady could want) seemed just the thing to take her mind off her troubles. Frannie had no money, but going along would be great fun. She might even be of help to Mrs. Arundell if she grew flummoxed about which bonnet to purchase, or which fabric better suited her light complexion in candlelight.

Sebastian's mother, however, had other things in mind. She announced, while stirring a cup of chocolate, that she'd decided to bespeak a gown for Frannie.

"Well done!" Edward exclaimed. "Every lady ought to have a new gown at Christmas. No family wants to present a shabby appearance, eh?"

Frannie blushed.

Sebastian scowled. "Are you implying that Miss Fanshawe is in danger of that?"

With a comforting glance at Frannie Mrs. Arundell hurriedly said, "Frannie has never looked shabby, dear heart."

Edward cleared his throat and quickly amended, "Well I only meant, a lady delights in the latest fashions and being all the crack."

"Of course," agreed Mrs. Arundell, "and what with meeting your cousin and the local gentry, a new gown is just the thing to bolster any lady's confidence."

Sebastian's look was not promising so she added, "It will be my Christmas present for her, if that settles your mind."

"Dearest," began Sebastian, but Mrs. Arundell held up a hand. "Do you doubt Mr. Harley's success in securing her fortune? He and his men have learned that a goodly annual sum came to Frannie's mama each year, and therefore they say it can only continue, and then there's the trust fund to follow. I assure you," she added with a smiling glance at Frannie, "Mr. Harley will not rest until 'tis settled, and it shall be done to everyone's satisfaction."

Frannie frowned. Mrs. Arundell surely did not understand the matter could never be solved for "everyone's" satisfaction, for the Fanshawes would hardly be satisfied if Frannie were indeed assigned the trust. Nor, if the matter was settled to *their* satisfaction, could it be equally so to Frannie's. She was about to object but the boys' mother gave her a quelling look. Shaking her head as if to dismiss the notion that further discussion was necessary, she said, "Let us not speak further on it—money, we all know, is a vulgar subject."

But Frannie could not remain silent. Mrs. Arundell's intention was generosity itself, but all Frannie's fears of being found less than respectable one day made her loath to accept it. She said, "Ma'am, I thank you, but I have two gowns I have not yet worn. They are too fine for casual evenings at home, and I have not had need of them. They will answer perfectly for Gloucestershire."

"My dear," she replied, putting one hand upon Frannie's and patting it. "I have examined your wardrobe. I own, those gowns you mention are very agreeable, but you need one that is especially fine for our visit."

Frannie wondered if the lady still had hopes of making a match between her and Sir Hugo. Her heart sank. "Ma'am," she ventured, "I maintain, my gowns are sufficient; I have no desire to bespeak new ones."

"Nonsense," returned the lady, smiling. She turned to the men. "Is our Frannie's attitude not refreshing? She is the farthest thing from a grasping female!" Turning back to Frannie she added, "But as Edward noted, all women must adore a new gown. And since this is my gift to you, there is nothing in it to dislike." Frannie opened her mouth to object, but the boy's mother put a finger to her lips. "Not another word, my dear! I won't hear it."

Mrs. Arundell had made up her mind. Frannie turned a perplexed stare upon Sebastian, a silent plea. She saw thoughts roiling in his eyes. He wiped his mouth with a napkin and set it down. Now he would set Mrs. Arundell straight—that nothing was certain as far as Frannie's trust fund was concerned and that they ought not put out extra expense for one not entitled to the trappings of wealth. But to Frannie's concern he said to his mother, "So be it, dearest. Frannie is become a part of our family circle," he added, giving her a look of benign approval, "so naturally we ought to furnish her a new gown under the circumstances." Mrs. Arundell thanked him prettily, and then cast a dazzling smile at Frannie.

"Thank you, sir," Frannie said in a small voice. Would they regret this generosity if she was discovered to be illegitimate? Would Mrs. Arundell rue the day she came to stay with them? Oh, that fateful day when Edward had nearly run her down on Monmouth Street! If the worst were true, and the Arundells were forced to reject her, she could almost wish that Edward's curricle had not missed.

Ninety minutes or so later the carriage containing Frannie and Mrs. Arundell pulled away from the house on King Street. "I have a particular gown in mind for you," the lady said, turning earnestly to Frannie. "And I know just the right modiste for it. Lady Russell uses her exclusively and swore me to secrecy—but I can tell you, I'm sure, for you won't go gadding it all over town." She produced a copy of the latest *Bell's Court and Fashionable Magazine*, opened to an earmarked page, and pointed at a beautiful confection of peach satin, elaborately embroidered with pearls and spangles, short puffed sleeves, and a train at back. The neckline was square, with a standing lace collar—the kind the Empress Josephine had favored and which was still all the mode—and overall, dazzlingly elegant.

"That is too fine a gown for *me*, ma'am, and certainly for Gloucestershire!" Frannie said.

"But you'll use it again for the Season next year!" Mrs. Arundell smiled sweetly. "You see, I haven't entirely forgot economy."

Frannie was now deeply suspicious that the older lady's plan was to make her the wife of the baronet. But surely she *should* not wish for it—not when her son stood to inherit the baronetcy as long as Sir Hugo was obliging enough not to have sons of his own. And even Sebastian had pointed out the obvious, that Frannie might indeed supply those sons! Mrs. Arundell had seemed to come round to this logic. Yet no other explanation presented itself. Why did she wish to see Frannie gowned so expensively and with such pomp and style? The gown could almost be considered ostentatious.

As if reading her thoughts, the older woman said, "We leave for Bartlett Hall in two weeks, my dear. I already have two new gowns fit for the best company, but you are in need of this. A lady can never be too well dressed, you know."

"But ma'am, a lady can be *over*-dressed for an occasion, would you not say? Edward assures me the baronet's gatherings promise to be thin of fashionable company." She glanced again at the beautiful illustration on the page. "This would be proper for some great town mansion of your London acquaintance, I grant, but surely not for the country."

"Frannie, dear," said Mrs. Arundell with a little smile. "You must trust my judgment. I know how to get to the top of things, but you my dear, in your quiet style, with your quiet manners, are simply not going to climb Mount Olympus without my help."

Frannie frowned. Gaining the summit of Mount Olympus, she could only presume, meant getting a husband. And the husband that Mrs. Arundell had in mind must be Sir Hugo.

"I am indeed grateful to you," Frannie said, "but—"

"But let us not speak more of it. Come, come, dear—" For they had drawn up on a busy street lined with highbrow shops and well-dressed patrons coming and going. A footman opened the door and handed them down, Mrs. Arundell first, and then Frannie. As they walked toward a seamstress's shop, the lady leaned toward Frannie. "You must allow that I am in the best position of knowing how to please the man, for I know him best!"

These words were nails in a coffin for Frannie. There could be no further doubt. Mrs. Arundell's object was now crystal clear. She clung to the ridiculous notion of matching Frannie with the baronet. Looking greatly troubled, Frannie had no choice to but follow the lady into the shop. The French modiste was soon speaking to them with experienced ease of fabrics and styles, which ones were all the mode, and which were *faux pas*. Mrs. Arundell produced the dreaded illustration of the richly embroidered gown, explaining that she wanted it copied for Frannie. The Frenchwoman seemed delighted, all smiling approval. She said something in French to two shop girls who descended upon Frannie with zealous fervor, drawing her away for measurings.

When they exited the shop a good hour later, Frannie had resigned herself to the inevitable, eye-catching gown. Her one, tremulous hope was that, if she needs must wear it to please the lady, that it would be fetching enough to catch Sebastian's eyes. For the baronet, she had only one thought, and that was to avoid him as much as possible, as much as was in her power. But if Sebastian should look with approval upon her, with something approaching admiration—ah! That would make Christmas special indeed.

CHAPTER FOURTEEN

The next morning's *Maritime News* column brought the encouraging announcement that *The Golden Sovereign* was expected to dock in London the following day! What they did not expect was the announcement by Sykes, entering the parlour after a cursory scratch at the door, that a Miss Catherine Fanshawe awaited Miss Frances Fanshawe's pleasure. Only Frannie and Edward were home. Mrs. Arundell was on a morning call, and Sebastian was out to unknown destinations. Frannie looked in surprise at Edward, who said, "Another Miss Fanshawe? *Delicious*." But at Frannie's look of uncertainty, he asked, "Do you not wish to see her?"

"My heart *longs* to know her, I assure you. But I fear she comes not on friendly terms." Her insides were already aquiver. Had the young woman come to relieve her mind of the same resentment displayed by the mother? Had she come only to scold, or worse, threaten?

Edward gave her a look of concern. "Leave it to me. I'll sound her out. If she's here to have a pet at your expense, I'll spare you." To Sykes he said, "The first parlour." And with that Edward was on his feet and out the door before Frannie could make the smallest objection. Her insides churned uneasily. She came to her feet and paced the room. At the window she observed a nondescript carriage at the kerb, no doubt Miss Fanshawe's. If only Sebastian would return from wherever he'd gone. He would handle this young woman if her intentions were unkind.

But in a few minutes a short knock at the door was followed by the entrance of Edward and their guest, who had one hand upon his arm. Upon spying Frannie, the young woman nearly stopped at the threshold with a look on her face as though she feared she would receive at Frannie's hands what Frannie feared from hers.

Frannie left the window and Edward made introductions, giving Frannie a bright look and a furtive wink as the girls made their polite curtseys. She felt she'd been holding her breath but now relief settled upon her. If Edward was reassured, then she could be also. She might even hope for friendship to come of this!

"Please, have a seat," she said with a polite smile, motioning with a hand at a wingchair, while she took one opposite, so that the two young women faced each other. Miss Fanshawe registered the kind look with apparent relief, nodded, and took her seat. Frannie said, "May we offer you some refreshment, Miss—Fanshawe?" She'd hesitated over the word, never having had cause to address another Miss Fanshawe before. Catherine shook her head. "Thank you, no, Miss Fanshawe," (spoken with a tremulous smile). "I will trespass upon your privacy only for a few minutes."

More relief filled Frannie at her kind tone, and because Catherine evidently accepted her as a relation.

Looking toward Edward with concern, Catherine cleared her throat. "Mr. Arundell has informed me that you may not wish to speak with me privately, only I must tell you, I fear our conversation may be…delicate."

Frannie said, "I understand." For surely they would wish to speak of the trust, and of the shrouded mystery of their connexion, both delicate matters to be sure. She leveled a quelling gaze upon Edward. "Dear Edward, please allow me to speak with my—my cousin—privately."

Edward came to his feet and made a deep bow to Catherine. "A great pleasure to make your acquaintance, Miss Fanshawe. I hope we may see more of you?"

Catherine's cheeks flushed. "I—I hope so, sir. Thank you."

He turned to Frannie and bowed. "Ring if you need me," and then, facing her in a way so that Catherine could not see his face, made a raised brow and motioned imperceptibly toward the visitor. Frannie had no idea what this was meant to signify and merely smiled sedately. "Thank you. We won't be long, I'm sure."

"Indeed. I only need a few minutes of Miss Fanshawe's time," added Catherine hurriedly. After the double door had shut behind him, Catherine turned to Frannie. "Do you know *how* we are related?" she asked, coming right to the point.

Frannie blushed. "To be honest, I'm not quite certain. I believe your father is my uncle."

"Yes," Catherine said. "That is my belief as well!"

Both young women had been sitting stiffly erect, but with that one thing established, that each considered the other a close relation, tension dropped from the atmosphere as if bright sunshine had shooed away clouds. They studied each other benignly and with undisguised curiosity.

Smiling shyly, Catherine said, "You are the only female cousin I have."

Frannie said, "Do you have male cousins? Do I also have other cousins?"

Catherine chuckled. "No, I'm sorry. I should have said you are my only known cousin. Until now, I thought I had none."

"As I thought also," Frannie said, nodding. "But my mother was your father's sister, I believe?"

Catherine's eyes clouded. "Was? Is your mother—?"

"Passed from this life," Frannie said, with admirable self control. "For nigh eighteen months."

"I'm sorry." Catherine's blue eyes filled with sympathy.

"Thank you," said Frannie. "But she left me with quite the mystery…" Here she hesitated. Should she say outright that the biggest mystery of her life was the identity of her father? It was a shameful thing to own. "The trust," she said at last. "Do you know about it?"

Catherine bit her lip, blinking. "This is the reason I have called. I wanted to let you know that I remember a day when a woman called upon Papa. I believe it was your mother."

Frannie gasped. "Indeed?"

Catherine nodded. Her face grew pensive as she thought back to the day. "It was in Papa's study; they looked over some papers together. She said something like, *it must be this way*, and that someone would be disinherited if she didn't obey some sort of agreement."

"There was an agreement?" asked Frannie eagerly.

Catherine licked her lips. "I believe those papers hold the details of the trust. Apparently your mother left them in my father's safekeeping. I searched Papa's study, but I couldn't find them."

"But your father still has them, I suppose?"

Catherine nodded. "I believe so. I seem to recall your mother saying she must not use a solicitor." Here her brows furrowed. "But Papa told me never to speak of it, not even to mention the incident to my mother." She gave Frannie an apologetic look. "Mama heard, though. I found her listening at the door."

Frannie said, "My mother never spoke of having a brother, or told me of any family at all. I always found it strange. And she said my father died when I was young."

"I was told Papa's sister ran off to America." Again she looked apologetic. "After a tragic love affair." She gave Frannie a searching look. "You do not speak like an American."

"We lived in Lincolnshire," Frannie said. There was an awkward silence then until she added, "My mother evidently felt it incumbent upon her to cut off all society with her friends."

"It must have been a stipulation of the agreement," said Catherine, "for certainly a woman and her child are in need of friends." Gently she added, "Although unmarried women may disappear to some country village when there is a child..."

Frannie's eyes shone. "I was never given to understand anything else but that my parents were in fact married!"

"I am glad of that," she said, "only 'tis curious that your mother kept her maiden name," she replied, in that same gentle tone.

"I believe that too was part of the agreement," agreed Frannie. "But it is irregular, I grant."

"Yes, indeed!" Catherine said, staring at Frannie. "If you were not aware of the trust, I should think you were a Fanshawe that had nothing to do with our branch. But you evidently know about it, though my fiancé and his family are the sole recipients of the secret to my knowledge." She paused and asked, "How did you find us if your mother never spoke of her brother or his family?"

"Your father's name and direction were given to me when

my dear benefactress, Mrs. Baxter, left this world, only weeks since."

"Another loss for you! I'm sorry." Sympathy again filled her eyes.

Frannie sighed. "Thank you. All my life, both she and my mother assured me that, upon my majority, I would come into a fortune. The trust. And that it came from my father's estate."

Catherine looked intrigued. "Then you must know who your father is?"

Frannie swallowed. "I am afraid that is the mystery behind it all. My parents were separated before I was old enough to understand such things. I was told he'd died at sea. But we received an annual sum on his account, enough so that I was always kept in the first style of fashion."

"And now you have reached your majority?" Catherine asked.

Frannie hesitated. "I have not. But I am in need of the funds. With Mrs. Baxter gone…you see." She lapsed into silence, unwilling to divulge the unhappy circumstances that had beset her since Mrs. Baxter's passing. Catherine seemed mesmerized, staring at Frannie. "Yours is a strange history," she said, nodding thoughtfully. "Truly, why your father would set up a trust for you to begin with, when he took no further notice of you…? When your mother failed, even, to use his name?" The questions hung in the air solemnly. The likelihood of how it could ever be sensibly—or respectably—explained seemed to grow more remote with each revelation. Instead, the stark realities seemed to point to only one thing: that Frannie had been born out of wedlock.

With brows furrowed, Frannie said, "I understand your astonishment, believe me, Miss Fanshawe. I find it all rather astonishing myself. Indeed, most perplexing. I can make no sense of it." She looked across at her frankly. "We are hoping your father will untangle the enigma."

Catherine nodded. "I believe he can." Again a silence fell, until suddenly she added, shifting in her seat, "I beg your pardon, cousin, but—would not a marriage license contain your father's name?" Her question was not shaded in judgmental tones, but only of curiosity.

Frannie sighed. "I am certain it would, if only it can be found…" Her voice trailed off. She was suddenly desirous for the interview to end. How much she longed to be welcomed as family by the Fanshawes, but how estranged she felt! How ashamed. Why would they want her for a legitimate relation when for nineteen years they had seen fit not to know her or her mother? She said, "I am, as you might imagine, quite distressed over this…"

"Yes, of course!" the other replied, very kindly. "I am sure it will be found. My mother refuses to believe we are cousins and would rather torment herself with the notion of there being infidelity on my father's part. She sits upon pinpricks waiting for an explanation." She shot Frannie a gleam of wicked amusement. "If she were right, we would be half-sisters!" She shook her head, smiling. "I confess the notion of having a sister never crossed my brain before!" But then she grew sober and said, "I know it isn't true because I saw your mother with Papa, and I heard what I told earlier, talk of an agreement. I believe they may have mentioned your father's name…"

Frannie's heart quickened.

But she finished, "Only I cannot recall it… Harry, perhaps?... I'm sorry, I'm not certain."

Frannie said, "Your mother regards me as an impostor and a thief! But I assure you—!"

Catherine shook her head. "There is no need! Please, I know how it is." She looked away and then back, calmly. "My mother's heart is much set upon the trust. That is why she behaves monstrously to you. I daresay her behaviour may yet grow worse, for if Freddie—Lord Whitby, that is—cries off when he learns I have no funds to bring to the wedding, well, Mama will be in rare form." She swallowed.

Before Frannie could interject a word, she continued, "My father's return will silence her, for he will explain it all. But in the meantime, she persists in believing it must belong to me." She hesitated, deliberating. "Papa replied with a mysteriously unhappy letter after he received word of the betrothal. I see now 'twas because he knew it might not stand when the truth came out—that I have no fortune awaiting me." She paused, her face scrunched in concentration. "Now I think on it, he wrote that 'Old Swenson,' that is Lord Whitby's father, 'would *sink the ship* soon enough.'" She looked up apologetically. "Sink the ship—that's sailor speak for put an end to it."

She swallowed and continued. "My betrothal to Lord Whitby was accomplished with the promise of that fortune, and—and—as I did not know of your being in England, I saw no harm in hoping it was true." Tears sprang to her eyes.

"Of course you didn't," Frannie cried. Gently she asked, "Are you in love with him?"

Catherine looked away and licked her lips. "I am *fond* of him. I daresay I expect to love him once we are wed." But a little smile formed and she added, "Though I must say, he is a bit of a fribble." She looked up. "Mama will be furious, for surely he will cry off, now."

Frannie's eyes clouded.

Hurriedly Catherine added, "But I assure you, I *will* come clean to him."

Frannie held up a hand. "Say *nothing* to him. Not yet. We do not yet know the particulars of the case. Not until your father's ship docks, shall we know what's what." She spoke eagerly, for it seemed now that the whole sordid mystery would finally be solved. She leaned forward conspiratorially, leaning with hands upon her skirts. "And if it does turn out in my favour, I promise you, I shall assist you in whatever way I can."

Catherine sniffed, giving Frannie a wide-eyed look of hope. "I daresay I should never have asked it of you, but you are kind to make the offer."

Frannie smiled. "You are my *only* cousin. I could do no less in good conscience." The girls came to their feet and stood smiling at each other with surprised gladness. "I'm very obliged to you for coming," Frannie said.

"Oh, but I had to!" cried the other. "As soon as I learned your name, I knew there was nothing I wanted more than to know you!"

"Because you are good and kind," said Frannie. "I know only too well that you might have refused to know me." She glanced at the door, hoping Edward wasn't endeavouring to eavesdrop. "And you might have fought for the trust, especially since your marriage may depend upon it." She frowned. "Indeed, I do not wish to be responsible for coming between you and your future hope—"

Catherine shook her head. "If Lord Whitby cares for me, I am sure he will do what he can to preserve the betrothal, no matter what his papa wishes." She stared ahead unseeingly. "And if he does not, 'tis better I know that now, isn't it?" She shook her head again. "I cannot fault a man who wants a wife with a good dowry. Whitby is agreeable and I had no horror at the prospect of marrying him. But I will learn what his feelings are now, shan't I?"

She looked so melancholy that Frannie vowed silently that if indeed she was ever to possess a fortune, she would do what lay in her power to ensure Catherine's marriage. Though if this Lord Whitby's interest in the match was purely mercenary, perhaps her cousin would do better to look elsewhere. But that was hers to decide. Not every woman, like Frannie, dreamed of marrying for love.

But suddenly her cousin looked up, smiling. "My father is the 1st Officer of a ship. Though my prospects without the expectation of the trust may not be of the aristocracy, I may be introduced to a bright young sea captain, yet! Many take prizes and do quite well for their families, you know."

Frannie smiled back. Catherine had an infectious, bright air, but it was by no means without sense. "If my father returns tomorrow as expected," Catherine said now, leaning forward in her seat as Frannie was, "We will shortly undo this mystery. Depend upon it, dear Miss Fanshawe—dear *cousin*—my father will confirm our connexion, and we shall know each other henceforth and have coses together and dinners and whatever you like! Now I have found a near relation, I'll not lose you!"

Frannie's lips curved into a grin, and she stood up to take the hands of the other girl. "I pray it is all just as you say! Dear cousin!"

"All your worries will be past," she said, smiling. "You will wonder no longer about your parentage." She paused. "How does it go? *The crooked shall be made straight, and the rough ways made smooth.*"

The following morning Frannie arose before the sun, determined to accompany Sebastian to meet Mr. Fanshawe's ship. Any ship by name of *Golden Sovereign* must be dignified. She imagined the sight of it on the horizon, growing bigger as it approached, its masts and riggings coming proudly to a halt like a fashionable lady ready to accept a dance at a ball. But more thrilling yet was to think that the mystery of her parentage, of her whole life, was about to be solved!

A peek at the street from a window assured her Sebastian hadn't left yet. The coach was at the ready, a groom holding the reins. But as she approached the morning room to see if he was having a quick breakfast before leaving, he came from it and met her in the corridor. He looked her quickly up and down, put his hands on her shoulders gently and said, standing only inches from her, "I see you've risen early and are in walking out dress. I'm afraid you cannot accompany me to the docks."

Surprised by his nearness, by his touching her, assured by the spectacles that this was gentle Sebastian only behaving brotherly toward her, she tried to quell the strong pull she felt for him. With a shock, she realized she wanted to be closer still, to feel his arms about her. She couldn't help but search his peculiarly sensitive eyes, looking sweetly earnest, into hers. She dropped her gaze, afraid that her longing would reveal itself.

He mistook her reaction for disappointment not to meet the ship. Lifting her face gently by the chin, he said, "I have only your best interest in mind. Ships are often delayed at sea and may even be days late. If it does come to port, Mr. Harley and I and a land agent will be there to meet Mr. Fanshawe the moment he steps off the plank." She nodded, still mesmerized by her face being only inches from his. "By the time you see me next," he added, "the mystery surrounding the trust and your parentage will be solved."

What he did not tell Frannie was that he was endeavouring to spare her in case Fanshawe had the worst sort of news. Perchance Frannie's mother, as he feared, had never married; perhaps the trust fund, despite Mrs. Fanshawe's hopes, was non-existent. Nothing was certain, and if only bad news was forthcoming, Sebastian would rather break it to her himself with all the gentleness he could muster, than let it crash upon her at the cold and bustling water's edge like an icy, wind-swept wave. No, he could not risk letting her hear it in the coarse language of a seaman, or of finding Mr. Fanshawe as implacable and unfriendly to her cause as his wife. Sebastian would be the first bearer of the news, the breaker, so to speak, between the harsh ocean and the shore of Frannie's heart.

Frannie *was* disappointed, but she saw the wisdom in staying home, and felt Sebastian's kindness in requiring it. She hadn't considered how uncomfortable and long might be the wait at the dirty and busy London docks; and what if Mr. Fanshawe was much like his wife? Imagine the scene if he met her with the anger and resentment of his spouse. She would be publicly humiliated, mortified beyond her present mortification. It was more than she wished to bear.

She thanked him for taking such trouble on her behalf.

Sebastian said, "But of course. You are part of our home now, dear Frannie. Your concerns must be ours as well." She held her breath. Sebastian had never called her by her Christian name before. She had heard him refer to her by name when speaking to his mother or Edward *about* her, but never had he used her name in conversation *with* her. And he had said, *dear* Frannie.

And then something unexpected and breathless and astonishing happened. He leaned in toward her and his mouth hovered for two seconds near her own. He moved slightly and planted a small kiss—on her cheek. Her heart soared. He bowed, and, after reassuring her that her troubles were nearly at an end, he strode quickly off. She was left in the corridor, stunned with joy.

She returned to her bedchamber replaying the scene over and over. Had he almost kissed her on the mouth? Had he wanted to? She thought at first that he had. But it happened very quickly and in the end he'd only kissed her cheek. Like a brother. Or like any affectionate relation. What had he said? "You are part of our *home* now." He might have meant it the way a servant becomes part of the household, a trusted, much-liked servant—but not an equal.

She tried to replay the scene with a different interpretation but could not convince herself the gesture was anything more than detached affection, perhaps even pity. He was too familiar with the ways of humanity to expect a completely felicitous ending to Frannie's dilemma, and felt sorry for her. He expected she was to face a crushing blow to all her hopes. In fact, she realized now that was probably the motive for his keeping her home. He wanted to spare her for as long as possible, the poor, baseborn child!

On an impulse she fled her room, rushing into the corridor and down its carpeted length to a window overlooking the street. She watched while Sebastian's coach pulled away. With a pang, she realized another disappointment about not accompanying him to meet the ship. She could not yet set eyes upon Mr. Fanshawe—her *uncle*. He, more than any human being on earth, possessed the information she wanted more than any fortune—the identity of her father. And even if he proved to be ignorant of the circumstances of her birth or—horrors!—resentful of her appearing, he was nevertheless her mother's brother and nearest relation. She had such curiosity about him. Did he look like Mama? Did he share her mannerisms? *Oh, Mama! How I miss you!* A tear slid from one eye and made its way down her cheek. She did not wipe it away. It was the one that Sebastian had kissed.

But why, why, Mama, did you leave me such a tangle?

Frannie could not return to sleep amidst all her musings and anxieties of the coming day. She resigned herself to an early breakfast alone in the morning room, for Edward and Mrs. Arundell had not yet risen. While she waited for coffee, Tipps placed the *Morning Chronicle* before her. She didn't often get to read it first, as it went from Sebastian to Mrs. Arundell to Edward, if he were interested, before reaching her hands. But she went straight in search for the maritime news. Sure enough, *The Golden Sovereign,* a mercantile clipper ship, was expected to dock, and with holds filled with carpets and spices, China tea and Indian silks.

Next to the listing of arrivals was an article enumerating the numerous sea hazards that must be skirted by the captains of such ships. Their treasures were tempting prizes for enemy military vessels and privateers if, by bad luck, they crossed paths at sea. The newspaper assured its readers that Britain had lost fortunes during the war, and that no ship set sail without the horror of capture hovering about its masts. Even in peacetime, pirates roamed the ocean waters in search of civilian vessels to commandeer and strip clean. Frannie sent up a prayer that no such disaster had waylaid *Golden Sovereign.*

Eventually the others joined her. The whole household, it seemed, had risen early. Frannie could not help glancing often at the clock, thinking of whether or not the ship had come in. At length Mrs. Arundell said, while buttering a slice of toasted bread, "Watching the time won't bring your news back any sooner, dearest. Why do you not amuse yourself in the library as you like to do? I'll see you have a nice fire and perhaps I'll join you shortly."

Frannie thanked her and was soon in her favourite room with a book, but the morning crept by with excruciating slowness. She might have enjoyed knowing that the library was completely hers for the day with no worry about keeping Sebastian from it. But she continued to check the clock often. Mrs. Arundell came in after an hour with a sewing basket, claiming she had the headache and would make no morning calls that day. "I've had one of my prodigious inklings!" she announced at length, her eyes intently upon her sewing. She turned and looked at Frannie with bright eyes.

"Indeed, ma'am?" asked Frannie politely.

The lady smiled. "I was reading this morning's collect— you do recall that I am fond of the prayer book of a morning?"

Frannie nodded and smiled. "Yes, ma'am. I admire that in you."

Mrs. Arundell said, "Of course; because you, too, read it, do you not?"

Frannie nodded. The little black book with its wispy, delicate pages, was a cherished keepsake of any devout Anglican, and she was no exception. In the past she had attended chapel with her mother and Mrs. Baxter, and was happy to find that Mrs. Arundell and Sebastian were church-goers.

"Well, as I was reading, I had a prodigious inkling," she said, jabbing a needle into the seam of a cast-off chemise, destined for the poor box. "You know I have remarkably accurate inklings. Things are going to turn up trumps for you, my dear. When Beau returns—or perhaps soon afterward—he will have the best of news for you, I am certain!"

Frannie's eyes lit with hope. "Was that your inkling? About me?"

Mrs. Arundell nodded. "You could not be so sweet and genteel for nothing, and such a blessing to me with my hearing device! You must be the daughter of a nobleman just as your mama said, and a fortune awaits you, I am sure."

Frannie thanked her, swallowed, and returned to her book. Mrs. Arundell would be disappointed indeed if things did not turn out so felicitously. But the older lady continued to chat of what she'd read in the morning paper, the Regent's recent scandalous expenditures, how shamefully cruel he was to his estranged wife, and even his daughter. Any mention of Princess Charlotte always got Frannie's attention, so that the chatter proved an effective distraction to stop the flow of worries that eddied around her soul like water bubbling over stones in a riverbed, ceaseless and unrelenting. But soon the older lady left the library saying she must lie down in her bedchamber until her horrid headache passed, and that no, there was nothing Frannie could do for her.

In minutes, Frannie's earlier apprehensions returned in force, clouding about her brain like a flock of noisy birds settling all in one tree. By late afternoon she was on tenterhooks, and almost considered that she too, had the headache.

Finally, she heard the sounds of an arrival and, knowing it must be Sebastian, hurried to meet him in the corridor. She stood at the top of the stairs and waited as he gave Sykes his things, her face a picture of tragic certainty that only bad news was to come. Mrs. Arundell's "prodigious inkling," had lost its reassuring sound in the midst of her fears. Sebastian saw her, stopped for a second, then lowered his head and quickly ascended the steps. At the top, he took her hand and said, "I'm afraid we failed you. We never laid eyes on Mr. Fanshawe."

He motioned her into the parlour. Frannie sat across from him, now looking breathless as well as tragic. Sebastian sighed, and suddenly she realized he looked weary. She rang for a servant to order refreshments. She was about to hear of an adventure, she was sure, for he must have put forth a deal of energy having it. When a maid appeared, she ordered tea, but then glanced at Sebastian and added, "And a glass of Madeira for Mr. Arundell."

The maid curtseyed. "Tea for two, mum?"

"Yes, for both of us, but the Madeira for Mr. Arundell only." When she turned back to Sebastian he had a raised brow and a little smile. "Thank you."

She smiled shyly, still startled by the absence of spectacles on him. She mostly saw him at home when he wore them more often than not, and the difference in his bearing and air was not possible to ignore. Unbidden, her mother's words crossed her mind, *handsome devil!* Her pulse quickened. Sebastian sat directly opposite her giving her his full attention and looking far too handsome. The memory of that kiss to her cheek brought heat to them now. She must focus on the matter at hand! She was about to learn what transpired that day, what misadventure had taken so many hours and brought him home in a state of weariness.

While the maid brought in the tea service and his glass of wine, Sebastian explained what happened. "Mr. Harley's land agent got on board as soon as the gangplank was clear enough for him to snake past the passengers disembarking with their trunks and bandboxes. He was told where to find the 1st Officer (Mr. Fanshawe, that is) but the man had already packed his belongings and left. The cabin was empty." He paused to take a sip from his glass and waited while Frannie poured tea into her cup. She glanced at him to see why he paused and found him studying her. He continued his tale. "Mr. Harley and I never left the dock and kept a keen eye, watching for his exit, but we saw no officer. Upon making inquiries, all we got was Grub Street news." To her questioning look, he said, "Lies." He grimaced. "Seamen will cover for their own, you know. He no doubt stripped off his officer's garb and passed for a member of the crew. We might have spoken to him directly for all I know, but no one gave him away."

He took a breath and continued. "We made our way to the Customs House, for 'tis the responsibility of the first mate to settle accounts there. But that office was backlogged, and kept us waiting an incomprehensible amount of time, before informing us that Mr. Fanshawe had long since been there and left." He rubbed his chin, "I daresay that having a land agent with us must have given the impression that we were out to nab the man for debt. If I had to do it over, I'd inquire about him at the office alone, or send Mr. Harley. A land agent is a plague for debtors; they're all well known. Fanshawe was no doubt alerted to his presence and ran like a rabbit."

"He is in debt, then," said Frannie.

Sebastian nodded. "Very likely."

"Shall we call upon him at his house?" she asked. "Without a land agent?"

He gave her an indecipherable look. "Ah. Now we come to the matter. This was yet the biggest disappointment. What should have been an easily accomplished meeting at the dock turned into a convoluted chase that has yet to find success. Not only was he not at home with his wife and daughter," he said, shaking his head, "which any sea-faring man must be eager for, but a servant assured us the whole family had gone off to an unknown destination! We know not to whom they ran, or where."

Frannie's brows furrowed. "But recall, Miss Fanshawe came to see me only yesterday! She said nothing of their going away and was most agreeable!"

Sebastian drew spectacles from a pocket and absently wiped them with a handkerchief. "She may not have known. I suppose it was Mr. Fanshawe's doing entirely."

"But why should he avoid you when he knows not your mission?"

He sniffed and stared at his spectacles before leveling his gaze upon her. "Harley's looking into it. We'll see what his debts are." He gave her a bracing look. "I almost hope he is indeed in the duns, for that would answer as to his eagerness to avoid us. If he is not, if his affairs are in order, it can only look suspicious, and I fear, must have to do with the trust. In which case we must think him a blackguard."

"How could he have known about your coming?"

"Harley and I discussed that. No doubt his wife got word to him before the ship reached port. She is cunning and desperate for that fortune." He put on the spectacles and became the mild-looking bookish gentleman. "She might have sent a note by an outgoing ship—for one sea captain is always pleased to deliver messages or letters to another—or by smuggling a word to him even while we waited on the dock."

His lips firmed into a line. "Depend upon it, we will find the man. He cannot evade us forever." While she watched, he tipped his head and emptied his glass. After putting it down, he said, "We took the precaution of calling upon the captain at his home, Captain Jennings, his name is. We had first to discover his direction, but that was easily accomplished once the home office understood we were not endeavouring to arrest one of theirs."

Frannie's eyes glowed. "You did all that on my account?"

A glimmer of mirth shone from his gaze. "I believe I am almost as eager to understand your mysterious history as you are."

"Thank you," she said, but couldn't help wondering if he meant he was eager to understand whether she was respectable or not. It was a lowering thought.

"The captain was reluctant to help," Sebastian continued, "but eventually he gave us to know that he tries always to set sail with the same 1st Officer if he can help it. So we will find out when Captain Jennings next goes to sea, and, if we have not already discovered Fanshawe on land, be ready to nab him before the last mooring rope is loosed. The ship that carries him will not set sail without our seeing him first."

Frannie thanked Sebastian earnestly. She was sure she hadn't meant to put him to such trouble, nor Mr. Harley or any land agents. But she was equally certain, and could only thank him again on account of it, that without their help, and particularly Sebastian's, she would be without hope or means in the world. Sebastian stood, bowed, and said, "I am pleased to be of assistance." With a little smile he admitted, "I enjoyed the chase, if you must know. I fancy I now understand to a small degree what makes a man become a Bow Street Runner." To Frannie's answering smile, for with his spectacles on Sebastian did not look the part of a wily Bow Street man, he added, "I'll leave you to your own amusements."

"Won't you have tea?" she asked, with a glance at the

unused cup.

He hesitated. "A quick cup, then. Only because you've ordered it."

He watched as she poured and thanked her afterwards, their eyes meeting as she handed him the porcelain with hot liquid. "One would think you'd been to finishing school," he said, with a little smile. Frannie beamed with pleasure. "Not finishing school, but my mama felt the importance of social graces, and, as I am a gentleman's daughter—as she often reminded me, though she evidently told me precious little else about my father—she hired fine governesses."

"Which explains your love of literature?" he asked.

She smiled sheepishly. "It explains only my appalling lack of familiarity with literature. My governesses only taught me useless things like how to pour tea, and how to walk and talk properly, and I had dancing masters to teach me to dance. But literature and mathematics were sadly neglected, as was history. My French is nominal at best, and Latin" she said with a little impish grin, "is Greek to me."

He smiled and sipped his tea. "But those 'useless' graces, as you call them, are not useless in society. Many ladies must have a servant pour, for example," he said, with a glance toward the tea pot, "because they are clumsy at it themselves, to the point of spilling. And if you can dance nearly so well as you pour tea, you will enchant everyone who watches." Their eyes met as he spoke. Frannie felt breathless. He finished his tea in a gulp, thanked her again with a polite bow, and left the room.

Frannie remained in her seat, glowing from Sebastian's unexpected praise. First, the kiss on the cheek in the morning, and now this! But did it signify? Did any of it signify? That, she could not be sure of. Sebastian was known as an unintentional tease, according to Edward. What had he said? That his brother's manners toward the softer sex raised hopes everywhere he went, and dashed them with equal ease, for he never followed up what had appeared as a flirtation, with an offer.

No, thinking on it, Frannie had to allow that Sebastian no doubt thought he was being only polite, not flirtatious. Kind, not admiring. His was the sort of attention that one got purely on the basis of availability. If Sebastian was present, he would be attentive. He would be kind, even offering compliments above the normal exchange, simply because he wished to please others. He was generous in nature. The only occasion when he seemed otherwise was if Edward was involved. Edward called his brother a 'starched shirt,' but it was only to Edward that Sebastian was cold or stiff.

Sadly, she concluded that she must not read affection into anything Sebastian said or did towards her, though coming from another man it might indeed be construed as such. She must harden her heart, for it yearned more and more, it seemed, in his direction each day. More and more she thought only of where he was, when she would next see him, whether he would read to them of an evening, and—most of all— whether he took notice of her not only on account of his mother's affection for her. She tried to avoid such thoughts, remembering that she might yet be deemed illegitimate—how she loathed that word, now!—and had no right, no right at all to set her cap at a future baronet. Even were he not in line for the baronetcy he would be a world above her.

Suddenly her musings ceased. Sebastian's voice, in the corridor! It was followed by Mrs. Arundell's higher tones. In a moment, the door opened and she swept in. "Upon my word! Such a conundrum!" She surveyed Frannie. "You must be downcast now. In the blue devils, I expect." She came and sat across from Frannie, who could not help missing the son who had sat there earlier. With kindness in her eyes she continued, "We thought it was all to be sorted at last, only to find it a deeper muddle! But I must tell you, Frannie dear, that my inklings are never *wrong*. And I have a prodigiously strong one about you and your fortune. I am known for having prodigiously strong inklings, you remember." She paused and waited for Frannie's nod to indicate that yes, she remembered. Then she continued in her sweet, soothing tones, "You must see this as only a setback; a further waiting period, but not something that should dash your hopes."

Frannie nodded. Sudden tears sprang to her eyes, for despite the kind words she realized that Mrs. Arundell was right; all the mystery of her past was now yet *more* perplexing, since Mr. Fanshawe had purposely escaped notice. It was a deeper muddle than before, a deeper muddle that put Sebastian that much further from her reach.

The older woman smoothed her skirts before settling dancing eyes upon Frannie. "So," she said, patting her hands on her knees. "We must have no melancholia, my dear. Beau will not rest until 'tis all sorted." She sat back with a mischievous sparkle in her eyes. "We Arundells are seldom players in a real-life mystery! I warrant you have brought a diversion to us, and Beau appears quite equal to the challenge; he even relishes it, I think."

To Frannie's puzzled look, she hurriedly added, "Oh, I am not making *light* of your troubles, or would have you believe for a moment that *he* does. We feel your suspense. Only—"

Here she paused and searched for the right words. "You are not in it alone." The cast of her eyes was affectionate. "It will all end handsomely, you'll see. If I weren't utterly certain of that, I should be in the doldrums for you. But it will end in your favour, dearest."

Frannie could not take offense at the strange delight her predicament was affording the mistress of the house, for she had called Frannie *dearest*. It was the favored term she used for her sons and therefore did not go unnoticed. Frannie managed a smile of gratitude with genuine answering affection. But she really could not let Mrs. Arundell suffer any longer beneath a delusion regarding her situation. She said, "Ma'am, I am much obliged to you. And all my prayers are that everything *shall* end as we hope, but—"

Mrs. Arundell's eyes strayed above Frannie's head to the clock on the mantel. "Frannie dear, there is no need at all to speak of it. I know all the particulars, I assure you. Now, come, 'tis time to dress for dinner."

With a heavy heart, Frannie followed the lady from the room, bade her goodbye at her bedchamber door and continued to her own. Could it be true that Mrs. Arundell was in possession of every particular of the case? Did she really understand how tenuous Frannie's claim to gentility was? To respectability? She'd have to speak again to Sebastian. He must ensure that his mother understood it rightly. She assumed, of course, that if Mrs. Arundell really grasped the uncertainty of Frannie's situation, that her attitude would reflect that knowledge. She would cease to put forth the foolish idea of Frannie marrying the baronet, for one thing. Most upper-class matrons wouldn't even want her in their home, let alone one with unmarried sons about. Perhaps

Penelope Arundell knew Beau, that is, Sebastian, too well to be worried. He'd never showed the least interest in marriage, even Edward attested to that. And for Edward she had no fear of Frannie probably because she was older than he.

That must be it! Mrs. Arundell cared not whether Frannie had a fortune or not, for it mattered not. Neither son was in danger. As for marrying the baronet, it was just as she said. She wanted an amiable, sweet girl for him, and Frannie seemed just that. It did not answer as to why the woman treated Frannie quite so well, almost like family. Frannie almost wished to ask her, point blank, *why*. But she supposed she must be thankful for it and leave it at that.

CHAPTER SIXTEEN

Earlier that day, aboard Golden Sovereign

Mr. Fanshawe's cabin boy scurried to get his officer's trunk packed. Golden Sovereign was soon to dock in London, and the 1st Officer had barked at him to "do it handsomely, now," which meant, make quick work of it. He wanted no needless delays. Another officer would have his cabin boy scurrying even faster, working harder, but Mr. Fanshawe, everyone knew, was light on discipline. Nevertheless, the cabin boy moved with speed. Every man and boy on board yearned to get home to his family.

A flurry of shouts signified contact with another ship, and though he shouldn't have left his task, the cabin boy went to take a peek. As he reached the quarterdeck, a crewman told him that an outgoing merchant ship had flagged them to deliver a message for an officer. A moment later, a note was thrust into his hand. "Fer yer master," said the seaman.

Minutes later 1st Officer Charles Fanshawe was reading the note. "There's trouble with the law," it said. "A monstrous legal claim is being threatened upon us. They'll be waiting for ye on the docks, I warrant. Land agents, I suppose. Disguise yourself and don't hobble it! Will explain all later. Yr loving wife."

He put the note away calmly, but with an inward frown. What on earth could have happened to cause "a monstrous legal claim" against him? Or that land agents—those relentless devils—should be awaiting him? Whatever it was, his wife was right in that he must evade them at all costs unless he wished to find himself in debtor's prison!

If she'd only stated the amount due, he might have faced the men with confidence. Captain Jennings had only just doled out his wages, and he felt surely it must be sufficient to quiet all creditors. How his family had got in the duns during his voyage was a troubling matter. But his wife's warning about the land agents was enough to make him—or any man in his place—determined to avoid capture. Land agents were ruthless, would pull a man right out of his chair at dinner or anywhere else, to bring him in for arrears. Until he found out more about this "monstrous legal claim," he had no choice but to skirt the clutches of the law.

He found a crewman willing to part with a change of clothing—temporarily, as it would have to be returned—and changed from his uniform to look like an average hand. The agents would be searching for an officer. He pulled a cap down at a jaunty angle over his face. After alerting the captain to his dilemma, he disembarked at the earliest possible moment with other seamen who had received their pay. He saw the men looking for him as he left. Keeping his face devoid of feeling, he quickly passed by. One looked like a gentleman, and perhaps he might have been reasoned with. But first he'd get home and find out what was happening. He paid a dray cart driver to drop him at the Customs House. A long line met him, but he managed to move swiftly ahead by sharing his dilemma—all good seamen loathed a land agent and sympathized—then, afterward, he paid a wagon driver to take him home.

When he reached his own sweet front door—infinitely glad to be home after five months at sea—he was ushered in by a frantic wife. Then he was hurried and hastened from the house, astonished to find his family packed and ready to beat a hasty exit from town! With barely a greeting after five months' separation, and his wife's assurances that she would explain all to him during the journey, he found himself in a hired chaise along with their trunks and valuables.

It was only with severe objections, before setting off, that he was able to return to the house and locate important papers in his study that had been much on his mind for months while at sea. He wished to assure himself that these documents were intact; but on account of his wife's being in such a deuced hurry, he merely shoved them into his waistcoat pocket and scurried back out to the chaise.

"Where are we off to in such a pell mell, scurvy fashion?" he asked with no little irritation, after seating himself in the vehicle.

"A place where they won't find us, I'm sure!" was the only information he received. Most disturbing. As the equipage rumbled away from the curb, his daughter Catherine spoke up. She'd been cast down since his arrival, though she had given him a quick embrace, a half smile, and a kiss on the cheek, in greeting.

"Papa, it is all a mistake," she said, looking quite tragical.

"I should hope it is," he agreed. Looking to his wife he said, "Let's have it. From the beginning. What is behind this odious retreat? Are we criminals that we should run from the law?"

"Do not mistake the matter," returned the lady in a redoubtable fashion. "There are those as would steal your daughter's fortune!"

"My daughter's fortune?" He looked to Catherine. "Do you have a fortune, daughter? One that I know nothing about?"

Before she could answer, Mrs. Fanshawe balked. "Don't sell me a dog! That'll make a stuffed bird laugh! I've heard whispers here and there. I know about the trust fund!" She leveled a steely gaze at him. "I think it's high time you start from the beginning. Lord knows, there should be no secrets between us on such a matter. Man and wife—and you've never seen fit to trust me with the particulars! I daresay Catherine knows more of the matter than I do! But I won't stand by and let her be shammed from her due!"

A frown had deepened upon Mr. Fanshawe's sea-weathered features. A soft-spoken, balding man of fifty-five, with kind grey eyes, he shook his head and peered out the window. He removed his cap. He turned a baleful look upon his spouse. "Is that what this is about? Upon my soul, my dear, you mistake the matter! There is a trust fund, yes, but our daughter is not the beneficiary, and I have no idea what you're talking about, her getting shammed by anyone."

Mrs. Fanshawe's eyes blazed. "Do you dare tell me you put aside a fund for someone else's child?" She let out an awful wail. "Lord help me! You've fathered a child out of wedlock! You—you horrid man! You sinner! I should ha' known! I knew you was too good to be true, so gentle and kind and—and a devil! A blackguard! A cur!"

Mr. Fanshawe seemed accustomed to letting his wife release her energetic objections before countering them with his own. But finally he said, "Lucy, my dear!" He fixed his gaze upon her. "I have never dishonoured my vows." The look of gravity upon his face must have broken though the cloud of indignation that was suffocating his wife's brain, for the torrent of name calling ceased abruptly. Crossing her arms and still glaring at him, she said, "How do you explain the existence of the other Miss Fanshawe!"

The 1st Officer's face lightened, grew curious. "Have you met her?"

"She's come to the house twice now," she said with a firm nod of the head. "She's after the trust."

He looked thoughtful. "And you turned her away?"

"Of course I did. It belongs to our Catherine! I am certain it should, in any case."

"And this is why you had me disguise myself and avoid the land agent? This is why we are on the run from our home, our fireside, and all our comforts?"

"I told you it was all a mistake, Papa," put in Catherine just then. Her face was less troubled than it appeared earlier, as she saw that her father was in a good way to settling the matter justly.

"Well!" demanded his wife. "Who is she if none of your get, eh?"

He sniffed. "She is Margaret's child," he said quietly. "How could you not realize that?" There was an abrupt silence, and suddenly Mrs. Fanshawe was blinking back tears. She looked out the window.

Mr. Fanshawe said, "My dears, I suggest we turn about and go home. No one's to go to debtor's prison."

"They threatened King's Bench!" his wife cried.

"None here needs must appear before the Bench, I assure you," he returned in a strong tone. He turned and struck the wall so that the coachman shortly pulled up the horses. They came to a stop.

"No, no, no!" Mrs. Fanshawe cried. "I cannot bear it. I shan't return this day!" When their sole footman appeared at the door, she cried, "Keep us going! Keep on!"

Mr. Fanshawe said, "Why am I to be denied the comfort of my home when I can assure you that no one will drag me to King's Bench or debtor's prison?"

"I need a holiday," she said, dolefully. "And depend upon it, you won't see home again until I understand every particular of this business!"

"Very well," he said. As they drove on, he explained the matter to his wife and daughter, beginning thus: "You see, my dears, it all began because my father's fortunes suffered a severe loss, leaving Margaret with no dowry… "

Ten minutes passed while he told his wife and daughter the sad tale of his sister's marriage, including the conditions of the trust. Mrs. Fanshawe had grown rather white, but Catherine, with large, compassionate eyes, asked, "Papa, who did your sister marry? You must know that Miss Fanshawe desires very much to know her father! And I should like to know also, as he is my uncle."

"Eh?" asked her mother, eyeing her with stark concern. "How do ye know what Miss Fanshawe desires?"

Catherine coloured. "I'm sorry, Mama. I called upon her."

Her mother's eyes widened as her features clouded. "Cavortin' with the enemy!"

Mr. Fanshawe said, "Now, now, m'dear; nothing of the sort. Recall, she is your niece."

"And my cousin," said Catherine. She added, with pleading eyes, "I longed to know her, Mama." She turned back to her father. "She is in great suspense. Who is her father?"

He eyed her gravely for a moment. "'Tis no one to you, no one of our acquaintance."

Catherine sighed and leaned back into the seat. "Poor Miss Fanshawe!"

Her mother scowled. "Why do you feel for her?" she asked, drawing out the word her for the space of two syllables. "Do you not comprehend that if the trust is hers, your betrothal falls through?"

"I regret, my dear," Mr. Fanshawe said to Catherine, "that I predicted as much from the moment I received your letter telling me of the arrangement."

"Poor Miss Fanshawe, indeed!" cried his wife. "Poor Miss Catherine Fanshawe!"

"My cousin promised, if she comes into the trust, that she would help me," Catherine offered. In truth the idea plagued her that she must accept help from someone so new to her acquaintance, but a relation was family, and it might appease her mother.

"Did she give you a sum? A set amount?" asked the mother.

Catherine recoiled. "No, Mama! I would never have asked it of her! She was all generosity to make the offer at all!"

Her mother scoffed. "Offered to help, my eye! She'll sing a different tune once the blunt's in hand, I warrant you."

"Mama, my cousin was all amiability. She wants nothing more than to be included in our family. We are her relations. And she has none other."

"Where'd you meet her?" her mother asked with narrowed eyes.

"I called upon her on King Street. At the home of Mr.

Arundell, who left his card."

"And why is she living with Mr. Arundell, I wonder?" she asked with a bitter edge.

"She must live with someone," said Catherine. "She lost her mother a year ago August, and—and—another lady, a dear friend."

"A year ago August?" asked Mr. Fanshawe wistfully. "I wish I'd known. I saw my sister only once since she left the papers detailing the trust into my care." He sighed heavily. "I had every intention of contacting her as soon as I got to shore."

"And why would you contact her now?" demanded his wife.

"A report reached my ears that concerns her…I thought I'd give the papers back now, as they'd be safe in her hands."

"The papers? You have them still? With the terms of the fortune?" asked his wife eagerly. Catherine's eyes were also fastened upon him.

He nodded.

Her eyes gleamed with hope. "If we hold the papers, we hold the fortune, Mr. Fanshawe," she said, smiling now. In a quick gush she added, "That fortune belongs to our girl, yet!"

He shook his head, frowning. "No, m'dear. I have only held the papers in trust." He winked at Catherine. "I've held the trust in trust," he murmured, smiling.

She smiled back. "'Twas good of you, Papa."

But his wife, scowling, cried, "You kept it all these years. I daresay you must be entitled to something for your trouble at the very least!"

He shook his head, his lips pursed. "Dear heart, there is nothing in it for us. You must reconcile yourself to that." As the coach left the vicinity of London, rumbling past an empty turnpike gate on the rutted road, Mrs. Fanshawe began to cry. Soon she was outright sobbing. Between sobs, she wailed, "You ha—have ruined your daughter, Mr. Fanshawe! Ruined! All the fat is in the fire, now! Catherine shan't be married to His Lordship! She is all done up!" She turned and pummeled his chest with one fist while the other held a handkerchief to her nose. He grasped her hand and kissed it. "We are no worse off than we've ever been, my dear."

She stopped hitting him but continued crying brokenly, and then fell against him. He patted her back, his eyes meeting Catherine's. His daughter's countenance assured him that she was not nearly as cast down at the prospect of her losing her betrothal as her mother.

Catherine nodded. "It's alright, Papa."

CHAPTER SEVENTEEN

Frannie tried not to lose heart despite the Fanshawes' hasty and mysterious departure from town. It might have been a coincidence, beginning with Mr. Fanshawe's leaving the ship without being seen. He might have hurried home for any number of reasons. The family could have been called away on account of a sick relation on Mrs. Fanshawe's side. She simply could not countenance thinking the worst of the family, when Miss Fanshawe, her cousin, was all amiability and sweetness.

She'd told Sebastian everything she'd learned from Catherine's call. He was sorry, he'd said, to have missed her for he would have liked to question her himself. He'd said, "Perhaps with Catherine's help we'll unravel this tangle yet. Her father, it seems, may not be depended upon." Looking at her thoughtfully he added, "I should have preferred to have it settled *before* we leave for Bartlett Hall—it would be to your advantage for Sir Hugo and any other of his guests, to know you at once for an heiress. Though it is not in fact an *inheritance* at stake, it is a respectable fortune by anyone's standard."

Frannie silenced the protest that flew to her lips. She did not wish Sir Hugo to know her for an heiress, nor for being the owner of a fortune. She did not wish to find favour with the man at all! And now her heart ached, for was not Sebastian implying that he too, like his mama, thought she would answer the baronet's search for a wife? Despite all he had sensibly pointed out about his chances of being disinherited if Sir Hugo got himself a young bride? As she mulled over this lowering idea, Mrs. Arundell breezed into the library with the information that the modiste had arrived with Frannie's new gown.

"And with five days yet before we leave for Gloucestershire!" she purred. "Come, Frannie dear, for the fitting." She glanced at Sebastian. "You may come also, Beau. You'll be first to admire Frannie's new gown."

He lowered the book in his hand and surveyed her above his glasses. He looked so fetching, Frannie thought, when he stood thus, with his dark hair in short waves, and neat, manly attire. His brows looked particularly thick, his eyes green-brown but clear and piercing as usual.

"And subject Miss Fanshawe to further scrutiny than your own?" he said. "I am certain she will look lovely in this gown. She could never look a fright." For his mother's benefit he added, "I am especially confident as you had a hand in choosing the frock." He gave Frannie a short nod.

Frannie knew not whether to be relieved, for facing his scrutiny did seem worrisome; or disappointed, for perhaps he did not care how she looked in a new gown, or for that matter, any gown. However, he'd also said she "could never look a fright." That was praise she supposed, of a sort, though certainly not high praise. Indeed, Sebastian never seemed to take the least notice of her appearance in a way of personal interest, whether she took pains over it or not. Mrs. Arundell had appointed a maid to help with Frannie's hair, but he seemed to take no notice of that either. She and the maid, Clarice, were both fully grateful for the new appointment, however.

For Frannie's part, it relieved her of trying in vain to achieve a proper hair style, as she'd never been required to do her own hair before. Her former maid Eliza, who she'd had to discharge after Mrs. Baxter's death, had done it.

Clarice, the new 'lady's maid,' was enchanted with the situation, for now she ranked higher than a parlour maid and had less laborious duties. If she raised her nose slightly when in the servant's hall these days on account of this elevation, could anyone blame her? The housekeeper, Mrs. Spencer, perhaps, did. She admonished her to mind Romans chapter twelve, verse three, and not to think of herself too highly. Clarice merely pursed her lips, though the chambermaids snickered, and even Mr. Tipps, the butler, nodded gravely at her.

Mrs. Arundell's lady's maid, Betsey, passing by—for she was too lofty a personage to eat with the others—stopped and sneered at Clarice. "You're only helping a poor orphan!"

"'Ere, she's no poor orphan, I'm sure!" replied Clarice fiercely.

"She is, that. I 'eard it right from 'er mouth!"

Every servant stared at Clarice pityingly. As the colour rose in her cheeks, she said, "She ain't! She eats wi' the family! I'm to do 'er hair! No poor orphan would be given such attentions!"

Tipps dipped a piece of bread in his bowl of stew. "I daresay our Clarice must be right in this matter. The family treats Miss Fanshawe with respect." He cleared his throat and nodded toward Mr. Sykes. "Mr. Sykes, I believe, can affirm this."

The valet nodded. In his peculiarly gloomy voice, he

intoned, "She is in a good way to inherit a fortune."

Betsey scoffed, shrugged disdainfully, and went her way.

Clarice was smiling, her reputation wonderfully restored. "Thank 'ee Mr. Tipps and Mr. Sykes," she said, not hiding her elation.

The rest of the servants, though still determined to regard Clarice as an unmitigated upstart, accepted defeat and resumed eating. Time would tell, they seemed to be thinking.

The new gown fit nearly to perfection, needing just the slightest taking in below the bust. Mrs. Arundell looked on with satisfaction at Frannie while the modiste flitted about her. But noticing the look on Frannie's face, she frowned. "You do not look pleased. Are you not pleased?"

"Mademoiselle is not pleased?" repeated the modiste lightly, but with her brows furrowed in concern.

Frannie said, "To be sure, the gown is more beautiful than I imagined!" She peered down at the peach satin with its delicate pearls and spangles. Her only displeasure, which she needed somehow to make clear to Mrs. Arundell, was the reason for the purchase: to make Frannie more appealing to Sir Hugo.

"Come, move before the looking glass," ordered Mrs. Arundell. Frannie obediently went and stood where she could see her reflection. The peach gown contrasted dramatically with her dark hair, making it look black as night. The square neckline and standing lace collar accentuated the perfect bare space for jewellery. "I have a necklace from Mama that will look just right with this," she said, observing the patch of skin. The necklace was one of the few items Frannie had *not* been willing to part with in order to cover Mrs. Baxter's debts. It was something her father had given Mama—she hadn't thought of it until now, for she always kept it safely hidden in an *etui*—the embroidered jewel case she had painstakingly sewn by hand, to contain it. That case was in her trunk, right there in her bedchamber.

"Let's see it!" cried the older lady. Frannie opened the trunk, and after rummaging down, for she kept it well out of sight, drew out the little case. She opened it, took out the necklace lovingly, and held it up. All three women admired it. The modiste said, "Ah! *Un beau rubis*!"

"Indeed!" said Mrs. Arundell, taking the necklace in her hands and examining the blood-red jewel closely. "This is a fine gemstone, Frannie," she said, "unless I am much mistaken." She looked at the girl brightly. "From your mama, you said?"

Frannie nodded and allowed the lady to put it around her neck and clasp it from behind. "It was given her by my father."

Mrs. Arundell turned her around by the arms and smiled up at her. "You see? Your father could afford such a gift only if he were a gentleman of means. 'Tis just as I said!" She turned the girl around to face the looking glass. "Now take a look at yourself."

Frannie peered at her reflection and had to give a little smile. She said honestly, "I feel like a princess!"

Mrs. Arundell chuckled. "I believe a princess *could* wear that gown or that necklace, but it looks splendid on you!"

The seamstress removed the matching plumed headdress

from a bandbox with fingers adept at handling delicate fabrics and bonnets. She came and placed it securely on Frannie's head, pinning it into place.

"My, but that is a regal look, is it not?" said Mrs. Arundell, beaming with pleasure. "I daresay I have transformed you. Even with your quiet manners, you will now draw eyes wherever you wear this."

Frannie smiled weakly. "Thank you, ma'am, but it is never my ambition to do so."

Mrs. Arundell leaned in confidentially. "I noticed that about you, dear. You are almost *too* retiring. Gentlemen aren't enraptured by women who are *too* quiet." She paused and gazed at Frannie affectionately. "And some are slow to appreciate what is before them and must be coaxed to take notice." She stood back again and smiled. "Fortunately for our sex, we know ways in which to nudge such men! I warrant this gown, the way you look in it, will do the trick."

Frannie's heart sank. Perhaps now was the time to put an end to this. Surely Mrs. Arundell had Sir Hugo in mind, for, having failed to marry, was not his the character she described as "slow to appreciate" the opposite sex? "Ma'am," she said, her large eyes troubled. "I must tell you—I have no wish for the match you have in mind."

The lady's face fell. "No wish? Why ever not? I wouldn't put it forward for just anyone, dearest. You are really my idea of the wife he must have. You observe economy; you are not overly loud; you enjoy strengthening your mind with reading, and above all, you are amiable!"

Frannie's distress grew. How could she explain it in terms the lady would accept? To cavil on account of her uncertain social standing or the jeopardy of her position was useless.

Mrs. Arundell refused to believe Frannie could be anything except of good stock.

"Ma'am," she said finally, "there is such an age difference, for one thing—"

"Oh, that is nothing! That is nothing, I assure you!" With pursed lips she said, "Frannie dear, I warrant you *just* need more time. Now be a good girl and get out of this dress— Madame will help you—"

"*Oui, Madame!*" said the Frenchwoman. Instantly she was at Frannie's back to undo the fastenings of the bodice, but a knock at the door made her freeze, waiting.

"Since it distresses you, we'll speak no more on it now," continued the older woman with a kind smile. She lifted her little delicate nose up. "Every young woman is fearful of marriage to some degree, I suppose, though *I* was not." She turned away. "Come in," she said, in a tone meant to be heard outside the room.

A moment later the door opened to reveal Sebastian, bespectacled, with a note in his hands. He entered the room with barely a glance up from the note but saw Frannie and his head came up. He held the note out to his mother, all the while surveying Frannie. She gave him a shy little smile.

Mrs. Arundell took the note. "Thank you, dearest. Who is it from?"

"Sir Hugo." He looked toward his mother. "He merely sends his hope that we are still coming as planned, and instructions as to where to stopover to bait the horses, and for meals." Looking back at Frannie he came toward her. "This is the new gown?"

She nodded, watching for his reaction.

He circled her, while the modiste stood back, smiling.

"What good taste you have, Mama," he said, and then, when he was back in front of Frannie, added, "You look splendid."

"Thank you." Though his words were praise, his voice was curiously flat. She hardly felt flattered. Perhaps he did not really think she looked splendid. Perhaps there was something about the gown he disliked.

Sebastian apologized for interrupting them, bowed, and left, not looking back at Frannie once. Mrs. Arundell smiled at her, though. "I am so glad he stopped in!" She went toward the door. "Until dinner, dearest!" She stopped and turned back to level a mischievous grin at her. "I can hardly countenance waiting for you to be thus *unveiled* at the Christmas ball!"

After she'd gone, her last words hung in Frannie's mind as heavy as the tolling of a death knell. "*Unveiled* at the Christmas ball." For Sir Hugo's benefit, no doubt! And suddenly, an idea formed that gave her hope.

After Madame had carefully packed away the gown in papers, the headdress in a huge bandbox, curtseyed her goodbye and gone, Frannie took the bandbox and withdrew the delicate headdress. She found scissors, took a lacy shawl from her wardrobe, and cut a good piece of it. Now she would execute her idea.

She stayed in her room, sewing piece after piece of the lace onto various bonnets, all her simpler headwear such as wide ribbon bandeaus, and her only tiara.

There will have to be an unveiling indeed, she decided, if Sir Hugo was to be graced with a single, unobstructed glimpse of her face. Why hadn't she thought of it sooner?

CHAPTER EIGHTEEN

Charles Fanshawe, with his wife and daughter, eventually stopped for the night at a country inn. Mrs. Fanshawe had cajoled him into making the stop, claiming it was too much for her poor soul to be expected to return home, they'd travelled too far to make the journey back that day, and if her husband had any sensibility at all for a poor woman's nerves and constitution, they must stop.

After a substantial inn supper, Mr. Fanshawe thought himself entitled to peace. But his wife, as it were, began a new campaign against his having it. Instructing the inn keeper to keep her husband supplied with a steady infusion of his best ale, she reasoned upon him thus: He must reveal the identity of the benefactor of the trust, first of all. For as yet he had kept this personage's name strictly to himself, and a body had a right to know. Secondly, they must find this man and prevail upon him to include their daughter in some disbursement of funds, for hadn't they kept his secret all these years? Mr. Fanshawe must see that he had been monstrously abused otherwise; he had been keeper of the trust and should rightly be rewarded for his discretion, his honesty, his help.

Mr. Fanshawe resigned himself to a long evening during which his wife would relieve herself of every complaint concerning the business that she could devise. He listened with a disinterested air, but focused instead on enjoying the ale, which was excellent. Sometime during the third pint, however, his wife's petitions began to sound sensible. He had done the man a great service, hadn't he? He'd been silent for nigh two decades about the business when he might have gadded it about, even to the newspapers. The newspapers, he could not deny, were always amenable to printing a scandal.

Was not a secret trust fund scandalous? A secret marriage and runaway bride? Mr. Fanshawe began to feel the injustice of his position. Why, he had ought to have received some small stipend for his extraordinary discretion in the affair, if not solely for his keeping of the papers. He had guarded the secret, not even leaking the man's name to his own family. He was a paragon of virtue! The name of the solicitors was another well-guarded secret which he had kept. Was he not shamefully abused to have gone without reward until now? Surely he must see that it was time to contact the family and set the case to rights. He had hobbled the business altogether, but now he could seek redress.

"He must see his way to rewarding your efforts," his wife said reasonably. "What man, once he knows how you safeguarded his wife and child's welfare could fail to see as much!"

"Indeed, indeed!" cried her husband, sitting back in his chair. Why, he was the victim of monstrous ill-usage by his sister, for she had put the papers into his hand for safekeeping all that time ago. Left him with the burden of it, hadn't she? Forced him to lie to her husband, insist she'd gone off to America when in fact she was hidden only as far as Lincolnshire! Why had he not seen it before?

Catherine sat by all this time, frowning and silent, while her mother plied her father with persistent, wheedling pleas. She almost interrupted Mama on numerous points, but knowing that anything she said to counter her arguments would be summarily dismissed, she had saved the effort. But now she cleared her throat. "Papa, it grows late. Shall we go to our rooms now?"

"No!" cried her mother sharply. "Your father is entitled to enjoy himself. He's earned more'n that, if you ask me."

"Mama, whatever you convince him of now, he will likely forget entirely by morning!"

Her mother stared at her.

Mr. Fanshawe muttered, "To bed, to bed, m'dears!" He tried to rise from his chair and was surprised to find himself immediately returned to his seat as though a great weight forced him down. "I believe I'll sleep here," he said, closing his eyes.

Catherine stood and got the attention of the innkeeper, and soon two porters were there to help Mr. Fanshawe from his chair and up the wooden steps to his room.

As soon as he was placed safely in bed and the porters gone, his wife turned to him. Poking him in the side, she said, "Who is he, sir? The benefactor of the trust?"

"What? What? Eh?" said the man.

She kept at him. "His name, sir! Who is the founder of the trust?"

Mr. Fanshawe opened red, bleary eyes and tried to see his wife. She looked like a blur in the candlelight. A shadow of a woman. But a shadow that would give him no rest until he told. He spoke to the shadow. "Sir Malcolm. There's the name for ye."

Sir Malcolm! Greatly satisfied, Mrs. Fanshawe allowed her husband to sink back to unconsciousness. She was determined to gain an audience with this Sir Malcolm. Her husband was too soft by far, but she would convince the man of the merit of their claims and come away, she was sure, with something for her trouble. It would be no fortune, to be sure—that disappointment was not to be answered—but there must be some small consolation for the disappointment of all their hopes. Before drifting off to sleep, she planned the morrow's adventure, exactly what she would say when she gained her audience with this personage. Suddenly her husband started in his sleep. "He's dead now. Saw't in a paper we picked up at a port stop. He's been gone for three months."

His wife was thunderstruck. "He's *dead*?"

But her husband was once more in the land of Nod.

Again Mrs. Fanshawe's tears flowed, for now whom could she apply to? To whom could she press their cause? "There must be something we can do!"

Catherine heard the wails and knew her mama was vexed over the business of the trust. But Mr. Fanshawe's face was as clear and untroubled in his sleep as a child's.

For Frannie, all too soon, the day came for departure, two days before Christmas. The Fanshawes had not returned to their London abode, which meant Frannie's history was still a muddle, her fortune still no more than a distant hope. Sebastian reminded his mother and brother that Frannie would go by the name Miss Baxter during the visit. It was a simple kindness to her, he assured them, and, as an alias would injure no one, they could be agreeable about its use. Further, it would spare Frannie from uncomfortable questions regarding her heritage. As they had each been apprised of Frannie's wishes in this a fortnight ago, neither made an objection.

During the long, bumpy coach ride, Sebastian read to them from the newspaper, then from a novel. Mrs. Arundell paged through a copy of the *The Ladies' Monthly Museum,* while Edward dozed. If he began to snore, Sebastian would nudge him in the side. Each time, Edward came to with a start asking, "What, are we arrived? Are we there?"

Despite the travelling rug that the women had the advantage of in the carriage, Frannie's toes and fingers were numb by the time they stopped at an inn for an early supper. The horses must be allowed to rest, said Sebastian, who was adamant that he would not exchange his dependable beasts for any the inn offered. Nor would he risk harming them by continuing on. After a good meal, the innkeeper's wife led the ladies to their bedchamber, for they wished to retire at once. The gentlemen lingered afterward over port. They would be shown later to a separate chamber not far from the ladies. Sykes alone of the servants got to sleep in the same room as his master, while the footmen took turns sleeping and guarding the carriage and luggage.

"I loathe long journeys," Mrs. Arundell moaned that night while Frannie rested in a bed opposite hers. "But I must say I look forward to seeing the Hall, and whether Sir Malcolm and Hugo have had the sense to maintain it properly. Let us pray they have not taken it into their heads to redo any of the ancient parts of the house. Too many of our great houses are ruined by such ideas! 'Tis the ancient elements that give the best character."

"How ancient *is* the house, ma'am?" asked Frannie, for the first time curious about the Hall.

"I believe it was built in the Restoration," she said. "Sir Hugo's ancestor supported the monarchy and was rewarded with the land. He built the estate rather in the Baroque style, which was all the rage back then, you know. A more recent baronet built a modern addition, as did Sir Malcolm, Sir Hugo's father. I hope he limited his changes to that."

Frannie fell asleep to images of dancing in a grand baroque hall, but the face of the baronet, greeting them with a smile, resting his eyes upon her, tarnished the impression. She did not wish to think about Sir Hugo. She focused instead on Sebastian, realizing Sir Hugo's ball would be her first opportunity of dancing with him! Why hadn't she thought of this earlier? Her heart swelled with relief as dread of the visit vanished. She pictured the scene; her, in her expensive new gown and headdress; him, the ideal of manhood looking exquisite in eveningwear. Sebastian was strong but gentle, handsome but not flirtatious. He would take her hand, lead her to the floor with a smile, his eyes all admiring. Suddenly she shivered. She couldn't tell if it was from a draft in the room, or from the delicious anticipation of standing up with Sebastian, of having his entire attention. The memory of when he'd leaned in and kissed her cheek now floated in her mind. Except that in her mind's eye, he did not kiss her cheek. He kissed her lips. *Oh, vain thought!* But she fell asleep smiling.

When Frannie saw Sebastian at breakfast, she blushed and looked away as if he could read her mind. As if he could know that she'd gone to sleep dreaming about him. She must not allow that. She had no right, no right at all, to think of him. Oh, why, if the Arundells knew this much, did they not also know that she was utterly unsuitable as a bride for Sir Hugo? It made no sense.

She looked back at Sebastian and found him smiling gently at her, but this merely tumbled her heart further, for while his look seemed affectionate, she must not construe it as such. To her, Sebastian was all a muddle, a kindly elder brother of a sort that she must not think of—but every minute did.

Mrs. Arundell raised a cup to her lips while watching the others. She saw Sebastian smile gently at Frannie, whose look became one of sweet confusion. His grin broadened as if he knew he sent her heart tumbling, though the mother was certain her son was impervious to his effect upon the softer sex. But Frannie was such a humble, honest girl. It warmed her heart.

Edward interrupted the moment when, with half-closed eyes, he demanded to know what was taking so long to get coffee. He went on to bemoan how miserable a night he'd spent. "Your man," he said accusingly to Sebastian, "snores with the same sepulchral tones he speaks with, only twice as loud. The bed was nothing more than hay, if I'm not mistaken, and," he finished, glaring at his brother from his half-opened eyes, "I was too far from the deuced fire to feel it!"

"Hold your tongue, cub," chided Sebastian. "I slept well enough with the same snoring in my ears, and the same poor sort of mattress."

"Closer to the fire!" snapped Edward, loath to give up all points.

Sykes, who had appeared with an urn of coffee and began pouring, said, "My apologies, sir," in his gloomy voice. Edward raised red eyes to the ceiling. Frannie hid a smile behind a napkin.

"We shan't stay here on the return journey," said Mrs. Arundell, "though we were not incommoded by our beds, were we, Frannie?"

Frannie looked apologetically at Edward. "We were not."

In the morning, Mr. Fanshawe awoke with the headache. Despite this, his wife was quick on her feet and hurried the family to breakfast. She wanted an early start.

At table, she broached the plan which she had spent a good part of the night formulating. At first dejected to have discovered the man behind the trust had died, it soon occurred to her that all was not lost. "Now, Mr. Fanshawe," she began. "I gave considerable thought last night to our situation. With your sister gone, God rest her soul, and this nobleman gone— mercies upon 'im, I'm sure—there can be no harm in our bringing it all forth to the light of day."

"Bringing it forth? What are you saying?" her husband asked.

Catherine understood her mother at once and said, "If we are to reveal anything, we must speak to Miss Fanshawe first, Mama!"

"Pshsaw to Miss Fanshawe!" she replied. "I care nothing

for Miss Fanshawe. Your father 'ere was guardian of the secret concerning her. In fact, he is yet. There must be something in it for him. This Sir Malcolm must have an heir. A *legitimate* heir, I warrant."

To her father, Catherine said, "Sir Malcolm—was he Miss Fanshawe's father?"

He shook his head. "No, m'dear, her grandfather. By rights, Margaret's girl should be known by that family name."

"And what is that name?" asked his wife.

He gave her a grave look. "I'll tell you only if you give me your word not to interfere."

"Interfere! Interfere in what, I ask you? I only wish to point out to 'im the great service you done 'im."

"He may not see it that way, my love." His kind eyes looked sadly at the two women at his table. "I kept my sister's whereabouts hidden for *her* sake, not his. From his perspective, indeed, he lost a wife and child with no explanation, no word of parting, no understanding of where he'd gone wrong or anything to explain their disappearance. I daresay he must have suspected his father had a hand in the business, but that would little ease his suffering, I warrant. It must have been hard for him." He leveled a hard gaze at his wife. "Rather than thank us, he may wish to drag us before the law!"

There was silence for a long moment. Finally Mrs. Fanshawe said with a strange gleam in her eyes, "We can do him a service now and earn his gratitude. For, if Miss Fanshawe knows him not, I presume he knows not her. We can enlighten him!" She turned narrowed eyes upon her husband. "Are you certain they were wed proper? Why would any woman married to a man of title not take her rightful place and name?" She turned earnest eyes to her daughter. "She would be a lady, then, a *real* lady!"

"But I told you why," he returned in a reasonable tone. "Sir Malcolm promised to plunge his son into bankruptcy, entail the estate, run up debts, reduce them to genteel poverty." He paused and sipped his coffee. "Margaret told me she'd made enough mistakes; would brook no guilt for ruining her husband's life and inheritance. Said it was best all around to comply with his demands. It was a sacrifice, to be sure."

"Poor Miss Fanshawe!" cried Catherine again. "To think she might have been raised as the daughter of a baronet—"

"The granddaughter of one until three months ago," he clarified. "Her father has only just assumed the title."

"A baronet!" cried his wife. "Surely we must see this man! There is something in it for ye, Mr. Fanshawe! Would he not wish to know his rightful brother-in-law? 'Twould be a Christmas gift, moreover, to let him know 'is daughter is in London, alive and well."

He gave her a look of reproof. "We shan't intrude upon him just now. It may not be the proper time to give him *that* information, but I'll write to him, letting him know that if he wants to know more about his long-lost wife and child, I am ready to supply it." He paused. "He came to me when she disappeared, you know. I had to do as Meg wished; tell him she'd gone to America." His grey eyes creased with long forgotten sorrow. "'Twas an unpleasant business. I should like very much to set it all straight, tell him everything I know." He nodded. "And most of all, how his own father is to thank for it."

His wife frowned at him. "If you hold off, he'll learn about his child some other way; she will get the fortune; and we shall have naught. Is that what you want?"

"I like it, Papa," said Catherine approvingly. "And may I write to Miss Fanshawe? She is longing to know anything regarding her family history."

"I daresay there's a mistress of the manor by now who won't be eager to take in this waif!" huffed Mrs. Fanshawe.

"She is the legal child of the present baronet of Bartlett Hall," said Mr. Fanshawe quietly. "I do not believe there is a new mistress." To Catherine he said, "Hold off on your letter to Miss Fanshawe. Until I hear from him."

"Who *is* this man, the current baronet of this place?" demanded his wife with a sneer.

Mr. Fanshawe looked down at his cup. Quietly he said, "His name is Sir Hugo."

After congratulating herself for extracting this much from her husband, Mrs. Fanshawe excused herself to make a few inquiries of the innkeeper. She returned shortly, beaming with suppressed excitement. "I should like very much to see Bartlett Hall, Mr. Fanshawe," she said enthusiastically, "for the innkeeper assures me we are no more than an hour distant by coach! And what do you know? The baronet is hosting a Christmas Open Hall! Is that not providential?"

"To what do you refer to as providential, Mrs. Fanshawe?" asked her husband, who failed to see the source of her private joy. "That we are in the vicinity of the Hall, or that the baronet is opening it to his tenants? For I little see how his entertainment can concern us."

"'Tis providential on both accounts," she insisted. "Not only may we take a drive past today to catch a glimpse of the big house, but the Hall shall be opened with music and refreshments for the tenants and townsfolk tomorrow! We can enter along with other common folk; we'll see the manor and beg an audience with the baronet!"

Mr. Fanshawe eyed his wife and then looked at Catherine. "If Cat has no objection, I see no harm in a drive past," he said, for he was not above curiosity regarding the grand estate that his sister had been coerced into giving up her right to. "But Christmas approaches apace, m'dear. I'm sure you've got a pudding and other good things set by. You'll want to be home, no doubt."

In a conciliatory tone she said, "We shall of course enjoy our own Christmas dinner and fireside, sir. But that is two nights away, yet! The open hall is tomorrow. Your holiday shan't be ruined, and we may get a Christmas present from the baronet, I've no doubt."

"You must tell Sir Hugo what you know," agreed Catherine, who, upon reflection, considered that even if they could not enlighten Miss Fanshawe beforehand, certainly Sir Hugo would wish to know his daughter. "If we indeed attend this open hall, he will make an appearance and you must speak to him, Papa! It cannot be a coincidence that he opens his home tomorrow, just when we are in the vicinity, and when you have such intimate knowledge of his family that any feeling man must be in want of."

She glanced at her mama, who was vigorously shaking her head in agreement. "Besides which," Catherine continued, "if you speak with him, it shall all be settled, and I'll know what to say to Whitby after church on Christmas Day." Her words held a shadow of sorrow, and an uncomfortable silence ensued. Mrs. Fanshawe said, "Do not speak to Whitby of the lost fortune, my dear. A disagreeable thing it would be to break such news to him on Christmas!" She turned to her husband and cried, "For Catherine's sake, you must procure some *good* from this, sir!"

Mr. Fanshawe's mild wrinkles creased as his lips firmed in a line, but the most he would commit to procuring was, "If the baronet welcomes our news, perhaps he will see his way to some recompense."

"Either way, I must speak to Whitby and inform him," said Catherine.

"Of course," agreed her father.

But suddenly Mrs. Fanshawe gasped and put a hand to her heart. "My dear sir! It just occurs to me. There is also a ball tomorrow night for the upper gentry only, which will follow the open hall festivities. Let us forgo this open hall of the farmers and land workers; we are not of their class. We must attend the ball! The baronet will needs must greet you then, and you can arrange a private little cose to tell him all."

Even Catherine had to smile at this suggestion, for what young woman could despise such Christmas merriment as a ball?

To press her point, Catherine's mama added, "And think of all the eligible young men who may be there for our Cat. If Whitby cries off, this is her best chance to look elsewhere!"

Mr. Fanshawe saw that his idea of forgoing a meeting entirely in favour of writing Sir Hugo a letter, was going the way of a passing wave. It looked powerful, formidable and sound, but like the *Golden Sovereign* cresting such a roller, his wife and daughter refused to let it stop them. The ladies saw by his silence that they'd won the day. Mrs. Fanshawe said cheerfully, "Cat and I must attend to our evening dress, but I see no objection to taking a drive past the Hall today, to catch a glimpse of it, so long as we are settled back in our rooms before dinner. We'll have plenty of time to get our apparel in order."

Mr. Fanshawe cleared his throat. "We have no invitations for the ball, and the man is entitled to his privacy!" His words fell like a judge's gavel, producing silence, and dousing the spirit of excitement in his wife. A frown settled upon her features, but after a moment it cleared and she declared, "So we shall attend the open hall and you must finagle an audience with Sir Hugo then. But in any case, we shan't be deprived of a drive past today."

In half an hour their meal was finished, another night's lodging secured, and horses freshened for the drive were straining at the reins of the coachman, stamping their feet to be off. The family set out.

"Is it an annual tradition for great houses to open their doors at Christmas to the surrounding countryfolk?" asked Catherine.

Her father said, "Many of 'em do; 'tis a way to thank servants, tenants, and farmhands, sort of like a harvest home to show some goodness to the local villagers. All the nobility should be generous in such a fashion, I think."

Mrs. Fanshawe winked at Catherine. "It forebodes well for us if this baronet is generous."

When, an hour and five minutes later, the Fanshawes' hired chaise rumbled onto the grounds of Bartlett Hall, they saw with surprise that another coach had turned onto the drive just ahead of them.

Mr. Fanshawe kicked the wall and the coach soon came to a stop.

"What are ye doing, Mr. Fanshawe?" asked his wife.

In his quiet voice he replied, "That is either the baronet's carriage ahead of us, or his guests arriving. We shall not intrude today." To the postilion who appeared at the window, he gave instructions, but there was not room enough on the drive for a turnabout. When they arrived at the front of the Hall, all strained to get a good look at the Palladian style mansion as they kept moving, following the circular drive back toward the turnpike. The coach ahead of them had slowed to a stop before the great front doors. They rumbled past. Mr. Fanshawe saw a well-dressed gentleman peering curiously at them from the window of the vehicle. He nodded respectfully, though he knew him not.

By the time the Arundell's carriage turned into the drive of Bartlett Hall, Frannie was undeniably curious, even excited. She'd never been to the home of a baronet before and knew that even the good taste and elegance of the Arundell's townhome would not compare to what lay ahead. As they turned into the drive, another carriage followed.

"Could that be our carrier with the servants?" asked Mrs. Arundell, craning her neck to get a look. "I hoped they'd arrive before us, as we sent them on ahead."

Sebastian turned to peer out the back window. "They should be hours behind us, regardless. That plodding equipage of a carrier moves at a snail's pace!"

When the long, tree-lined drive ended and the house came into view, Frannie was not disappointed. Though not a student of baroque architecture, she knew at once that the stately exterior with its three stories of bricked façade dressed with stone, many long windows, wide, fanned stone steps and circular drive, must be ancient indeed. It was an orderly arrangement, but ornate. A pair of tremendous Greek urns with evergreens stood to either side of the steps, above which led to a ponderous front door. The only feature Frannie did not approve of was the hipped roof with its four huge chimneys, towering over the house like top hats that were too high. Two liveried footmen now emerged from the door and came toward them.

It might have cheered her under other circumstances to arrive at such an impressive domicile, for the additional beauty and elegance that must be inside could only excite her sensibilities. But no amount of grandeur could elevate the dread that once again returned to her now they were arrived; the anticipation of pleasure reverting to that former state which had plagued her ever since Mrs. Arundell had first suggested she would make a good wife for the baronet. The pit of her stomach suddenly felt hollow.

The carriage slowed to a stop. As it did, the one following continued on, sailing past at a good trot. "They must have taken a wrong turn," said Sebastian.

"I do hope the servants have already arrived with our things," murmured his mama. "I must have my extra hearing device on hand." She looked at Frannie, who had, in company with Edward, procured an additional hearing device as security in case of loss. "One can never have too many hearing devices," she said with a small frown.

In the confusion and bustle of disembarking, the ordering of trunks, the gathering of wits, Frannie moved along with the others, though woodenly. Sebastian gave her a little encouraging smile, which turned to a look of concern. "Are you well, Frannie?" This should have cheered her, for he had only begun calling her by her Christian name that week, and it still gave her a thrill. But she could not muster a reply of assurance besides allowing that she was fatigued.

Soon they were ushered inside while footmen unloaded their trunks and bags. Frannie handed over her travelling bonnet, but she had prepared for this moment. Beneath the bonnet she had on a light muslin cap to which she had sewn an intricate lace veil. She coaxed it out and smoothed it down, covering her face to the lips.

As they climbed the stairs to the first floor, Mrs. Arundell, who had been busy giving over her things and questioning the servants, turned to glance at her. "Frannie, dearest! Why 'tis a fetching cap, but Sir Hugo will hardly see you behind it. Why should you wear it?"

"I beg to be allowed, ma'am," she said with sudden feeling. "It warms me."

Mrs. Arundell blinked at her, surprised at the near desperation in her voice. But she was kind-hearted and merely said, "Well, of course, if you wish. But I should enjoy above all things showing you to Sir Hugo at your most advantageous."

Frannie said nothing, relieved that her little ploy had worked. If there was anything she did *not* wish, it was to be shown to Sir Hugo at her most advantageous.

Sebastian, who was escorting his mama, looked around her to gaze at Frannie with a question in his eyes, but thankfully said nothing, and turned away again.

Edward, whose arm Frannie was upon, opined, "I, for one, think it dashing. Nothing like a little mystery surrounding the softer sex to make a man look twice, eh?"

Frannie's heart froze. Did the Arundells think she was being coy? That she wanted Sir Hugo to look twice? Oh, dear! That was precisely what she did not wish. "I assure you, that is not my object," she said, grieved that it could be construed as such.

When they followed the butler into the mansion, Mrs. Arundell sighed with satisfaction. "I always did enjoy this house. Even the corridors, so wide and spacious, as you see," she added, motioning with an arm at the cavernous passageway lined with illustrious looking portraits of past baronets and their wives. Frannie could just imagine walking this corridor by candlelight at night, the glow of a candelabrum illuminating each large artwork briefly as one passed so that ghostly faces would peer out momentarily and then disappear like phantoms.

The butler came to a stop before a door. "This is the finest parlour," whispered Mrs. Arundell, smiling, "and not in the Baroque style. Sir Hugo assured me that he has kept up a careful blending of English style with French taste, and above all, a 'chaste contour and simplicity of effect.'"

The door opened to a well-appointed parlour, its large windows pouring in afternoon sun, and with a welcoming fire in a large grate. Frannie thought the "chaste contours and simplicity" neither chaste nor simple, noting the effusion of Grecian pilasters, Romanesque plasterwork, and Japanned objects in the room. But the mantel was dressed in cheery holly, berries, and pine boughs in anticipation of Christmas, and the candle sconces sported more. As they disbursed into the room, a large, red-faced man came to his feet. Sir Hugo. Frannie made a beeline to the hearth, spreading her hands out to warm them while the others shared greetings. She moved beside a standing fire screen that was off to one side with silk cord and small tassels, wishing her veil had such tassels to hide behind.

But too soon, "Frannie, Frannie dear, come, my love!" called Mrs. Arundell. Frannie had no choice but to go and curtsey to Sir Hugo as she was introduced. "This is Miss Baxter, Miss Frances Baxter, a particularly dear acquaintance stopping with us," she said. "'Tis a comfortable arrangement, for I cannot do without her," she added, as if to explain Frannie's visit, but she succeeded only in giving it an air of mystery. Better for her to have said nothing at all, Frannie thought.

Sir Hugo stared at her. He had gone rather white. "Did you not say that night at the ball, Penelope, that she was your cousin?"

Mrs. Arundell tittered with laughter. "To think you should recall such a thing! Why, it was only a lark, my dear sir."

Still staring hard at Frannie, he was overcome by a fit of coughs, and turned away. While the others were solicitous of him, Frannie saw a chance to escape his scrutiny and took a chair near the fire.

Sebastian approached her with a thoughtful look. "This is the second time I have seen Sir Hugo react strangely at sight of you," he said, mildly. "The first time, when he came to escort Mama to the ball, I thought it must have nothing to do with you, but only my mother. Tonight, however, it seems evident that he must know you?"

Frannie's eyes widened beneath the veil. "I *assure* you, this is our first acquaintance!" She swallowed, unsure of whether to share her own surmise; that Sir Hugo was just as conscious of the family's expectations regarding the two of them as was she, and that he was equally disturbed by it. *I should not have come!* She thought. "Perhaps now," she added shyly, "you may agree that my coming was ill advised. Perhaps I should return to London—"

"Why, my dear girl, I was suggesting nothing of the sort," Sebastian said. "Perhaps there is no coincidence in it. Sir Hugo is easily befuddled by most any female, I think."

Meanwhile, Sir Hugo seemed to have recovered, and refreshments were brought in for the travellers. Sebastian encouraged Frannie to take some tea and a slice of seed cake, but she sat down uneasily, wishing only to escape to a place of solitude. While the others chatted, she admired the ornate carving of the sofa wood, the chairs, and couch, as well as the golden scrolled frames of numerous portraits and bucolic country scenes on the walls. Twice, however, she chanced to spy Sir Hugo staring at her. Both times she looked hurriedly away, noting that he seemed as disturbed by her presence as she was by his. A veil, it seemed, offered little protection against being noticed. Sebastian's keen eyes missed none of it.

He approached her at length. "You must be eager to get settled, to rest, perhaps, before dinner?"

"I am indeed." Gratefully, she looked up at him. How thoughtful Sebastian was.

He turned to the company and announced that he would escort Miss Baxter, with the help of a servant, to her appointed bedchamber; he was sure she was fatigued by the journey. He looked expectantly at his mother. "And you, ma'am?" he asked. "Are you ready to take rest?"

Sir Hugo immediately piped in with, "Of course, Penelope! You must be in want of it, for delicate ladies and long journeys do not well go together, I comprehend." He spoke in a low tone, timidly meeting her eyes. Mrs. Arundell looked perplexed for a moment, and then annoyed. She exclaimed, "Why, Hugo, you haven't changed a jot! You never did enjoy entertaining, and I daresay you are hoping we shall retire at once so you may be rid of us!"

"Mama," began Sebastian, but she held out a hand. "Say nothing, Beau! I understand your cousin." Turning back to the baronet, she said, going right up to him and with a little challenging look, "Whatever possessed you to invite us? I can see you still prefer solitude, your own company over any other, even your relations."

Sir Hugo, who was perpetually of a sanguine complexion, turned even redder. "Penelope—but no, to be sure. You are quite wrong, there. I am heartily obliged you have all come. And to ask me—when, when you must know"—he made a little helpless gesture with his hands. "I wrote of my intentions."

Frannie's heart froze at those words. Ready to cry, she looked away in mortification, her face crestfallen. His *intentions*—she knew what that meant! Without realizing it, she drew in a deep, sighing breath.

Sebastian took her hand. "I think my cousin has it right. Long journeys and ladies do not always meet happily. Come, I shall accompany you to your room."

"Yes, yes," Sir Hugo said, overhearing this. He hurried to the bell pull. When a servant appeared, he was instructed to show the guests to their bedchambers. Mrs. Arundell said with peculiar determination, "I'll not go yet, if you don't mind, Hugo."

"Not at all, ma'am!" Sir Hugo said with a relieved look, restored to almost his usual color. Beside his large bulk, the boys' mama looked diminutive. But his eyes strayed again to Frannie with a most particular and worried look.

"If there's a drink to be had," piped up Edward, "I will linger also."

"Of course, of course," said Sir Hugo.

Sebastian helped Frannie to her feet. She curtseyed to the company and allowed him to lead her from the room, her throat still tight with unshed tears.

"I'll see you at dinner," said Mrs. Arundell. "And you, Beau, are you also done in?"

"I will return after seeing Frannie to her room."

Frannie, not *Miss Fanshawe.* It still thrilled her. The word rang in her heart and mind like a little sun shower amidst a torrent of rain.

His mama smiled. "Good man."

Frannie accepted Sebastian's arm as they followed the housekeeper to the quarter of the house where the bedchambers were. Sebastian purposely slowed their pace, however, so that soon there was enough distance between them and the servant for a private conversation.

"Frannie dear," he began, sending another shot of warmth into her heart. Gently he continued, "Are you certain you haven't met Sir Hugo before you came to us?"

"I have not," she said, surprised at his question.

He smiled wryly. "Why did you don a veil, then? I haven't seen you wear one in all the time you've been with us. Is it not to avoid recognition?"

He must have felt the hand upon his arm tighten. "No, not that at all!" she said in a little choked voice, and blinking back tears. How it pained her to know that he wanted her to marry his cousin! *Why* should he? He had once said himself that he would be disinherited if Sir Hugo had a son of his own, and surely he must see that Frannie, if she wed the baronet, could provide that son. Why should he so wish to be rid of her, that he would gladly endanger his own inheritance?

All these thoughts roiled in her brain and yet she could speak none of them. If she dared to express even one, they would all come rushing out. She would never be able to hide her anguish of heart, the anguish that came from wishing Sebastian would want her to be *his* wife, not the baronet's.

"What makes you wear it, then?" he persisted.

Frannie swallowed her heart. She sniffed and replied, "Surely you do not expect a rational explanation for every accoutrement a woman deems indispensable."

He smiled. "But you have never found this particular accoutrement to be indispensable before."

She was silent. They ascended a set of stairs, for the bedchambers were on the second floor. She looked down at the carpeting.

"Tomorrow is Christmas Eve," he said. "We shall have the ball tomorrow night. Then we shall have a happy Christmas, I trust. And on the following afternoon, I will return to town to find Mr. Fanshawe. I'll find him, wherever he has gone, I assure you, and wrest the truth from him, come what may." In a gentler tone he added, "Your agony and dread of what is unknown shall be removed forever."

"No, Beau!" she cried, without realizing it. Something rippled in his eyes, a quick flash of warmth, but then was gone. She had hardly time to comprehend it as she hurriedly added, "You mustn't interrupt your visit here on my account! I have waited months to learn my history. Surely we can wait until after Twelfth Night." As soon as she spoke, she realized he might want the information in order to reassure the baronet that she was an eligible bride, a bride bringing a sizable dowry. To his steady, thoughtful gaze, she added, "The—the baronet need not concern himself with me!"

His brows furrowed. "The baronet need not— ? Come, we're all of one family," Sebastian said kindly. "Any concern of yours must be ours." But he fell silent, for the housekeeper stopped ahead of them at a door and waited politely for them to reach her.

To the gentle warmth in his eyes, hers answered only with anguish, for was he not saying that the Arundells wished to know her history as much as the baronet, for they were his family? He stopped at the door to the room, raised her hand and kissed it. "I hope you find some rest. I'll see you at dinner." With a bow, he turned and left.

Frannie could hardly attend to the housekeeper, who ushered her into the room, pointed out the lovely prospect from the window, the closets with fitted shelves, the comfortable four-poster bed and japanned writing desk. A chambermaid was at work raising a fire in the grate.

Frannie was asked if there was anything she needed, and then was finally left alone in the sizable room. It was high-ceilinged, and intricate plasterwork and roundels stared sightlessly back at her. The wallpaper was a delicate floral, the bed and bedclothes properly plush. It was all elegance and beauty, but she sat upon the bed dejectedly. In the next moment, she threw herself down.

And sobbed.

Sebastian was certain Frannie was hiding something of her history, something that seemed—incredible as it was—to have to do with his cousin. She wasn't telling him what it was, and it perplexed him. Her sensibilities had seemed heightened since they'd left King Street. She was never a gad-pie, but her silence during the journey was greater than her usual reticence. Perhaps it was only this—the tiresome journey—that wore upon her senses. Not all could withstand the rigors of travel. But he recalled Sir Hugo's countenance upon seeing Frannie on both occasions and felt surely there was something more afoot. He must find it out.

CHAPTER NINETEEN

Frannie did not join the family until a maid fetched her for dinner. Clarice had joined her in her chamber, filled with raptures for the stately dwelling. While she put away Frannie's things, she chattered on about the size of the kitchens, the staff, even the cavernous servants' hall. Frannie listened with gradually growing amusement. She'd given the meeting with Sir Hugo some thought, and came away with good reason, she felt, for hope. The baronet seemed downright alarmed at the sight of her, which meant he was no more pleased with the notion of marriage to her than she was to him. If he did not desire it, she was safe.

Nevertheless, after Clarice had done her hair up and put a tortoiseshell comb in place, she had her remove it in favor of a thin tiara to which she'd attached a lace veil. Pulling the veil down, Clarice clucked her tongue. "A veil at table, miss? In the way of yer food?"

Frannie sighed. The veil was precariously close to her mouth. She removed the tiara, folded the lace twice round the rim, and replaced it. Now the veil reached the tip of her nose but no lower. She caught Clarice's reproving eyes in the looking glass. The maid immediately vented her thoughts.

"'Tis fetching, to be sure, miss." Her face creased as if in pain. "But for a cheerful dinner afore Christmas? *Why*, miss? Why hide yer pretty face?"

"It isn't Christmas yet," Frannie said defensively. But she

thought back to Sebastian's asking her if she wore the veil to avoid recognition. With a deep sigh, she removed the tiara with its offending lace, and pursed her lips. "A turban, then. The one with tassels. And the largest tassel must drape over my face."

Clarice's expression of satisfaction lasted while she changed the headdress, arranged Frannie's curls again so they framed her face, and then stood back, allowing Frannie to judge her handiwork. The tassels hung to one side, just as Clarice thought any self-respecting tassels of a turban ought to. Frannie frowned, adjusted the turban, and then nodded with satisfaction as her face became half-obscured by the tassels. She felt less tragic since realizing the baronet did not welcome the match, but one could never be too careful.

Clarice frowned. "The mistress won't like it." She shook her head. "Will ye play Snapdragon?"

"Dear me, no!" Frannie had to laugh. The child's game was often played at Christmas festivities, but not since early days in the village had she participated in such a thing. With no children in Bartlett Hall at present, the idea of bending over the flaming pan of raisins and flaming rum made a ridiculous scene in her mind.

"That's well, or ye'd end up afire from your 'ead down," said Clarice, still frowning with disapproval. "Sure, there will be some festivities," the maid went on, "and that tassel will block your view."

Frannie thanked her for her concern. And wore the turban as she liked it.

Sebastian was standing outside the large dining hall when she arrived. She gave a short, polite curtsey and he leaned forward in a bow, but he stared at her. When she would have entered the room, he put out a hand. "Frannie, dearest, forgive me, but your maid was neglectful." He reached up and with both hands gently adjusted her turban so that the largest tassel now hung just in front of her right ear. Afterward, his hands lingered for a few seconds while he studied her face. They were no more than inches apart. Her heart fluttered.

"That's better," he said, his gaze fastened upon hers. Something flitted across his eyes. "Or were you still attempting to hide?" She could not tell if he was annoyed or amused. She stared at him, but no response came to her lips. Her only thought was, *Sebastian is a beautiful man.* And then he dropped his hands and nodded his head, motioning her into the room. She halted long enough only to flick open her fan and put it before her face as she entered.

Spying Sir Hugo at one end of the long table, she contrived also to bow her head so that the tassel might at least partially fall over her face. She would keep her head down as much as possible, she thought. But chancing to meet Edward's eyes, she saw him studying her with a look of slight perplexity. When Sebastian took his seat across from her, she refused to look up at all. Could they not see, could not the Arundells see, that she had no wish to be a spectacle in front of Sir Hugo?

But from the moment of her entrance, Sir Hugo stared at her. Mrs. Arundell said, "Hugo, upon my soul! You look at dear Frannie as though you'd seen a ghost!"

Frannie was forced to look up then, with quite the most tragic look upon her countenance.

Sir Hugo wiped his face with a napkin. "I beg your pardon. She does indeed remind me of—of an old acquaintance," he said. "Pray, where did you find Miss Baxter?"

Mrs. Arundell's face grew curious. "Of whom does she

remind you?" She turned and gave Frannie a meaningful look, as if to say, *Imagine if Sir Hugo can shed light upon your situation!*

He said only, "Where is her family from?" looking at Frannie for the answer.

"Lincolnshire, sir," she said as if admitting to a crime. Her face grew rosy. This was the very circumstance she did not want scrutinized! She darted a look of consternation at Sebastian, hoping he would rescue her from further scrutiny.

In a cheerful tone Sebastian said, "Sir Hugo, as the founder of our feast, do you care to do us the favour of opening our meal with a dinner blessing? Or whom shall we call upon, sir? It is, after all, two nights before Christmas. 'Tis fitting to be in mind of the Giver of all good things, do you not think?"

Sir Hugo stared for a moment. "Oh, er, thank you, sir, certainly, certainly." He cleared his throat and folded his hands, and the rest of the table closed their eyes and folded hands. Sir Hugo prayed in a surprisingly firm tone, "Blessed are you, O Lord God, King of the Universe, for you give us food to sustain our lives and make our hearts glad; through Jesus Christ our Lord. Amen."

Frannie and the others said, "Amen." She looked up with surprise at Sir Hugo. His customary timidity was wholly absent when he prayed. Indeed, he might easily give a sermon with such a tone, she thought. She recognized the prayer from the prayer book, but knew it was not the *shortest* mealtime prayer in it. And Sebastian's instinct was right on the mark, for now the scrutiny upon her was forgotten as covers were removed and the food admired. Footmen circled the table to spoon helpings onto plates, and the conversation moved on. Her eyes met Sebastian's—he sat across from her—and she shone a small smile of gratitude at him. That he only nodded gravely at her did not seem very curious; Sebastian was often serious or deep in thought.

Sebastian caught Frannie's look of relief, but he was determined that he would later get to the bottom of it all. Seeing his cousin's reaction to Frannie yet again convinced him more than ever that there was a shared history between the two. The idea vexed him, though he did not know why.

The ladies retired after dinner to the best parlour, where a roaring fire and hot negus awaited. The men lingered at table over port for only a short while, but it was illuminating for Sebastian. He asked the baronet, "Sir, I could not but notice that you seem to have had a previous acquaintance with Miss Baxter?"

His cousin reddened and gripped his glass. "No, sir, but as I said to your mother, she puts me strongly in mind of a previous acquaintance." He paused. "I should like very much to know her history, if you could see your way to enlightening me." He shot a furtive glance at Sebastian. "What is her mother's name?"

Edward spoke up. "She's an heiress, sir!"

Sebastian cautioned him with a look.

"An heiress!" said their cousin, rubbing his chin. "Who is her father?"

Sebastian cleared his throat. "May I ask, first, sir, the name of the woman she reminds you of?"

The baronet stared at his nephew. "I warrant we should join the ladies," he said, making a move as if to rise. Sebastian nearly choked on his sip of port. He lowered his glass and, sputtering, cried, "My dear sir! Was this lady's friendship so loathsome to you that you cannot speak of it? I daresay you appear vexed whenever you see Miss Baxter."

Sir Hugo sat back with a sigh. "She brings me to mind of a sad chapter of life, sirs." His broad chest heaved as another sigh escaped him. "'Tis a chapter I do not wish to open tonight. If you would enlighten me on her family history, however…"

Edward looked at Sebastian expectantly, leaving it to him.

"Her history is obscured by strange circumstances," Sebastian said. "There is reason to believe she is entitled to a large fortune in the form of a trust, left to her, we believe, by her father."

Sir Hugo's eyes bulged. "What is the name of her father, sir?"

Sebastian hesitated. He pressed his lips together. "That, sir, is the point of obscurity. Her parents were separated when she was quite young, and—"

Sir Hugo exclaimed, "Separated, you say? On what account?"

Sebastian said calmly, "The reason is uncertain."

"That, sirs, is strange indeed!" He seemed to deliberate upon his next words for a moment. Then, levelling a direct stare upon Sebastian, asked, "*How* are you acquainted with Miss Baxter?"

Edward's brows rose. He looked to his brother as if he

thought, *how will you get out of this one?*

Sebastian said, "I am shortly to discover all the circumstances of Miss Baxter's history that at present seem befuddling. Our solicitor is on the case, I assure you. We have located a relation who will clear any doubts regarding the trust. When 'tis settled, you shall have that history in its entirety."

Sir Hugo sighed, nodding and lifted his glass to his lips. Draining it, he nodded again and then rose heavily from the table.

CHAPTER TWENTY

The evening was spent at whist. Since the company made an odd number, Frannie volunteered to sit out, and indeed insisted upon it, though both Sebastian and Mrs. Arundell offered to give her place after the first game. Nor would she even join them at the table despite entreaties to the contrary, for she could not ignore the unsettling gaze of the baronet. She determined to remain, as much as was possible, out of his line of sight, having lost count of how many times she chanced to look up to find his eyes upon her. His look was no longer one of alarm, nor did he grow white when he studied her. In fact, he twice attempted a small smile, but Frannie looked hurriedly away both times. She hoped he wasn't becoming agreeable to the idea of a match between them. Such a thought made her retire early.

The company regretted her going, Sebastian saying that were he not in the midst of a rubber, he should insist upon escorting her. All three men rose and bowed politely, though she kept her eyes down when curtseying in Sir Hugo's direction.

Had she stayed, she might have seen that Sir Hugo twice forfeited a trick, much to Edward's chagrin, to give it to his mother, who was partnered with Sebastian. Both times the eyes of the baronet and the matriarch met above the cards, Sir Hugo with a little smile, and Mrs. Arundell returning the gesture.

The next day was Christmas Eve. The servants were in a bustle, scurrying to and fro in hasty last-minute preparations for the open Hall that day for the townsfolk. When Clarice did not come to wake Frannie or respond to the bell pull, Frannie realized her maid had been conscripted to help the house servants. That meant Frannie could not take breakfast in her room, though she had taken advantage of that option the day before. A meal in her room was one less over which she must face the baronet. Having scarcely said a word to him since their arrival, nor he to her, she wished to keep it that way.

She slipped into a morning gown, put on a veil with a wide head band, and arranged her hair. She grabbed her prayer book in hopes of reading the morning's collect at breakfast, for most of the company, she felt sure, would still be abed. With any luck, she could be in and out of the morning room before the baronet would make an appearance.

When she reached the room, she was surprised to find both Sebastian and Edward already there, though not, to her relief, Sir Hugo. Mrs. Arundell too, was absent. Sebastian was reading the paper as usual, and Edward pouring himself coffee from the sideboard when she entered.

"Pray, do not rise," she said to Sebastian, who had started to rise in order to bow a greeting. Edward, however, gave a short bow with a smile, asked if he might pour her a cup, and to her grateful nod, did so. He placed it before her and then resumed his seat.

Sebastian asked, "Is it your ambition to attend today's Open Hall festivities?"

Frannie lowered her cup hastily. "No." Judging by the heightened tension and fuss of the staff, she expected it to be a crush, and moreover wished to avoid introductions at all costs. What would she say of herself? *Pleased to meet you, I'm the toad eater of the family, like the poor relation.* Spending the day anywhere *but* near the Hall seemed her only hope of peace.

"Well, *I* shall be there," said Edward carelessly. "Entertainment's what we lack. I should very much like to see what sport or diversions may arise."

Sebastian, lowering his head to regard his brother from above his spectacles, said, "What do you anticipate? I believe the townsfolk come in expectation of food, ale, and dancing, nothing more."

Edward eyes lit. "Food, ale, dancing! Sport enough for me, sir!"

Sebastian shook his head and returned his gaze to Frannie. "I'll take you for a countryside drive, if that suits you."

"Very much, thank you!" Her heart soared at the thought that he would spend his afternoon with her to entertain her.

"Mama may like it as well," Edward chimed in.

"Mama is welcome to join us," his brother said.

At that moment Mrs. Arundell swept in, her colour high. "Mama will not join you, dearest, though I thank you for the thought. Sir Hugo has asked me to preside with him over the Open Hall. I daresay he finds it a challenge. Sir Malcolm did not invite the townsfolk these five years, Hugo says. He is unused to it."

Sebastian nodded. "Whereas you, dearest, will be in your element."

She smiled contentedly. "I shall be of *some* use to him, I

am sure. There are things only a woman can properly see to, you know, especially when it concerns hospitality." She looked around brightly. "I do hope, Beau, you won't neglect Frannie for a minute."

"Not in the least." He looked at Frannie, his eyes deep and thoughtful.

"Thank you, ma'am," Frannie said. "Mr. Arundell has promised a drive through the countryside." She looked back at him. A shimmer of pleasant anticipation ran through her.

The boys' mother smiled. "Good of you, Beau. Only do not be out too long. You will both need to refresh yourselves and dress for tonight's ball."

Edward looked on with rather a desultory air. After his mother had gone, and Frannie to fetch her bonnet and redingote, he said, "One word, big brother, if you please."

Sebastian looked up from his paper, one brow raised.

"Your manner toward Frannie borders on the...*familiar*, I might say?"

Sebastian's brows furrowed. "Do you have a point?"

Edward snorted. "My point, sir," he said as if it should be utterly obvious, "is that you are well on your way to inheriting a baronetcy; whereas I am, as always, without certain means. I gave you to understand my hopes regarding Frannie. I trust you have not forgot."

"I told you not to think of it."

"You told me to *wait*. To wait until we discovered the truth about the trust! I have done my part. I have kept my wishes to myself. But you are *encroaching*, if I do not mistake myself."

Sebastian shook out his paper, then folded it. He came to his feet. "No Arundell could possibly align himself with such uncertainty as lies in her case. My word to you is the same.

Wait. In fact, I think you should look elsewhere."

Outside the room, Frannie stood just at the doorway, blinking, her face a picture of dashed hopes. She'd left her prayer book on the table and was returning to fetch it just as she heard Edward say, "I gave you to understand my hopes regarding Frannie. I trust you have not forgot." Sebastian's answer, though it did not surprise her in the least, ripped at her heart like a tear in stockings that, once begun, would grow and spread. "No Arundell could possibly align himself with such uncertainty as lies in her case."

She turned and fled. *Why does my heart ache?* She asked herself. It made perfect sense, what Sebastian said. She understood utterly why she was not fit for an Arundell. Indeed, it was this very fact that made her marvel that anyone would think the baronet should want her for a wife. Yet even Sebastian seemed to. None of it made sense.

After reprimanding herself for daring to raise her hopes regarding Sebastian, she went to wait in the huge entrance hall. People were already arriving, beginning to fill the rows of long tables that had been carried in for the event. A huge ball of mistletoe hung in the center of the room. High upon one wall over an arched doorway was the baronet's heraldic badge bearing the red hand of Ulster. Frannie recognized it from an illustration in the Arundell's library. Holly stems and berries decorated the mantel of an enormous hearth, a leftover, she was sure, from the earliest days of the manor.

Still smarting, she reflected gloomily that Sebastian's offer of a drive was merely his way of being polite and helpful. Despite the look in his eyes that sent her heart pulsing, his words to Edward rang in her ears. *No Arundell could align himself….*She must not think anything of his attentions on this day—or any other.

When Sebastian appeared, he smiled and offered his arm. Outside, the family coach stood waiting in the drive, a footman standing smartly at the back as chaperon. Their own coachman, Gilley, sat atop the board. But around them a steady flow of town arrivals in all manner of conveyances, from creaking family coaches to wagons and carts piled with boisterous guests, spilled out and marched gaily past them to enter the hall. Simply clad mothers in coats hardly thick enough for the cold, holding the hands of red-cheeked children, surveyed her with eyes bright with interest. These were the sort of people she had used to converse with often, as errands or goodwill missions took her into the village. Now their country clothes looked clean but shabby. Living with the Arundells had inured her to finery, so that what she used to see as ordinary now stood out as common.

Sebastian handed her into the vehicle and took a seat across from her. They started off slowly, as they could move only as the arriving horde of laborers and townsfolk made way. Sebastian drew a travelling rug from beneath his seat and leaned over to place it on Frannie's lap. He had ordered warm bricks for their feet, and she had the further protection of a muff and lined bonnet.

The coach passed yet more people en route to the Hall, and Frannie marveled at what a crowd Sir Hugo must feed. She looked at Sebastian curiously. "Will you continue this practice as the next baronet?"

Sebastian smiled wanly. "*If* I am the next baronet, I certainly will." They continued on, getting only as far as turning off the drive onto the road when there was a loud crack. The coach lurched and sank forward to one side. It came to a stop.

Frannie's hands were inside the muff. Unable to stop herself, she hurtled forward, straight into Sebastian's arms. After he held her for a second, looking deeply at her he said, "Are you all right?"

She stared into his beautiful but unreadable eyes. *She was in his arms, practically upon his lap.* His look was exquisite. "I am, thank you... I *beg* your pardon."

"Not at all," he said slowly, still looking into her eyes. His gaze dropped to her mouth, but the edges of his lips turned up—was he trying to stifle a laugh? The thought made her grin and suddenly they both chuckled. Smiling, he gently extricated her from his lap, and helped her to her feet. The footman, brushing himself off, opened the door, which now sat at an odd angle. Frannie drew a hand from the muff and allowed Sebastian to help her carefully from the equipage.

Outside they saw the cause of the mishap. One of the front wooden wheels was cracked completely in two. Sebastian examined the broken parts on one knee and exclaimed, "Good thing we weren't moving fast." Turning to her he said, "Or that this didn't occur in some God-forsaken place during our journey here." He gave orders to the coachman, sent a footman scurrying back to the estate ahead of them to fetch two grooms, and offered his arm to Frannie.

"Our drive must wait. I hope you don't mind a bit of a walk instead?"

"Not at all," she said. The clouds were low and grey, the

air cold, but doing anything in Sebastian's company appealed to Frannie. He moved her hand from his forearm to entwine her arm with his so they were warmer against the cold—and closer together. Frannie felt protected despite the weather, and looked up to study his face. If only she could think this familiarity, this easy closeness, *meant* something to him. If only! But of course she must not think it, though even as the wish assailed her, he glanced down at her warmly.

They walked briskly, being hailed and addressed by the last stragglers of arrivals who were coming by foot to the hall. Sebastian gave his name and relation to Sir Hugo to anyone who asked it, unhesitatingly, and with true warmth. He asked their names in turn, which she could see pleased them mightily. *He will make an excellent baronet*, she thought.

All too soon they were back at the estate and handing their things to Sir Hugo's butler. Loud merriment from the Hall greeted their ears to such a degree that, turning to her, Sebastian cried (to be heard above the din) "Let us find a quieter room—perhaps Sir Hugo's library!" Frannie nodded her agreement. The butler heard what he said and pointed down a corridor to the left, which led away from the grand hall. Sebastian grabbed her hand and hurried them off, almost running. She started to giggle. *Edward is indeed wrong!* She thought. *Sebastian is no starched shirt!*

They reached a quieter wing of the house. He put a finger to his lips and tried a door. Opening it, he peered inside and then shut it again. "A small parlour." He tried a few more doors, each time shaking his head afterward and moving them on. Finally, he opened one and said, "Ah! I believe we have found it."

He stood aside and motioned Frannie in. She entered an

interior room that was at first almost too dark to see in, but one corner emanated with a small glow from a candelabrum on a table. Only one of its candles was lit, but she veered toward it, Sebastian behind her. He took the lamp and held it up, and then they could see a wall lined with built in shelves, and the spines of books staring out at them. Pointing the light in another direction, they saw a settee in one corner off behind a folding screen, and another door at the far end. "This isn't the library proper; it's a connecting room. Perhaps it leads to Sir Hugo's study." He made a move to head to the door, but suddenly they heard sounds approaching from that direction. Sebastian placed the light back upon the table, took Frannie's hand and moved her behind the screen. Whispering he said, "Let us discover who is in this part of the house today. It had best not be a visitor."

With her heart beginning to pound, Frannie felt breathless in the gloom standing so close to Sebastian. "Shusshhh," he said into her ear, his breath warm and delicious upon her skin. His hands held her arms lightly, keeping her right in front of him.

The door opened. No sound but that of a light step hurrying across the room. When it reached the table with the candle lamp, it hesitated, and Frannie saw that it was Mrs. Arundell!

She almost cried out, but Sebastian immediately tightened his hold on her arms, a signal not to speak. Mrs. Arundell stared at the candelabrum. "Oh, dear," she murmured. She blew it out, and then, slowly in the dark, made her way to the door, opened it, and was gone.

Now the darkness was deep. Frannie turned, facing Sebastian, their bodies only an inch apart. "Why did you not let me speak?" she asked. Sebastian hesitated. "I suppose I thought it awkward for her to find us here." She could feel his breath upon her face. He paused. "I apologize, dearest. I was thoughtless to bring you somewhere alone. If Edward, or the baronet, found us—" He shuddered, and pulling her hand said, "Come."

This crushed her heart. And suddenly she was distraught. She refused to move, and overcome, cried determinedly, "I have borne with this for as long as I can, sir!" Her voice was raw with feeling. It mortified her, but she could not hide it. Her face at least was hidden in the dark, which was some comfort.

"Borne with what?" he asked quietly from the darkness.

"With this—this—*impossible* idea!" A sob escaped her. "I do not—*want*—to m-marry your cousin!" Sebastian was utterly still for a moment. Suddenly his hand grasped one of hers, and he dragged her toward the table and stopped. "Wait," he said. She heard him fumbling for a second and then a single candle came to life. His face, staring at her in stark surprise and consternation, came into view. "Whatever made you think the baronet would marry you?"

Frannie was almost speechless. "*You* did! Your *mother* did! She told me, numerous times," she cried, with an emphatic nod of the head, "that my future was settled to her mind, that it would all be settled at Christmas! And that I would make a proper wife!" A tear slid down her cheek. "I *tried* to explain to her what you know only too well!" she said, looking up at him tragically, her large eyes seemingly magnified by tears. "That I am not *fit* to be any man's wife! That my fortune may well be nonexistent, that—"

She was here stopped from continuing as he took her arms,

and said, "*Dearest!* My mother does not wish for you to marry Sir Hugo! Nor do I!"

She blinked up at him. "What? She doesn't?

"No."

"*You* don't?"

He shook his head. "Not at all!"

"But your mother, surely, does. If you could conceive of how often she told me my future would be settled at Christmas! She had one of her inklings about it! She seemed to believe that all I must do is sail down tonight in my new, elegant gown and I will strike love into Sir Hugo's heart! As if none of my history would matter then, though *I* never thought as much."

He smiled. He moved a stray tendril of hair off her face. "Is that why you've hidden behind veils throughout this visit?"

She sniffed and nodded. "I did not want him to see me long enough to form a favourable opinion!"

He let out a breath of a laugh. "You confounding girl."

But Frannie was still confused. "What did your mama *mean* by it all if not that she wanted the match?"

He smiled again. He leaned his head in toward hers and lay his forehead against hers. A rush of warmth filled Frannie's heart with sudden hope. He said, in a low, husky tone, "She wants you to marry *me*, dearest."

Frannie gasped. She moved away enough to stare up at him. She felt as though a thousand candles were lit at once in her heart, which was suddenly light as a feather. And yet, how could it be? When she was hardly respectable? "Oh, dear! I told her more than once I did not desire the match, but I thought she meant— " Here she stopped, for it struck her that even though Mrs. Arundell may have wanted her to marry Sebastian, it did not mean that Sebastian wanted it.

"You thought she meant my cousin."

She nodded.

"And now that you know what she meant? What is your reaction now?"

Frannie blinked. "I am quite confounded…I should never have presumed…I am sorry, indeed, for your sake. For I know how you feel and you are perfectly right in it. I cannot conceive why your mama would desire to have me as a daughter in law!"

Sebastian smiled. "Perhaps because she knows her son desires you for a wife."

Frannie's breath caught in her throat in a huge lump. But no, he could not possibly mean… "You mean Edward, of course."

"Do you wish to marry Edward?"

"No!"

"I did not mean Edward. I meant myself."

Frannie stared at him, her eyes widening with the thought. But this could not be! Blinking, she said, "I heard you tell Edward that no Arundell could align himself to a case like mine."

He nodded ruefully. "I believed it, too. I think I believed it until a few moments ago. Until you said you had no wish to marry my cousin!"

She said, "But surely you must still believe that I am not fit…you recall that I may have *nothing*? That my parentage is uncertain, that—"

"Shuusssshh," he put a finger to her lips. He put his arms about her and drew her up to him. He lowered his head and kissed her, at first tentatively, then firmly and more deeply. Frannie threw her arms about him, feeling as though it must be a dream! She wanted to cling to him and never let go!

Their lips came apart and she said, "'Tis only right that a future baronet have a respectable wife; a wife with a dowry."

He gathered her even closer in his arms. "I want a respectable wife with a dowry only if that wife is you." He kissed her again, quite soundly. Frannie felt tears of joy on her face, though she welcomed his kiss with equal fervor, savoring his touch, his arms about her, and the affection she felt free to acknowledge now, rushing up to fill her heart.

He broke the kiss lingeringly, his lips warm and full upon hers. Then he murmured, "You *will* marry me, Miss Fanshawe; my Frannie, won't you?"

She felt ready to burst. "With all my heart!"

CHAPTER TWENTY-ONE

In the great hall, the Charles Fanshawe family sat at one of the many wooden tables lined with merry, laughing townsfolk. Catherine and her father were content to eat, drink, and enjoy the waits, the amateur musicians playing and singing carols and reels; but Mrs. Fanshawe had in mind only that of finding the baronet and securing an audience with him. They'd had a late, slow breakfast at an inn, followed by a long wait to procure fresh horses. Upon their arrival, they'd learned that the baronet had been greeting guests earlier but now had gone from the hall. The consolation was an assurance that he should in all likelihood return "afore everyone departed."

And then he did reappear, standing across the large room, nodding at guests. Mrs. Fanshawe caught sight of him. With eyes blazing, she cried, "That must be him! The baronet. Let us request an audience *now*."

Mr. Fanshawe said, "M'dear, allow the man to enjoy the day. I will write to him, I vow." Her eyes widened for a moment as she stared at her husband. "We must see him betimes, sir! That other creature, *Miss Fanshawe,* knows not that he has the purse strings of the trust, or I warrant she would not have come to *us*. But how long can it remain hidden when she has that Arundell gentleman, and solicitors, snooping on her behalf? They'll settle it all without ye and then they'll be naught in it for our Catherine." Her dark eyes flashed at him. "We must reach him before her, and do him the service of reuniting his family before 'tis done without us."

Mr. Fanshawe stared at his wife. He rose and headed toward Sir Hugo. But at just that moment Mrs. Arundell came flitting up to the baronet and called him away. By the time Mr. Fanshawe arrived in the vicinity, the man was gone. He asked a footman if he might have a meeting with Sir Hugo, but when the servant learned that the Fanshawes were not local residents, was given no great assurance that it would occur. He returned to his wife and daughter and relayed the matter.

"He left just ahead of ye," said his wife grimly, her eyes upon the arched exit through which Sir Hugo and a fine lady had disappeared. She turned to her husband. "I'll settle the matter. If he wants more of it from yer own mouth, I warrant he'll have ye fetched."

Mr. Fanshawe looked alarmed and made to rise.

"No, sir! Stay out of it!" she cried. "I'll know what to say to the man. I will ensure the union of our daughter with Lord Whitby." She stood, straightened her gown and hair and added, "With it bein' Christmas Eve, I daresay there could be no more propitious time to find a man in a charitable spirit."

Mr. Fanshawe did not argue, having drunk plenty of ale and was feeling no pain. Moreover, his wife would give him little peace until the feat was accomplished, and she'd make his precious shore life miserable if he were to attempt another audience and fail. He held up his mug for a passing good fellow to fill, gave thanks and cheers all around, he was sure, and took a deep draught.

Mrs. Fanshawe had no trouble at all, amidst the crowd and jollity, to slip from the public room and pass beneath the elaborately arched doorway through which she'd seen the baronet leave, into a narrower connecting corridor. She walked along, marveling at the luxury of the place. At length, she saw a young gentleman approaching.

Edward Arundell, returning to the public area from a water closet not open to the townsfolk, saw a stout matron coming his way. As they neared one another, he thought she wore a challenging look, one that bordered on impudence. His eyes narrowed. "Have you lost your way?" He stopped before her, wondering that no servant had already intercepted her.

"I must see His Lordship," she said decisively.

Edward's lip quivered, for the baronet was not a "lord," but all he said was, "Is he expecting you?"

"He'll *desire* to see me," she said, with a knowing air that could not but intrigue young Edward.

"Why is that?" he asked.

Her lips pursed and she raised her head importantly. "I have information of a personal nature for him."

This Edward considered doubtful. "What is your name?"

"Mrs. Fanshawe," she said, nodding her head.

"Fanshawe?" Edward came sharply to attention.

"Are you a relation of Frannie's, that is, er, Miss Frances Fanshawe?"

"I know all about *her,*" she said, with a sagacious and haughty eye.

"Sebastian will wish to see you," Edward said eagerly.

"Here now, I shall speak only to 'is Lordship."

Edward surveyed her. He didn't know where Sebastian was, but he must not let this woman escape. If she did indeed have knowledge of Frannie's history, he'd hear no end of it if he let her slip away. Besides which, it might lead to Frannie's finally coming into her fortune. "I'll take you to the baronet," he said, coming to a decision.

"Much obliged," she said with satisfaction, bowing her head, but with that same impertinent expression curling her lips.

As he led the way, Edward remembered that Frannie was going by name of Miss Baxter, and how befuddling it would all seem to his cousin, who surely knew nothing of a Miss Fanshawe. But he'd just seen Sir Hugo and his mama consulting with servants outside the baronet's study. He'd let them sort it out, and find Sebastian afterward.

A turn in the corridor brought them into sight of Sir Hugo and his mother, still speaking with the butler and housekeeper. Mrs. Arundell was giving last-minute instructions regarding the coming ball that evening, and, being a guest, had secured Sir Hugo's presence to impress the servants that her word must be followed. She looked up, saw Edward and a woman, and turned to the servants. "That will be all. Come to me if there are any further questions." Turning to Edward, she said, "Yes?" with an expectant air, not looking at Mrs. Fanshawe.

"Mama, Cousin, I have a Mrs. *Fanshawe* here," he said with peculiar emphasis and looking chiefly to his mother. Mrs. Arundell's eyes widened. "Fanshawe?"

"F-Fanshawe!" repeated the baronet, turning with sudden interest to the lady.

"Ay, and I needs must speak to 'ye, Yer Lordship, privately, if you would, about *Miss Fanshawe.*"

"To the baronet about *Frannie?*" asked Mrs. Arundell, putting a hand to her heart.

"Do you mean, Miss Baxter?" Sir Hugo asked.

Mrs. Arundell said, "Oh, dear," and put two fingers to her lips.

But the baronet's expression cleared and he murmured, "Frannie, yes. Of *course*." With a much concerned look, and pursed lips, he said curtly, "I must see this lady, Penelope. If you don't mind—" He drew a handkerchief from a waistcoat pocket and wiped his brow, which seemed suddenly to have broken out in a sweat.

"If *you* don't mind, I'll come along!" she said decisively.

"I will only speak to 'is Lordship!" cried Mrs. Fanshawe. Mrs. Arundell surveyed her, taking in the red cheeks, the worn shoes, the quality of her gown, the belligerent expression. She nodded shortly, but with pursed lips. "I'll wait, then," she said to Sir Hugo.

Sir Hugo, looking shaken, motioned the woman into his study. Once inside, he offered her a seat and sat down heavily behind his desk as if his legs had gone weak.

In the corridor, Mrs. Arundell looked at Edward in surprise. "Find Beau! He'll want to know about this!" Edward nodded and headed back to the great room. But he didn't expect to find Sebastian. He'd taken Frannie driving, the *usurper*, and would likely be miles away by now.

Mrs. Arundell, after watching Edward 'til he rounded the bend, crept silently to the door of the study. She adjusted her hearing device, and carefully put her ear against the keyhole.

Frannie and Sebastian, in the little ante room which connected to the study, heard the sound of voices coming from within. "My cousin's voice!" Sebastian said. "Let us apprise him of our happy news."

Frannie hesitated. "But will he approve? Surely he will want to know what I can bring to the match."

Sebastian smiled. "Only minutes ago you feared he wanted to marry you! Now you fret that he shan't approve of you for his heir?"

She grinned sheepishly. "I always marveled that he *could* approve of me, and wondered why your mother did."

"All you need, dearest, is *my* approval, and that you have." He pulled her close against him once more and kissed her. Then, taking her hand, he moved them toward the door to the study.

Inside the study, the baronet rose to pour himself a quick drink, motioning for Mrs. Fanshawe to speak.

"I am the wife of Charles Fanshawe," she began.

The baronet nodded his head. "Yes, yes, as I suspected."

Behind the door, Sebastian froze. "Why, I believe it's that termagant, your aunt!"

"She is a shrew!" whispered Frannie, "But what business could she have with Sir Hugo?"

"She may be in search of us," he said, though doubtfully. "Let's hold off going in until we hear what she wants."

In the study, Mrs. Fanshawe repeated, as though to be certain the baronet understood the connexion, "Charles Fanshawe's wife, *Margaret's brother.*"

"Have you been in contact with Margaret?" he asked urgently.

Here Mrs. Fanshawe hesitated, giving him a cautious look. "She's gone these eighteen months, sir."

"Eighteen months! She left England above eighteen years ago, madam."

"Nay, sir, she's *gone*. To the grave, sir! She's dead these eighteen months."

He stared. Quietly he said, "I was given that news. But how did you learn it? You had word from America?"

The lady hesitated. "From Lincolnshire, sir. But that's not what I'm here for."

But now he set his drink down and stared at her with consternation. "Lincolnshire?" His face grew exceedingly red. "Here in England? All this time! It cannot be." He looked at her sternly. "What has Lincolnshire to do with it? Your husband swore she'd left for America!"

"Yes, sir, that he did; thanks to your father!" She shifted in her seat and nervously wiped her palms on her gown. "But it were a lie. She lived in Lincolnshire, sir!"

He leveled a baleful gaze upon her, but soon his look became forlorn. His lips pursed. "Do you mean to say she never was farther from me than Lincolnshire? What—what do you know of her child?"

"She's the very reason why I come, sir!" she said with a nod, and swallowed. "My husband and I adopted her."

He looked thunderstruck. "Adopted her? You adopted Margaret's child?"

She seemed to grow slightly paler. A little more hesitantly she said, "We...we named her Catherine. Your father promised a trust fund to her, he did."

He stared at her down his nose. "I called upon your husband in search of Margaret, *my lawful wife*. You had a daughter already at that time, a daughter named Catherine, if I do not misremember."

The woman swallowed. "'Twas *her* daughter. The mother didn't want her."

There was the sound of a muffled noise, and suddenly the inner door to the study burst open. Sebastian and Frannie stood there, staring in with such expressions! Frannie was torn between joy and sheer astonishment—if Sir Hugo was lawfully married to her mother then he was her *father*! The man she'd been trying so hard to avoid—her father! But indignation too coloured her expression, for here was Mrs. Fanshawe trying to pull the wool over his eyes!

The lady rose from her seat in alarm, but her features became granite as she settled her eyes upon Frannie. "I was only telling 'is Lordship what we did for ye all these years," she said coldly.

Sebastian almost spoke. The words, "Sir, 'tis all a fetch and a gamon!" were at the tip of his tongue, but he waited to see what Frannie would do. She said, looking sorrowfully at her aunt. "Did for *me*?" She turned to the baronet. "What she told you is a humbug! I lived with Mama until her passing a year ago August. I only met Mrs. Fanshawe in my search for—why, I believe, for *you*, sir!"

Mrs. Fanshawe's face scrunched in anger. She put a hand to her hip and cried, "My 'usband did exactly what your mother told him! Had he revealed your whereabouts –and he might easily 'ave done so—then *you*!" She pointed at Sir Hugo. "*You* would have been out at the pockets! This fine estate," she said, turning her head to take in the dimensions of the room, "entailed! You'd 'ave had debt to yer ears! My 'usband did you a favour, sir, in keeping the agreement; all so's this one 'ere"—she turned and pointed at Frannie—"could come into the trust! I only aimed to ask for sommat for our trouble! My daughter's to be wed to Lord Whitby! If there's no trust for her, she'll not be equipt! The wedding'll be off!"

The baronet stared at Mrs. Fanshawe, his mind turning. Looking back at Frannie, he said, "Did your mother remarry? How are you Miss Baxter?"

Sebastian spoke up. "Her name is Miss Fanshawe, sir; I apologize for the confusion. Tracing Frannie's heritage has been our sole difficulty because her father's name—*your* name, sir—at Sir Malcolm's insistence, I gather, was blotted out on her birth record. Miss Baxter is an alias we hoped to use in society only until we understood the circumstances of her birth better." He gave his cousin a wry grin. "We had no idea, sir, that her real name could mean anything to you!" He motioned to Mrs. Fanshawe. "We have been searching for Mr. Fanshawe for weeks to get to the bottom of the mystery. This lady, however, was enraptured with the notion that the trust should be given to *her* natural daughter."

With large eyes, Frannie listened, nodding in agreement with what Sebastian said. Looking tremulously at the baronet she said, "I never should have asked the Arundells to disguise my name, sir. It was badly done. I beg your pardon. I am Frances Fanshawe." Her heart pounded in her ears and it seemed as though her hands shook.

With a look of sorrow mixed with dawning amazement, the baronet extended a hand toward Frannie. "Come here, child."

Frannie hesitated, but Sebastian gave her the smallest nudge. She went forward then, staring at Sir Hugo with a wholly different expression on her face than she had ever worn when looking at him in the past. She felt suddenly overcome with shyness—how could it be true? That Sir Hugo—Sebastian's cousin once removed, the man she'd done everything in her power to avoid—was her *father!*

His eyes were full with emotion, and he took her hand when she drew near.

"I knew it had to be. I knew from the moment I saw you that you had to be, you could *only* be Margaret's child. You are your mother's mirror image!"

"Then 'tis true?" she asked, while her heart beat strangely. "That you are my—my father?"

"I think it must be true. How old are you, my girl?" he asked.

"Nineteen, sir."

Tears sprang into his eyes. With compressed lips, blinking, he nodded at her, his eyes brimming with emotion. "Your mother was my lawful wife. You are my child!"

Frannie shot a brief glance of shining relief at Sebastian, even as Sir Hugo took her in his great big arms for a heartfelt hug. When he released her enough to stand back and meet her gaze, tears shone in his eyes. "I married your mother secretly on account of the baronet, my father. The plan was to give him time to accept the marriage. In the meantime, you were born. Your birth convinced me to face my father's wrath and bring my family to Bartlett Hall, but it was then you vanished! Your mother, I was given to believe in the single letter she wrote me, took you off to America. Your uncle Mr. Fanshawe confirmed to me that you had both gone." Here he swallowed uncomfortably. "I suppose I read that letter a thousand times. I suspected my father had a hand in the business, but what proof did I have? And I believed he knew nothing of the marriage."

Sebastian said gently, "He must have found out, sir. But why, after all this time, did *we* know nothing of it?"

"And why, sir, did I not know of your existence?" Frannie asked, now with tears rimming her own eyes. Sir Hugo took a deep breath, clasping her one hand between his two meaty ones. "Because, my dear, your mother contrived to keep it that way. I am sure Sir Malcolm required it of her. If I had known you were in England—oh! I am sorry to say I believed your mother, who claimed, by the time I received her note, that she'd have left the country with you." He surveyed her sadly. "I searched for you, to no avail. I was determined to do what I could for you, even if your mama had no wish to live as my wife."

His lips firmed into a line. "I see now that Sir Malcolm orchestrated it all." He shook his head self-reproachfully. "I should have faced his wrath to begin with. I thought—we both thought it better to wait for him to accept the match—but then it was too late." He sniffed and tried to smile. He cast small, sad eyes upon her. "Tell me, how did you fare all these years? How did you get by? Sir Malcolm said he settled a good amount upon your mother—I can only pray it was true."

"An annual sum came to us, sir, and kept me in genteel circumstances; I have been as modish as I care to be."

"An annual sum?" he said, his eyes glazing in thought. "So my father did not send your mother off with one payment?" He shook his head. "He knew all along how close you were, the blackguard! He told me upon his deathbed how he ran off my wife and child; but even then he gave me to believe you were across an ocean." He turned pained eyes to her. "But what's this about a trust?"

"According to my mother, sir, the annual payments were from the interest of a fund, a trust fund, that is in my name payable upon my majority."

Now Sir Hugo's brows rose. He lowered his head in thought. "That would be untoward generosity, coming from my father." He grinned ruefully, shaking his head. "Margaret demanded it, I am certain. Good for her!" But then he looked back at Frannie. "My solicitors disclosed nothing of this to me. We will look into it directly!"

Frannie sighed with relief. She wasn't a blow by! She was respectable! But suddenly it felt supremely less important than before, and the trust mattered to her not at all—she turned her eyes to Sebastian, who was approaching her as if with the same thought. *Their future* was all that mattered, now. Knowing he loved her was her supreme joy.

He came and took her free hand, lifted it to his lips, and kissed it. Then, turning to Sir Hugo, he said, "It seems, sir, that Miss Fanshawe is my second cousin once removed."

Sir Hugo smiled but said, "She is not, sir."

To Sebastian and Frannie's look of confusion he added, still smiling, "Miss *Arundell* is your second cousin once removed. She is my daughter, rightfully by name Frances Arundell."

Sebastian, grinning, said, "That is the very name, sir, that I have just now desired Miss Fanshawe to accept—as my wife."

Sir Hugo's face beamed. "Is this true?"

Frannie nodded happily, while Sebastian looked down at her with pride in his eyes. He gave a rueful grin as he turned to Sir Hugo. "I never dreamed I should require your approval for the match!"

Sir Hugo's large girth shook with mirth, even as a tear slipped from one eye and rolled down his cheek. "I have discovered my daughter and lost her again in one day. For how could I fail to approve?" He turned to Frannie. "This is the hand of Providence, my dear. You will be mistress here one day, taking your place in Bartlett Hall despite all of Sir Malcolm's machinations." Turning to Sebastian he added, "All my life I have not been able to give my daughter what was her due. It eases my heart, sir, that she will be mistress here. I regret deeply that her mother was not able to fill that role, to enjoy the rightful due that my father denied her."

Frannie could hardly comprehend it. Far from being the dubious natural daughter of an unknown gentleman, she was the daughter of a baronet and betrothed to Sebastian, the heir to the title! Her heart felt full to the brim.

CHAPTER TWENTY-TWO

Suddenly the main door to the study flew open and Mrs. Arundell burst in, her face beaming. She rushed to her eldest son, stopping only to shoot a triumphant smile at Frannie. "Oh, Beau, *dearest*! I *knew* she was perfect for you!"

"You knew it before I did," he said with a smile.

"But of course. I had an *inkling*!"

She kissed his cheek and went to embrace Frannie, but he spied tears upon her face. With furrowed brows, he said gently, "No need for that, ma'am." He drew out a handkerchief and softly wiped away the wetness.

"My tears aren't for you," she said. She turned to face the baronet. Her face went from happiness to sorrow. "You should have told me, Hugo! Indeed, you should have told me!" Her voice shook with emotion.

The room fell silent, as if each one knew the long-standing mystery, the second long-standing mystery that is, was about to be demystified. Frannie's parentage was the first, but it was settled. Her future, settled. But Mrs. Arundell's old grudge was still a tangle.

"Penelope," said the baronet, his eyes full. He almost dropped Frannie's hand, but raised and kissed it first, with a tender look. Frannie smiled at him, blinking back tears. She went and stood by Sebastian's side, who took her hand and grasped it between both his own.

Mrs. Arundell went and stood in front of Sir Hugo's desk,

facing him with large, tragic eyes.

He said, "I wanted desperately to tell you. I'm afraid I was too ashamed. When I met you, I had already secretly pledged myself to Margaret Fanshawe. We waited years to marry in hopes of gaining Sir Malcolm's approval."

"You ought to have told me," she said in a subdued voice. "I would have kept your secret."

"But that's it!" he said. "It was a terrible secret. I couldn't burden you with it. I was a mere cub at the time, only eighteen, and you were what?—only sixteen. I lived in fear that my father would discover my attachment. He desired I should offer for you, but I could not. My previous engagement, though it was in word only at that time, prevented me."

She looked at him across the desk, and by the expression on her face, Sir Hugo knew she was not yet appeased. He went around the desk and stood before her, and then took her hands in his.

She gazed up at him sadly. "I felt at the time there was a hindrance. I thought it must be me!"

He shook his head regretfully. "Dearest Penelope! If I had not already pledged myself to another, I would have gladly welcomed the match with you."

Here he paused, his eyes filling with sorrow, looking pleadingly at Mrs. Arundell. "I liked you very well, Penelope, and wished at times—well, it was too late. But I couldn't tell you of a secret betrothal until after I'd told Sir Malcolm. We were forced to wait years after you married Richard, and finally wed without having gained my father's approval."

She nodded but said, "Richard died in 1800. I've been an *ace of spades* a long time, sir," she said with a reproachful look.

"'Twas only when I learned from Sir Malcolm—he confessed it as he lay dying—that Margaret was gone, did I consider myself free to approach you, my dear; which I did, by escorting you to the Merrillton's ball, and inviting you here."

Mrs. Arundell bit her lip lightly and nodded. "I understand you," she said gently. Looking toward Frannie and Sebastian, she said, "And Providence has worked out a blessing in it." She turned her eyes back to the baronet. "Had you and I married then, neither of us would have our precious offspring!"

His eyes turned to gaze at Frannie, still standing beside Sebastian. "Thank God we do," he said, with a look of fresh appreciation. He turned back to the diminutive Mrs. Arundell. "But now, Penelope, you must put an end to my life's sorrow." She looked up at him, blinking.

"I was unable to ask you then, unable to approach you all these years. Say you will, at long last, dearest, be my wife!"

Her little mouth opened. She blinked. "Oh, all these long years, Hugo! After *all* these years!"

He took her hand and lifted it to his lips. "Well, m'dear? Well? I know I am a clodpate and ungracious, but please, am I to be the happiest of men?"

Mrs. Arundell stared up at him with wide eyes. She smiled. "I thought you would never ask me, you big, *wonderful* oaf! Of course I will."

His face lit with joy, and he took her slim figure into his meaty arms and drew her close for a kiss.

Sebastian said, "Happy day, indeed!" He put an arm about Frannie. "But I must disagree with my cousin about one thing; that bit about being the happiest of men. That blessing," he said, moving a tendril of hair gently from her face, "belongs entirely to me."

All this time Mrs. Fanshawe, clutching her reticule, had been squirming in her seat. She rose now and scuttled toward the door with her head down, daring not so much as a glance behind her. Sir Hugo tore his gaze from his future bride. "One moment, Mrs. Fanshawe! What did you mean by claiming you adopted my child?"

She stopped and turned to face the room. Swallowing, she looked with trepidation at Frannie. "We only did what 'er mother asked. We kept 'er secret!"

The baronet's face reddened. "For keeping a devilish secret, do you consider I should thank you? When I might have been told—"

"And yer father would ha' left ye with an estate entailed, and in debt! That's why she done it! Fer yer own good. Said she wouldn't be the cause of yer ruin. And without Mr. Fanshawe's help, I daresay you'd be low in the pocket, and with not a farthing to spare!"

"Had we not overheard you speaking to Sir Hugo," put in Sebastian with narrowed eyes and in a strong tone, "you and your husband would have 'helped' Miss Arundell out of her fortune, and worse, prevented her from knowing her father!"

She gave him a belligerent look, but it was laced with fear. In a second, without another word, she turned and slunk out of the room and made her way back to the great hall blubbering like a baby. She must gather her family and make a hasty exit. She had not only failed utterly to procure the slightest benefit for their daughter, but now feared that her bungled attempt at gain might lead to prosecution. That creature Miss Fanshawe might be of a mind to cause trouble for them seeing as how she, Mrs. Fanshawe, had misrepresented the case to the baronet.

She took her place by her husband but was forced to wait for Catherine who was among the horde of dancers. Gesturing frantically, she tried to get Catherine's attention. "Mr. Fanshawe," she said, "I desire we should leave *this minute!*" She looked at him searchingly a moment, assessing whether or not he'd enjoyed the baronet's ale a little too well and might not be amenable to a hasty exit.

Understanding the reason for her scrutiny, he said, "I'm all of apiece, m'dear; the ale's weak. Not at all the thing such as what we drink aboard ship." He reflected ruefully that the pleasant sense of inebriation he'd enjoyed earlier had already ebbed away, leaving as quickly as it came.

"That's a mercy, sir, for we must make haste!"

"What's this? In a hurry, now? Did you speak to Sir Hugo?"

"'Tis no matter now," she replied, turning back to the dance floor and resuming the gesticulations that she felt sure would gain Catherine's attention.

"What is the hurry, Mrs. Fanshawe?"

She turned to her husband, her face scrunched in an effort not to wail. "We're all done up! There's naught in it for Catherine, and her betrothal is ru—ruined!" She produced a handkerchief from within her bodice and blew her nose heartily. "She'll be an old maid, an ape leader!" She let out a shuddering sob.

He patted her hand, "There, there, m'love, cain't be as bad as all that."

"There's more, Mr. Fanshawe!" she cried, staring at him in

despair. "That other creature Miss Fanshawe is here! It's all out, now. They know each other for father and daughter! There's naught we can do for them. And I fear that creature will have the law on us!"

He looked thoughtful a moment. "Did they speak of the trust?"

Her eyes blazed. "His Lordship knew nothing of a trust! My hopes were raised all these years in vain. A fine husband you are, to raise a woman's hopes for naught! A trust, indeed! I suppose it don't, and never did exist!"

"But it does, my dear." He patted his waistcoat pocket.

She turned incredulous eyes upon him, blinking. "Do you mean to say, Mr. Fanshawe, that you have the papers of the trust upon you? On your person?"

He nodded. "I do." He thought back to the day of his homecoming, how his wife had wished to whisk him from the house, almost too quickly for him to step into his study to retrieve the vital papers which belonged to Margaret. Having discovered Sir Malcolm's passing while aboard ship, he was determined to return the agreement to her first thing. It could not be too soon for his liking, and he longed, moreover, to see his sister. He had barely time to stuff the pages into his waistcoat before his wife hurried him from the house.

Mrs. Fanshawe's countenance transformed in an instant. Tears vanished; her face cleared and she smiled. "Why, sir, you are the finest husband in the world! In the world, sir! Come, we must hasten to the baronet, for now we may do him a service!"

He looked out at the dancers. "Catherine is yet upon the floor. A very gentlemanlike young man is her partner. We mustn't leave without alerting her."

Mrs. Fanshawe followed his gaze and saw their daughter was indeed partnered with a very respectable looking gentleman—in fact—she gasped. "Mr. Fanshawe! That is the young man who took me to see the baronet!" She gazed at the dancers with a calculating eye. "And now he must do so again."

Frannie, Sebastian, Mrs. Arundell and Sir Hugo were just about to leave the study when there was a knock. The door opened; Edward poked his head in.

"Right, they're still here," he said to someone behind him, and then entered, followed by Mrs. and Mr. Fanshawe. The stout woman looked about with an air of triumph before settling her gaze upon the baronet. "Sir, we have something what should interest you, I daresay."

Her husband was standing almost behind her but he came about now and went toward the baronet, his hand extended. "Sir," he said, "very glad I am to see you well."

Sir Hugo accepted the handshake, though his heart ached at the knowledge that this man had known his wife and child were in England, all these long years. "What is this your wife refers to?" he asked.

"It is this, sir." Mr. Fanshawe put a hand inside his waistcoat pocket and drew out a small sheaf of papers yellowed with age and tied with a string. But Mrs. Fanshawe jumped to his side and grabbed them. Holding them up triumphantly she cried, "This here is what can solve the mystery of the trust fund! These are the very papers my husband's sister left in our keeping."

Sir Hugo's eyes gleamed. "The papers concerning the trust? Excellent. I must require them immediately." He held out a hand.

"Not so fast, Yer Honour, if you please," said Mrs. Fanshawe, quickly shoving the hand with the papers behind her back. She darted to the hearth and held it out precariously over the flames.

"I must require something in return," she said.

Sir Hugo said, "Of course, of course, no problem at all."

But Mr. Fanshawe, frowning at his wife, went to her. He held out his hand. "Mrs. Fanshawe, we will not extort Margaret's family. I am no such brother who would use my sister that ill."

"Think of Catherine's betrothal!" she cried pleadingly. "She must have a good future, sir! You are her father and must provide for her!"

Before he could reply, from the side of the room Frannie spoke up. "Dear Aunt Fanshawe, if those papers do assure me of a fortune, I wish to be of assistance to Catherine."

Mrs. Fanshawe turned to her in astonishment. "You wish to help our Catherine?" she asked in a small, incredulous voice, her face wrinkled in doubt.

Frannie smiled. "I do indeed, freely, and with all my heart."

Mrs. Fanshawe was suddenly faint. She put out a hand to steady herself, and her husband quickly put an arm about her. He helped her to a chair where she sat blinking at Frannie, her face distorted with the effort to hold back tears. Frannie moved toward her and took her hand.

"I give you my word on it, ma'am. I will do all in my power to help Catherine keep her betrothal."

The lady's tears now gave way, silently rolling down her face. She freed her hand only to take Frannie's in it and kiss it. "My dear, *dear*, niece!" she said, handing over the papers. "My darling Miss Fanshawe!" Frannie passed them immediately to the baronet, who had joined her by the chair.

Turning back to the lady she said, smiling, "I *am* your niece, but I am not Miss Fanshawe. I am Miss Frances Arundell, if you please." The truth rolled over her again like a great big victory banner. With a trembling mix of pride and humility, she said, "I am a baronet's daughter and the future wife of a baronet."

"Sir Hugo's daughter?" Edward's face froze in astonishment. "Did you ever hear of such a quiz!" he exclaimed, but then his face fell. "Wait. What's this? The future wife of a baronet?"

"Edward, dearest," put in Mrs. Arundell, hurrying to his side. "You cannot hold the smallest doubt that they must wed. Pray recollect I had an *inkling* of it, my love!"

In the great hall, the waits played their last number, "Hark, the Herald Angels Sing." The faintest strains could be heard in the room as Sebastian, taking one of Frannie's hands, squeezed it gently. "So there really is a trust fund, sir?" he asked, looking to Sir Hugo, who had rounded his desk while reading the papers.

Sir Hugo looked up with a sparkle in his eyes. "There is indeed! I daresay from the amount of the initial investment, something exceeding £30,000 must be accrued in my daughter's name by now, waiting only for her to claim it." He looked at Frannie. "Heaven be blessed that my father did this for you! His refusal to accept my choice of bride made him more generous than his nature would otherwise allow. He preferred to pay such a price rather than to enjoy the greater rewards of a happy family, and grandchildren about his coattails."

Mrs. Arundell went toward Frannie with open arms. "Did I not always say it would all work out? That you would get your fortune?" The women shared a quick but warm embrace.

Frannie said, "You did, indeed! But my greatest joy today is not the trust." She looked up to meet Sebastian's eyes, finding the warmth in them that melted her insides and made her long to be in his arms. As if knowing her thoughts, he stepped closer and put an arm about her.

"Nor is it that I have found my father, though I rejoice in that." Tears brimmed in her eyes as she added, "My greatest joy is that I am no longer unfit to be your wife!"

He raised her hand and kissed it lingeringly, his beautiful eyes locked onto hers. "You were never unfit for that, dearest."

TIMELINE Before the Story Opens

1786:   Sir Malcolm arranges for his son Hugo to meet Penelope Markham, the daughter of a wealthy nabob. Hugo likes Penelope very much but he makes no offer   for her.

1787:   Penelope marries Hugo's 1st cousin, Richard Arundell.

1788:   Sebastian is born to Penelope and Richard (he's 27 in 1815)

1796:   Frannie is born. She is raised by her mother, Margaret Fanshawe, and a lady, Mrs. Baxter.

1797:   Edward is born to Penelope and Richard.

1800:   The boys' father, Richard Arundell, dies.

1813:   Margaret Fanshawe, Frannie's mother, dies.

1814:   Sir Malcolm, Hugo Arundell's father, dies. Sir Hugo is now the baronet of Bartlett Hall.

1815:   Before dying, Mrs. Baxter tells Frannie that she is heiress to a great trust fund, and that her father is a nobleman.

1815:   **STORY OPENS** Frannie is broke after paying off what she could of Mrs. Baxter's debts. After calling upon the Fanshawe's of Cheapside seeking help, she is almost run down by Edward Arundell driving his brother's curricle.

Map: 1818 Map of Mayfair (Inset)

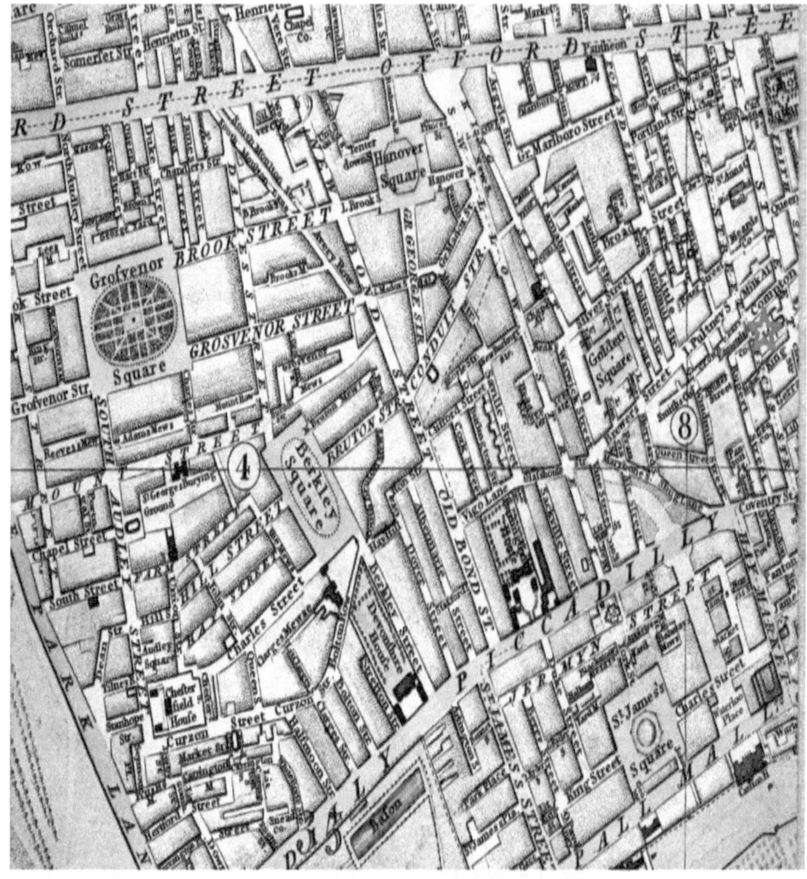

The Arundells live on King Street on the far right of the map. There is a faint star over the house.

CHAPTER ONE

Chesterton, Hertfordshire

England

1813

Something would have to be done about Ariana.

All winter Miss Ariana Forsythe, aged nineteen, had been going about the house sighing, "Mr. Hathaway is my lot in life!"

She spoke as though the prospect of that life was a great burden to bear, but one to which she had properly reconciled herself. When her declarations met with exasperation or reproach from her family—for no one else was convinced Mr. Hathaway, the rector, was her lot—she usually responded in a perplexed manner. Hadn't they understood for an age that her calling was to wed a man of the cloth? Was there another man of God, other than their rector, available to her? No. It only stood to reason, therefore, that Mr. Hathaway was her lot in life. Their cold reception to the thought of the marriage was unfathomable.

When she was seventeen (a perfectly respectable marrying age) she had romantic hopes about a young and brilliant assistant to the rector, one Mr. Stresham. It was shortly after meeting him, in fact, that she had formed the opinion the Almighty was calling her to marry a man of God. Mr. Stresham even had the approval of her parents. But the man took a situation in another parish without asking Ariana to accompany him as his wife. She was disappointed, but not one to give up easily, continued to speak of "the calling," waiting in hope for another Mr. Stresham of sorts. But no man came. And now she had reached the conclusion that Mr. Hathaway—Mr. Hathaway, the rector, (approaching the age of sixty) would have to do.

Her parents, Charles and Julia Forsythe, were sitting in their comfortably furnished morning room, Julia with a cup of tea before her, and Charles with his newspaper. A steady warmth emanated from the hearth. Mrs. Forsythe, being an observant mamma, had been growing in her conviction that the situation called for some action.

"What shall we do about Ariana?"

"What do you suggest, my dear?" Her husband reluctantly folded his paper; he knew his wife wanted a discussion of the matter and that he would get precious little reading done until she had got it.

She held up a folded piece of foolscap: the annual letter from Agatha Bentley, Charles's sister, asking for Alberta, the eldest Forsythe daughter, for the season in London. It had arrived the day before.

Aunt Bentley was a childless wealthy widow and a hopeless socialite. For the past three years she had written annually to tell her brother and his wife why they ought to let her sponsor their eldest daughter for a London season. She owned a house in Mayfair (could anything be more respectable than that?) and knew a great deal of the big-wigs in society. She had, in fact, that most important of commodities which the Forsythes completely lacked: connexions. And as Charles's family were her only living relatives, she was prepared—even anxious—to serve as chaperon for her niece

Much to the lady's frustration, Julia and Charles had annually extinguished her hopes, replying to her letters graciously but with the inevitable, "We cannot countenance a separation from our child at this time," and so on. Charles was unflinching on this point, never doubting his girls would reap a greater benefit by remaining beneath his own roof. They knew full well, moreover, that Aunt Agatha could not hope, with all her money and connexions to find as suitable a husband for their offspring as was possible right in Chesterton.

Why? For the profound reason that Aunt Bentley had no religion whatsoever.

And yet, due to the distressing state of affairs with Ariana, Julia wished to consider her latest offer. With the letter waving in her hand she said, "I think we ought to oblige your sister this year. She must be lonely, poor thing, and besides removing Ariana from the parish, a visit to the city could prove beneficial for her education."

Ariana's father silently considered the matter. His eldest daughter Alberta was as good as wed, having recently accepted an offer of marriage—to no one's surprise—from Johnathan Norledge. Ariana, his second eldest, had been irksome in regard to the rector, but to pack her off to London? Surely the situation was not so dire as to warrant such a move.

"I think there is nothing else for it," Mrs. Forsythe said emphatically. "Ariana is determined about Mr. Hathaway and, even though we can forbid her to speak to the man, she will pine and sigh and like as not drive me to distraction!"

Taking a pipe out of his waistcoat pocket (though he never smoked), Mr. Forsythe absently rubbed the polished wood in his fingers.

"I recall other fanciful notions of our daughter's," he said finally, "and they slipped away in time. Recall, if you will, when she was above certain her destiny was to be a missionary—to America. That desire faded. She fancies this, she fancies that; soon she will fancy another thing entirely, and we shan't hear another word about the 'wonderful rector' again."

Mrs. Forsythe's countenance, still attractive in her forties, became fretful.

"I grant that she has had strong…affections before. But this time, my dear, it is a complicated affection for in this case it is the heart of the ah, *affected,* which we must consider. It has ideas of its own."

"Of its own?"

Mrs. Forsythe looked about the room to be certain no one else had entered. The servants were so practiced at coming and going quietly, their presence might not be marked. But no, there was only the two of them. She lowered her voice anyway.

"The rector! I do not think he intends to lose her! What could delight him more than a young, healthy wife who might fill his table with offspring?"

Mr. Forsythe shook his head. "Our rector is not the man to think only of himself; he must agree with us on the obvious unsuitability of the match."

The rector was Thaddeus Admonicus Hathaway, of the Church in the Village Square. Mr. Hathaway was a good man. His sermons were grounded in sound religion, which meant they were based on orthodox Christian teaching. He was clever, and a popular dinner guest of the gentry, including the Forsythes. If these had not been true of him, Mr. Forsythe might have been as concerned as his wife. Knowing Mr. Hathaway, however, Charles Forsythe did not think a drastic action such as sending his daughter to the bustling metropolis of London was necessary.

Mrs. Forsythe chose not to quarrel with her spouse. She would simply commit the matter to prayer. If the Almighty decided that Ariana must be removed to Agatha's house, then He would make it clear to her husband. In her years of marriage she had discovered that God was the Great Communicator, and she had no right to try and usurp that power. Her part was to pray, sincerely and earnestly.

Mr. Forsythe gave his judgment: "I fear that rather than exerting a godly influence upon her aunt, Ariana would be drawn astray by the ungodliness of London society."

"Do you doubt her so much, Charles? This infatuation with Mr. Hathaway merely results from her youth, her admiration for his superior learning, and especially," she said, leaning forward and giving him a meaningful look, "for lack of a young man who has your approval! Have you not frowned upon every male who has approached her in the past? Why, Mr. Hathaway is the first whom you have failed to frighten off and only because he is our rector! 'Tis little wonder a young girl takes a fanciful notion into her head!"

When he made no answer, she added, while adjusting the frilly morning cap on her head, "Mr. Hathaway causes me concern."

Mr. Forsythe's countenance was sober. "'Tis my sister who warrants the concern. She will wish to make a match for our daughter—and she will not be content with just any *mister* I assure you. In addition to which, a girl as pretty as our daughter will undoubtedly attract attention of the wrong sort."

Julia was flustered for a second, but countered, "Agatha is no threat to our child. We shall say we are sending Ariana to see the sights, take in the museums and so forth. Surely there is no harm in that. A dinner party or soiree here or there should not be of concern.

And Ariana is too intelligent to allow herself to be foisted upon an unsuitable man for a fortune or title."

Too intelligent? He thought of the aging minister that no one had had to "foist" her upon. Aloud he merely said, "I shall speak with her tonight. She shall be brought to reason, depend upon it. There will be no need to pack her off to London."

Available Online or Wherever Books Are Sold

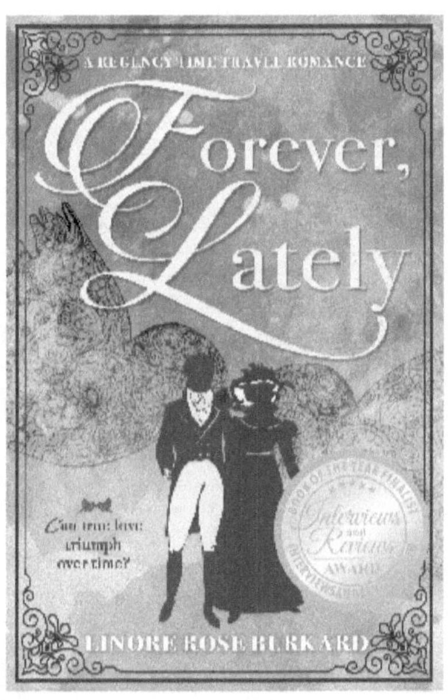

CHAPTER ONE

Love alters not with (time's) brief hours and weeks
But bears it out ev'n to the edge of doom.
Shakespeare

Julian St. John dug in his heels and spurred on Brutus, his thoroughbred of sixteen hands, as he approached the drive to his estate. A light rain obscured the moonlight, and he wanted nothing more than to return to his books and the fireside. He'd been dragged off by a messenger who'd claimed that a "proper lady" was on the road and in need of assistance.

He'd ridden all the way into the village and found no lady in need of help. Neither did he see the boy who'd appeared at his door claiming there was one. He didn't mind an urgent gallop—he was born for speed, and thrived on racing—but it was a fool's errand and he was tired. He secured his hat and again nudged Brutus with his heels. As he neared the turnoff to his own drive, suddenly the lights of a coach against the side of the road about fifty feet ahead lit up, looking dully at him like two sleepy eyes.

St. John squinted and slowed Brutus. The coach hadn't moved, so he spurred the animal gently towards it, wondering if his assistance was needed after all. But the sound of a whip and a coachman's yell brought the idle vehicle to life, and it barreled down the road—straight towards him. He moved

Brutus to the side but was astonished when the coach veered again in his direction. Was the coachman buffle-headed?

He spurred the animal's sides and maneuvered off the road and up a steep incline, and then turned to watch the vehicle. Unbelievably, it was still coming crazily at him, its lamplights brighter now, blazing like evil eyes. And closing in. This wasn't poor driving—the coach was *trying* to hit him! As it bowled towards him, the coachman's face materialised out of the haze, his eyes opened wide in terror.

A fence prevented St. John from vanishing into the trees that fronted his property, but just as the coach would have bowled into him, he shouted at Brutus, snapped his spurs, and cracked the reins—they missed a collision by inches as the sturdy animal lunged out of harm's way. The coach's horses hit the fence, whinnying.

Turning Brutus around, St. John patted his neck while surveying the vehicle as it came to a rollicking stop, balanced precariously on the incline. The messenger boy, he saw now, must have fallen from the coach, and was on his backside in the wet brush.

Taking a deep breath at the close call, St. John quietly reached into a coat pocket and pulled out a pistol. Good thing he rarely rode in the evenings without one. Good thing, too, that he was an excellent horseman or that insane coachman might have caused his demise. Brutus nickered nervously, so he patted his mane. "Good job, old boy," he said, never moving his eyes from the sleek black coach, silent and mysterious, but whose horses stamped impatiently. He cautiously approached. There was no sound as he made his way past the closed door, but he found the coachman huddled on his perch.

"How the devil do you explain your driving? Are you hocused?" he asked, thinking the man was in his cups.

"Nay, guv'nor. Followin' me orders, that's what."

"Orders from whom?" St. John demanded. "Who do you have in there?"

"T'mistress an' 'er sister," he answered sullenly.

St. John's heart sank—two women—if the driver could be trusted. "And you drove like a madman with women aboard!" The man shifted uneasily on his perch but muttered, "I follows me orders, guv'nor."

"And what were your orders, precisely?" he asked in a scathing tone.

Again the man shifted uneasily. "Ask t'mistress."

"Who is your mistress?"

The coachman gave him a guarded look. "Ask t'mistress," he repeated.

St. John turned away in disgust and urged his horse nearer the window of the equipage. He peered cautiously inside but saw only darkness. Dismounting, he kept the reins in one hand.

"Hello?" No answer. He readied his pistol. "If you do not answer, I warn you—I am armed." When still no sound came forth, he reached for the latch and turned it, eliciting a gentle click. Holding the pistol out, he swung the door open, and peered inside. "Hello," he said again, wishing the clouds weren't obstructing the moon so well.

He heard some movement and tensed. A muffled sob came from the far side of the coach. He shoved his pistol in a pocket—heavens, it *was* a woman—and was about to jump in when a female laugh, very close to his head, rang out, clear and distinct.

"Oh, Margaret," the voice scolded. "You've spoilt it! You needn't blubber; we are unharmed, are we not? And you can see St. John is equally unscathed."

Julian forced himself to take a deep breath before he spoke. "What the devil have you done?" he hissed at the speaker, who now pushed her face forward from the shadows, where the coach lamp illumined the lovely features of Clarissa Andrews in all her wicked, seductive beauty.

She smiled at him, turning her head demurely, only it wasn't an honest movement, for there was nothing demure about Miss Andrews. She was a vixen, a minx, a she-devil, and she'd been trying to get St. John beneath her power since the start of the season. She knew, as did all of London, that St. John, after thirty-four years of bachelorhood, was in need of a wife. He'd made an oath to the Marquess of Worleydon, his former guardian, and he meant to keep it.

"Allow me to congratulate you, Julian, on the excellent handling of your horse," she purred. "I am infinitely relieved you have kept yourself in one piece, you must know. I should have been utterly cast down had you been harmed."

Steely blue eyes glinted at her. He wished he could tell her to go to the devil, to plague *him* with her incessant fooleries, but he was too much a gentleman—by God, he would be a gentleman. So he said only, "You could have got someone killed."

"Yes, you," she agreed calmly. "But here you are, as handsome and alive as ever." She gave him a sweet smile, reminding him of what he found so vexatious in her. She had an innocent smile, delectable lips, but behind it all a black heart.

"Oh, come, Julian, you give me too much credit. No one was anything near being killed. You know it was naught but a lark, only a lark!"

"Only a lark?" His voice dripped ice. "Your coach came directly at me, and if I had been any less a rider, I would likely have broken my neck. My horse might have died as well."

She was thoughtful a moment. "We were not supposed to drive quite so close to you, I own. And why do you insist upon riding such an immense animal? We should have fared the worst, not you; only it did not work out the way I planned." She spoke with barely a moment's stopping. "And I warrant you would have come to rescue me in a moment if Margaret had not spoilt everything." She pouted at him from within the reaches of a richly beribboned bonnet. "I was perfectly prepared to swoon for your benefit. You would have come to my aid, would you not?" She looked at him hopefully, but he made no answer. He directed his next words to the opposite wall of the coach.

"Are you all right, Miss Margaret?" He couldn't see Miss Andrews's younger sister, but a sniffle came from the darkness.

"I—I think so. Thank you, sir."

"Margaret's perfectly well!" Miss Andrews cried, moving forward so her ample bosom, half revealed in the formal dress of evening wear, was not only plainly in sight, but she blocked any possible view behind her. St. John looked away, refusing to admire her.

Other men did admire her, for she could have made any wall in the kingdom proud with her portrait on it. She had dark, lustrous hair, an ovaline face with a well-delineated nose, and dark, long-lashed eyes. She also had slim ankles and small feet, which he knew from attending many a ball or rout in town. But St. John could not admire Miss Andrews'ss face or slim ankles, for her brazen impudence gave him a disgust of her.

In the past he would have taken advantage of her, welcomed her when she teased him with her alluring countenance and everything beneath it. At times he wanted nothing more than to take hold of her and…He forced his mind to concentrate only on her irksome behaviour. Tonight's escapade, what she called a 'mere lark,' was the latest in a string of vexatious attempts by her to gain his attention. And it was merely a hoax, another of her tricks, to put him in her path.

As he considered how best to give her a set-down, the jarring sound of a ring tone, quite close, made St. John turn in amazement and look around, not understanding the sound or its source. It was unrecognizable. But Claire Channing, the author writing St. John's story, did. She shut her eyes with a low groan, while St. John and the coach, the dark road, all of it, vanished, and she was back, sitting before her laptop, waiting for the call to go to voice mail.

"Good fiction creates its own reality."
Nora Roberts

Available Online or Wherever Books Are Sold

ABOUT THE AUTHOR

Linore Rose Burkard is a serious watcher of period films, a Janeite, and hopeless romantic. An award-winning author best known for Inspirational Regency Romance, her first novel (*Before the Season Ends*) opened the genre for the CBA. Besides historical romance, Linore writes contemporary suspense (The Pulse Effex Series, as L.R. Burkard), contemporary romance and short stories. Linore has a *magna cum laude* English Lit. degree from CUNY which she earned while taking herself far too seriously. She now resides in Ohio with her husband and family, where she turns her youthful angst into character or humor-driven plots.

Sign up for Linore's newsletter at **LinoreBurkard.com** to receive a free romance novella by Linore. (See below)

Free Offer!

Three French Hens
*A Novella Romance of England during the French
Revolution*

Young Mademoiselle Christine
D'Ornay and her family are exiles in England. The
dashing Lord Russell seems friendly, but the lives
of French aristocrats are cheap in an age of
betrayal. Can Christine and her family trust this
new friend? Or is he the enemy they fear most?

Receive this fiction novella FREE when you
sign up for Linore's Newsletter at
www.linoreburkard.com/newsletter

Limited Time Offer. Act Now!

A Short Glossary of Regency Terms

A

abigail: a lady's maid; any female maid (servant). Ex. "I see you've hired a new abigail."

Ace of Spades: a widow

ape leader: an old maid; based on a strange myth that single women who never bore children would end up leading apes in hell.

ague: (Pronounced ah-gyoo) Originally, malaria and the chills that went with it. Later, any respiratory infection such as a cold, fever or chills.

assembly, assemblies: Large gatherings held in the evening for gentry or the aristocracy, usually including a ball and supper. Almack's in London was the ultimate Assembly in the early part of the 19th century. A handful of high-standing society hostesses had autocratic power of attendance as they alone could issue the highly prized vouchers, or tickets.

Competition to get in was fierce. The Duke of Wellington was once famously turned away—for being late.

B

ball: A large dance requiring full dress. Refreshments were available, and sometimes a supper. Public balls required tickets; private ones, an invitation.

Banbury tale: A story with no basis in fact; A rumour; Nonsense.

banns: Banns of marriage were a public announcement in a parish church that two people intended to get married. They had to be read three consecutive weeks in a row, and in the home church of both parties. After each reading, (and this was their purpose) the audience was asked to give knowledge of any legal impediment to the marriage. If there was none, after three weeks, the couple were legally able to wed. To bypass the banns, a couple could try to get a marriage license instead. Without banns or a license, the marriage would be illegal. (null)

beau monde, the: The aristocracy and the rich

upperclass. The fashionable elite. In practice, anyone accepted into their circle, ie., a celebrity or an "original.".

blow by: Illegitimate child; other terms were, *baseborn* child of, *natural* child of...

blunt: (slang) Cash; ready money.

C

Carlton House: Given to the Prince of Wales by George III upon reaching his majority, Carlton House was in a state of disrepair (for a royal, at any rate). The house consequently underwent enormous alterations and changes, and was the London palace for the Regent. He spent a great deal of time there but eventually came to favour the palace at Brighton—an even larger extravagance. The Brighton "Pavilion" is today a museum, but Carlton House, unfortunately, no longer exists.

chamber: A private room in a house, such as a bedroom, as opposed to the parlour or dining room.

chaperon: The servant, mother, or married female relative or family friend who supervised eligible young girls in public.

chemise: A woman's long undergarment which served as a slip beneath her gown. Also, a nightdress. (Previously, the chemise was called a 'shift'.)

chintz: Patterned cloth, usually floral, with a pleasant satiny "shine" for texture.

chit: A young girl.

clubs: The great refuge of the middle and upper-class man in 18th and 19th century London. Originating as coffeehouses in the 17th century, clubs became more exclusive, acquiring prime real estate on Pall Mall and St. James's Street. Membership was often by invitation only. Among the more prominent were Boodle's, White's and Brooke's. Crockford's began to dominate in the very late Regency.

consumption: Pulmonary tuberculosis (TB)

corset: A precursor of the modern bra, usually meant to constrict the waist to a fashionable measurement, as well as support the high bust required for a Regency gown. It consisted of two parts, reinforced with whalebone that got hooked together in front and then laced up in the back.The garment could also be referred to as 'the stays.'

countess: The wife of an earl in England. When 'shires' were changed to 'counties,' an earl retained the Norman title of earl; his wife, however, became a countess.

cravat: (pronounced as kruh-vaht, with the accent on the second syllable). A loose cloth that was tied around the neck in a bow. Throughout the Regency, a fashionable gentleman might labour much over this one detail of his appearance, hoping to achieve a number of different, much-coveted effects.

curricle: Two-wheeled carriage that was popular in the early 1800s. It was pulled by two horses, and deemed rather sporty by the younger set.

curtsey: The acceptable mode of greeting or showing respect by a female. By mid-century the curtsey was less in evidence except for social inferiors like maids to their betters, or by any woman presented at court.

cut: An effective means of social discouragement that involved pretending not to know or see a person who was trying to be acknowledged. A woman might use this technique to discourage unwelcome attentions from a gentleman; but many others 'cut' people, too. Getting the 'cut direct' from a social superior was vastly humiliating.

D

Debrett's: A published guide to the peerage, often called simply, "the Society Book."

dowager: The name given to a widow of rank. Ie., if you were a duchess and your husband died, and your oldest son was married, his wife would become the duchess, and you would be dowager duchess.

draper (linen draper): Merchant who sold cloth.

drawing room: A formal parlour used in polite society to receive visitors who came to pay calls during the afternoon.

F

first floor: The second floor in the US. The English called the floor level on which one entered from the street the "ground floor." Entertaining was never done on the ground floor.

foolscap: A paper of certain dimensions, some varieties of which originally bore a watermark of a fool's cap and bells.

footman: A liveried male servant beneath the butler but above the boy or page. He had many duties ranging from errands to lamp-trimming to waiting table, or accompanying the lady of the house to carry packages when she shopped, or to deliver calling cards when making calls.

fortnight: Two weeks.

fustian!: "Nonsense!" "Don't be absurd!"

G

gaming: Gambling. Nothing to do with 'game' in the sense of hunting, or innocent playing of games.

gig: A one-horse carriage. Light, two-wheeled, and popular in the early century.

groom: The servant who looked after the horses.

Grosvenor Square: (pronounced "Grove-nuh") A part of Mayfair, considered the most fashionable square in London. Mr. Mornay's town house is in the Square.

H

hack: A hack was a general purpose riding horse, but the term might also refer to a "Hackney Coach" which was a coach-for-hire like a taxicab today.

have a pet: a tirade; a burst of temper .(to "freak out" in today's lingo.)

L

Ladies' Mile: A (horseback) riding road in Hyde Park for women.

lady's maid: The servant who cared for her mistress's wardrobe and grooming. A French lady's maid was preferred, and she was particularly valued if she could do hair in all the fashionable styles. A lady's maid was an "upper servant," and could not be fired by the housekeeper; she might also be better educated than the lower servants.

lorgnette: Used by ladies, the lorgnette was eyeglasses (or a monocle), held to the eyes with a long handle, or could be worn on a chain around the neck. The monocle used by a man was called a "quizzing glass."

laudanum: A mixture of opium in a solution of alcohol, it was used for pain relief and as an anesthetic.

livery: A distinctive uniform worn by the male servants in a household. No two liveries, ideally, were exactly alike. Knowing the colour of the livery of someone could enable you to spot their carriage in a crowd. The uniform itself was an old-fashioned style, including such things as a frock coat, knee breeches, powdered wigs, and a waistcoat.

M

mama: Always pronounced by the upper-class with the accent on the second syllable.

Mayfair: The ritziest residential area of London, in the West End, and only about a half mile square in size.

mews, the: Any lane or open area where a group of stables was situated. The townhouses of the rich often had a mews behind them, or close by, where they kept their horses and equipages when not in use.

modiste: (French) seamstress.

muslin: One of the finest cottons, muslin was semi-transparent and very popular for gowns; (beneath which a chemise would be worn).

O

on-dit: (French; literally, "It is said.") During the Regency it was slang for a bit of gossip.

P

Pall Mall: A fancy street in the West End of London, notable for housing some of the most fashionable men'sclubs. Carlton House faced Pall Mall.

pantaloons: Tight-fitting pants that were worn, beginning in the early

1800s, and which pushed breeches out of fashion except forformal occasions. They had a "stirrup" at the bottom to keep them in place.

parlour: The formal or best room in a modest home. Grand houses often had more than one; a "first" or "best," and a "second parlour."

peer: A nobleman, that is, a titled gentleman with the rank of either duke, marquis, (mar-kwiss), viscount (vy-count) or baron. The titles were hereditary, and the owners were entitled to a seat in the House of Lords.

pelisse: An outdoor garment for women, reaching to the ankle or mid-calf; and often hooded.

pianoforte: The piano. Genteel young women were practically required to learn the instrument.

pin money: A colloquialism for a woman's spending money. The allowance agreed upon in her marriage settlement, to be used on small household or personal (vanity) items.

R

regent: A person who reigns on behalf of a monarch who is incapable of filling the requirements of the crown. When George III's relapse of porphyria (most scholars agree this was his malady) rendered him incapable of meeting his duties, his son, the Prince of Wales, became the Prince Regent. The actual regency lasted from 1811-1820.

reticule: A fabric bag, gathered at the top and held by a ribbon or strap; a lady's purse. Reticules became necessary when the thin muslin dresses of the day made it impossible to carry any personal effects in a pocket without it seeming bulky or unsightly. The earliest reticules (apparently called 'ridicules,' as it seemed ridiculous to carry one's valuables outside of one's clothing) were, in effect, outside pockets.

rubber: In games like whist, a rubber was a set of three or more games. To win the rubber, one had to win two out of three or three out of five

S

season: The London social season, in which the fashionable elite descended upon the city in droves. It coincided, not unnaturally, with the sitting of Parliament,though the height of the season was only March through June.

smelling salts (smelling bottle): A small vial filled with a compound that usually contained ammonia, to be used in case of fainting.

spencer: For women, a short jacket that reached only to the high "empire" waist. For men, an overcoat without tails, also on the short side.

squire: 19th century term of courtesy (like "esquire") for a member of the landed gentry.

T

tendre: (French adj. *soft, tender;)* Regency slang for "a soft spot"; an attraction to.

ton, **the:** (pronounced 'tawn') High society; the elite; the "in" crowd; Those of rank, with royalty at the top. To be "good ton" meant acceptance with the upper crust, and opened most any door in fashionable society. Occasionally, those without fortune or pedigree could enter the *ton*—if they were an Original, for instance, having something either sensational or highly attractive about their person or reputation; or could amuse or entertain the rich to a high degree.

V

valet: The "gentleman's gentle- man." The male equivalent of a lady's maid, his job was to keep the wardrobe in good repair and order, help dressing his master, stand behind him at dinner if required, and accompany him on his travels.

Vauxhall: A famous pleasure garden, across the Thames from London, especially popular in the Georgian era.

W

wainscoting: Wainscot was a fancy, imported oak. The term 'wainscoting' came to mean any wooden panels that lined generally

the top or bottom half of
the walls in a room.

waistcoat: Vest.

Did You Read Book One of The Brides of Mayfair?

Miss Tavistock's Mistake

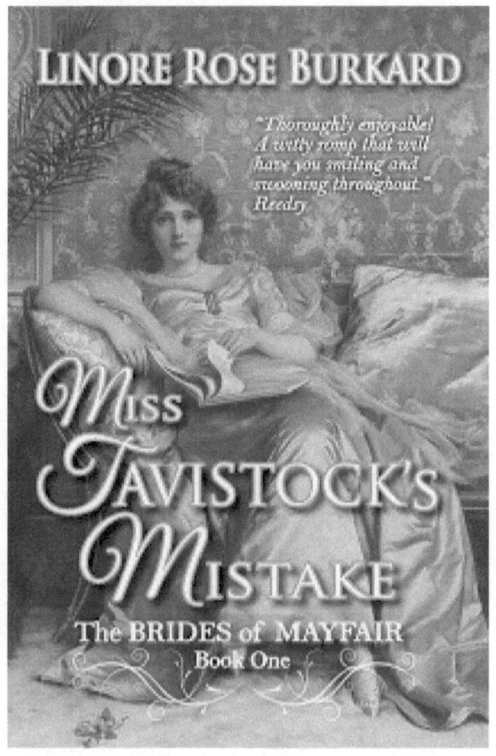

"Thoroughly enjoyable! A witty romp
that will have you smiling and swooning
throughout." Reedsy

New Cover! Available Wherever Books are Sold

OTHER BOOKS BY LINORE ROSE BURKARD

Award-Winning Inspirational Regency Romance

Available INDIVIDUALLY Online and Wherever Books are Sold

Book One: *Before the Season Ends*

Book Two: *The House in Grosvenor Square*

Book Three: *The Country House Courtship*

FOREVER, LATELY: A REGENCY TIME TRAVEL ROMANCE

READER FAVORITE AWARD WINNER from InterviewsandReviews.com

2019 BOOK OF THE MONTH WINNER

2019 BOOK OF THE YEAR FINALIST

Available Online and Wherever Books are Sold